THE NEW
INDIANS

THE NEW INDIANS

Joe Jessup

THE NEW INDIANS

This is a work of fiction. All of the characters, names, incidents, organizations, and dialogue in this novel are either the products of the author's imagination or are used fictitiously.

iUniverse books may be ordered through booksellers or by contacting:

iUniverse
1663 Liberty Drive
Bloomington, IN 47403
www.iuniverse.com
1-800-Authors (1-800-288-4677)

Because of the dynamic nature of the Internet, any web addresses or links contained in this book may have changed since publication and may no longer be valid. The views expressed in this work are solely those of the author and do not necessarily reflect the views of the publisher, and the publisher hereby disclaims any responsibility for them.

Certain stock imagery © Thinkstock.
Any people depicted in stock imagery provided by Thinkstock are models, and such images are being used for illustrative purposes only.

ISBN: 978-1-4917-5231-9 (e)
ISBN: 978-1-4917-5232-6 (sc)
ISBN: 978-1-4917-5233-3 (hc)

Library of Congress Control Number: 2014921366

Printed in the United States of America.

iUniverse rev. date: 1/22/2015

PINE RIDGE, SOUTH DAKOTA, 1968

The old Indian man sat on a new fold-up lawn chair in front of his dilapidated house of many colors. A faded sky-blue color covered the small square structure with window borders of weathered red and yellow paint. The roof was a patchwork quilt of black-and-green asphalt shingles. The east-facing screen door hung crookedly in the outer wall. It was unpainted and splintered with holes in the screen where hands and feet made contact.

A small black-and-white kitten came out of the house through the bottom hole in the screen door and rubbed against the old man's legs as he sat and waited. A skinny young boy with close-cropped black hair trudged hesitantly toward him from far down the dusty, barren street. The kitten jumped up on the old man's lap and began rubbing against his soft, round belly and worn cotton print shirt.

The kitten pushed harder against him and purred. Suddenly, it sat up and batted at one of his long silver braids that were tied off with thin red ribbon. That was more than the old man would tolerate. He softly cuffed the cat on top of its head and pushed it off onto the ground. The kitten bounced up and ran playfully back through the broken screen door.

The old man smiled a toothless greeting at the handsome young man.

"Good morning, Clyde! My grandson is growing up fast like the weeds between our houses!" He lifted up his right leg and displayed a clean white tennis shoe. "How do you like my new shoes? I bought them very cheap from Bobby Broken Horn. I thought maybe he stole them in town, but I've been wearing them all morning, and my feet don't feel hot in them yet.

"Some things that the white man makes—like this chair and these shoes—give comfort to an old man like me. And some things that an Indian makes—like this pipe—give a more lasting comfort in my old age. Let us smoke my pipe and then talk for a while."

The old grandfather pointed the long pipe stem straight upward toward the sky. Then he touched the bottom tip of the pipe against the earth. He signaled its recognition to the east, south, west, and north. He struck a blue-tipped kitchen match against a rock. It popped into flame, and he lit the tobacco inside the red stone bowl. He inhaled the smoke slowly and released it as if it carried a part of him with it out into the still morning air.

He handed the pipe to the boy, who carefully took it and offered it to the unseen forces with a frightened gesture of respect and unwilling practice. They each in turn silently smoked until the tobacco burned down into ashes.

The old man separated stem from bowl and blew the remaining ashes out and onto the ground. He pressed a small, pale-green bundle of sweet sage into the bowl and put pipe and stem back into an ornately decorated, white buckskin bag.

"Grandson, your mother told me that she had a dream about you and that you went away from us on a long journey. You are too young to be going out into the big world all alone.

"Sometimes our people leave here, and I never see them again. I often wonder if they are lost somewhere and they just can't find their way back.

"A long time ago, the spiritual leaders of our tribe decided to accept anyone into our family who had the smallest amount of our ancestors' blood in their veins. They were told by White Buffalo Calf Maiden that the Great Spirit wanted us to all stay together and that we would have more strength as a whole. In the old days, if you wanted to be 'Lakota,' nobody in our tribe would call you names like 'breed' or 'half-breed.' Those were foreign words to us!

"Grandson, I know that things have been difficult for you lately. You were born from the union of my daughter and a white man who left us, but you are a very important part of my family here."

The old man paused to watch a small gray lizard dart from the left eye socket of a buffalo skull resting on a mound of red dirt and facing the morning sun. The lizard ran beneath a pile of gray lava rocks near the round medicine lodge. Like the lizard, the old man tried to look in two opposite directions at the same time. One of his alert eyes gazed upon his grandson, who appeared restless and disturbed. His other keen eye watched for the nervous lizard to reappear.

The lizard could tell things that only the ancient ones knew about—secrets of the rocks and creation, when the earth was new, pure, and complete! Messengers could appear in many forms. Stillness, silence, native rituals, and the natural world could tell an old Indian man many things.

His grandson and the lizard both behaved nervously and restlessly. *Perhaps my grandson needs to seek shade from trouble. Lately, he had avoided the Sunday sweat lodge gathering, when the sacred stones were red-hot. Maybe he needs the guidance of the Buffalo Spirit and to seek a vision through both of its eyes.*

Clyde was agitated and couldn't stand the posture of sitting cross-legged and upright at attention any longer! His grandfather's silence could continue forever this way until he got some information out of him or fell asleep sitting up.

Clyde knew that in the Indian culture, youth was granted forgiveness of rude behavior after initial respect was given. He greatly respected his mother's family and his grandfather who helped raise him, but he had big problems with living here on the Indian reservation. He was ready to move on. He wasn't old enough for a driver's license and could get picked up any time for truancy. Clyde thought, *I can't believe this! I didn't tell anybody that I was running away!*

Clyde knew that the only way he could escape from his grandfather's powerful grip was to break the silence.

"Grandfather, why did my white father leave me here and never come back? My Lakota side tells me that the earth is round, but living here, it seems like the world is flat, and at the end of the reservation, it drops off sharply, where I fall off and get into trouble. I always hurt you and my mother. It seems like my world stops here! I've heard that my white father was a great cowboy! Could that be the other half of my world that isn't round yet?"

The old man directed both of his attentive eyes toward the lizard, who suddenly reappeared from beneath the sacred rocks and returned his gaze. Then it entered the right eye socket of the bleached-white buffalo skull and vanished from sight.

Far down the street, a truck backfired, and dogs began barking from all across town. The old man stirred the discarded pipe ashes in front of him with a charred stick and thought about the unusual behavior of the lizard.

"I am just an old man. The questions in your heart are of those of a young man who is restless and searching. I cannot answer all of your questions, but I can tell you that your white father was a good man. He tried to live and work around here so that he could be with you and your mother. I think he loved her very much.

"You think that living here is difficult, but it was very hard for your father. He was never accepted by the young men of our tribe. I think maybe he was too handsome and talented as a horseman. The single Indian men were very much jealous of him for being married to my beautiful daughter. But more than that, your father probably looked too much like Custer. I think he was a reminder to our people of too many lost regrets.

"Your mother tried to go with him when you were a papoose and live on ranches where he knew his trade with cattle and horses. Your mother loved your father but said that it was too lonesome when they traveled far away, and sometimes the white women whispered behind her back. She missed the love and respect of her own people.

"Your dad began traveling around to different ranches and rodeos without you and your mother, but he came back here from time to time and left money for us. Then after a time, we didn't see or hear from him again.

"One day, a cowboy who was a long rider came to our town. He knew your father well! He left us your dad's wallet that had some money in it, and he told us about how your father was killed by a wild bull. He said that your dad and his horse became tangled in a wire fence. The bull charged his horse, and they both went down. He said that your dad died with his spurs on and with his horse beneath him.

"Your mother and I decided that he died with honor in the white man way. I burned the sacred pipe to him as an offering on his journey."

The old man noticed the lizard sitting motionless in the center of the buffalo skull, sitting erect and facing the east.

"Grandson, if you leave us, I may never see you again, so I want to give you a road map to a place where you will always know where the center of life is, and from this place, you will always be able to find your way back.

"There is a place that the grandfathers call the Middle Ground. The Middle Ground is a place that is in the middle of each of us. If we can find this meeting place within ourselves, then we can become one with ourselves and even one with our Creator.

"We were each born with a left leg and a right leg to carry us in different directions on our journey. We were given a left arm and a right arm so that we could pick and choose things that are good for ourselves and for our relations.

"We were given two eyes to view our world with, but we only see one picture when we look out at our world. We were given two eyes so that we could look both ways and see two sides to things so that our true vision would see what is right and what is best for all.

"Each person is like two people who have two sides that are inside one body. The Great Spirit gave us our bodies like this so that we could look at ourselves and find a balance that would give us one clear picture.

"The Middle Ground is always there for us to meet ourselves and find out what is good or bad and right or wrong. If we can come to this meeting place and ask our two sides for the one answer, we will never become lost.

"When a man and a woman decide to be joined together, it is important that each of them know how to find their own oneness in the Middle Ground. If they have not found it or cannot find it, then it is like four people bumping around in different directions. This is why it is much easier for a single person to find the Middle Ground first!

"Grandson, I have given you a road map so that you can find yourself and so that you can find your way back to your people if you become lost somewhere.

"I have watched you ride the young horses around our town, and you have a special gift with them. When you leave here, go where there are many horses, and they will give something back to you. If you should become lost among the white people, let the horses carry your spirit with them while you try to sort things out.

"Always try to remember what we talked about during your last visits here with me. I have spoken. Ah-Ho!

"Now," said the old man, "come and eat something. You are thinner than a young jackrabbit that is hunting a mate where a wise pack of coyotes live."

Clyde looked at the ground and said, "Grandfather, I must leave here quickly. I found a maybe-job over in Shoshone country. There is a white man near the Wind Rivers who they say is a human being and owns many horses. The job may be gone before I can get there, so I must leave now to catch a ride out of here. It will take me halfway there."

Without another word or gesture, the young boy ran around an old government building partly dismantled and disappeared from the old man's sight. The remaining boards of earth-green siding bore witness to a youthful departure and unknown destiny.

The sun was moving now around toward the south and rising higher in the cloudless sky. The elderly Lakota man felt downward to his right side and found the latch on the new fold-out lawn chair. It was becoming a natural response to his reflexes now, like the distance of touch to his woman on a cold winter night—also a great comfort during these remaining years.

He pushed his weight to the back of the chair and pulled on the handle. He lifted his legs upward and tilted his back down to evenly meet the angle of the midday sun. He felt the sun's warmth enter and soothe his weary bones and caress his wrinkled brown skin.

The black-and-white kitten came blasting through the hole in the bottom of the broken screen door and ran up to the resting human being. He'd recently taught her to tread more lightly, so she carefully and quietly entered his domain, curling up against his soft, round belly and worn cotton print shirt.

"Small painted one, perhaps it will be my grandson who was born in the middle of two mighty nations. Perhaps it will be my grandson and others like him who bring back unity to the one great nation and return the spirit to our earth mother."

1

Wind River Mountains
Wyoming, 2012

THE TWO COWBOYS SAT ON TOP OF THE RIDGE IN DARKNESS,

waiting for the sun to spread its rays of light over and beyond to the
valley below. Like the drawing of a big curtain upon a stage, they
awaited the opening of a dramatic production they had witnessed
many times. The event was always special but especially so today.
To sit here on their horses and share this golden moment of sunlight
and anniversary was a silent episode in their lives but not without
personal unspoken feelings of mixed emotions.

Clyde remembered hitchhiking here from South Dakota, carrying
an old rodeo saddle and a rolled-up green army blanket across his
shoulder. Between several rides with Native Americans and many
miles of walking, he was dropped off at the last intersection leading
to the Bar-V Ranch. The Shoshone family warned him that the road
he was taking was along a steep grade with little traffic and that
he would most likely have to camp out all night. They gave him a
Hostess Twinkie. It was all they had!

He began walking up the winding gravel road in the shade
of majestic, tall pine trees. Miles from anywhere, he wondered if
he'd ever catch a ride. One of his prized cowboy boots flap, flap,

flapped against the hard, rough gravel road, and a painful jelly blister formed on the instep of his right foot beneath the torn sole.

Clyde knew that only Indians picked up hitchhiking Indians in cowboy country. His saddle and Western boots couldn't hide his deeply tanned skin and jet-black hair. Two pickup trucks had already passed him up, and it would be dark in another hour. Another vehicle was coming up behind him for a short time until it made a screeching noise, coughed, and became silent. He walked another mile and heard it coming again. He thought better than to turn around and give a clear picture of his Indian heritage, so he shifted his heavy, awkward saddle over his back and covered his hair, neck, and shoulders. He trudged onward.

The advancing vehicle whined, coughed, and sputtered in low gear. It seemed that it would never catch up to him.

The beat-up 1942 Dodge flatbed truck on bald tires was all that Fleebit could afford after spending two years of irrigating hay fields and building fences for the farmers around his hometown of Big Scratch, Montana. There wasn't a rancher around who would hire him to ride a horse all day. He was determined to go where nobody knew him and get a job as a cowboy. One day while loafing around in the feed store, he overheard two ranchers talking about the Bar-V Ranch, located in the Wind River Range of Wyoming. Their conversation suggested that it was a big spread and a real cowboy outfit.

Fleebit didn't have much money left after he'd bought himself a new Stetson hat, two pairs of custom-made, high-heeled cowboy boots with fancy stitches, new jeans, and fancy Western shirts with rhinestone snaps. If he was going to ask for a real cowboy job, he knew that he couldn't look like a farmhand.

When he paid out the last of his hard-earned cash to the junkyard owner, he could tell that the truck leaked some oil, but he had no idea that it regularly needed a transfusion to keep it alive. He didn't have a clue that the radiator had several bullet holes in it and that it was filled up with a case of Stop Leak. He found out when he turned up the long, winding, steep, high-altitude grade in the Wind River Range.

Fleebit could see someone walking far ahead, and he hadn't caught up with him yet. Each time he almost caught up with the hiker, his truck began overheating, and he had to shift down into creeper gear. He stopped again to cool the engine and empty his last remaining water jug into the radiator. It would soon be dark.

Fleebit climbed in and hit the foot starter. The old, dented relic backfired, screeched, and lurched ahead, finally chugging up beside a young man carrying a saddle on top of his head. Steam began hissing out of a .50-caliber bullet hole below the radiator cap.

Fleebit yelled out his side-view window, "Is there any water around here!"

Clyde dropped his saddle on the ground and looked at the tall, young white cowboy sporting a new Stetson hat and fancy, newly embroidered, button-down Western shirt.

"I hiked off through the trees a short ways back and found a spring. If you'll give me a ride, I'll hike back over there with a jug and fill it up for you."

"Sure enough!" said Fleebit.

Clyde placed his saddle and bedroll on the back of the splintered, oil-stained truck bed and headed off cross-country, toting a five-gallon jug through the dark pine forest. He thought, *That big, lanky paleface would have passed me by if he hadn't needed some water! From the look of his truck, it might be quicker to walk!*

When Clyde started back up the hill carrying the heavy water jug, the blister on his foot broke open. He tried to avoid stepping on sharp stones, but each step became more painful. By the time he reached the truck, his white sock was sticking out between the broken stitches of his boot, and it was red with blood.

The truck had cooled down now, so Fleebit filled up the radiator. When he poured in the cold springwater, it hissed and gurgled. The hot metal block of the engine emitted a mournful groan. The steel cast block trembled and vibrated. The loose air-cleaner cap snapped and shuddered like a cymbal in a drum set to a sad country song.

Clyde pulled off his right boot and pried open the passenger-side door that was dented and rusty. It took both arms to pull it open, so he threw his boot through the open window and pulled hard. The door creaked open halfway and stopped. Clyde squeezed in and used both arms to pull the frozen, creaking door closed.

Fleebit pushed his right foot down against the foot starter on the floor, and the oil-starved engine labored to turn over. The choke was still stuck open, and the rich gasoline mixture flooded the old carburetor. The starter finally caught, and the engine backfired. It popped like gunfire and exploded into flame.

Fleebit yelled, "Fire!"

Clyde tried to push the passenger-side door open, but it was jammed shut. Smoke engulfed the cab. In a desperate, angry rage, he threw his right boot out through the open window and scrambled out after it. He bumped his head on the door and landed outside the door on his bloody foot. He quickly grabbed his saddle and blanket from the back bed and hopped away from the roaring flame that was consuming the truck.

Fleebit grabbed a duffel bag that was strapped down to the rack behind the driver's seat and bolted upwind after Clyde.

"It's gone! It's all gone!" winced Fleebit.

Clyde picked up a hand-sized rock and threw it toward the burning truck. It bounced once off the flat bed, skipped, and crashed through the back driver's side window. "Yeah, a piece of dog crap is gone, all gone! What a tragedy! I've seen better discarded wrecks lying around the Indian reservation!"

Fleebit was distraught over the incident. He jumped up and down and frantically waved his hands in the air as though the fanning motion would put out the fire. "Dammit! You didn't need to throw that rock through my back window like that!"

Clyde picked up another loose rock that shone beneath the brilliant firelight and reached back his arm for the launch.

"I just walked a mile uphill with fifty pounds of water in a jug and crippled myself with a bleeding foot so that I could ride only four more miles to the Bar-V Ranch gate." Clyde launched the stone. There was a crash, and smoke billowed out from the new opening in the back window.

Fleebit suddenly realized that this belligerent pup was going after the same job as he was. It made him furious. "The Bar-V Ranch is a real cowboy outfit. I'm on my way there to take that job."

"Hell, they won't hire you; you're just a kid!"

"And that old saddle has seen a lot of use, but you sure didn't wear it out!"

Clyde became enraged and replied, "Yeah, and why would somebody hire a tall bonehead like you? Dressed in those fancy new clothes, it looks like you've watched too many Italian Westerns! I'll bet you can't even ride a stick horse! Man, you look like a dude!" Clyde spit at the ground. "Maybe you can afford to buy a ticket at a rodeo one day and watch me ride a big, rank horse in this saddle!"

There was a skirmish in the middle of the road amid the firelight of the burning truck, down an illuminated alley of tall pines on an isolated mountain road.

Fleebit tried using his extremely long arms to push Clyde away and shield himself from two wild, swinging fists. He slapped him back several times, but he kept coming. Fleebit shoved him away hard, causing Clyde to trip backward and fall to the ground.

Clyde jumped up and started collecting hand-sized rocks from the gravel roadway. He began throwing them at Fleebit with deadly accuracy.

Fleebit yelled out, "Ow! Ow! *Ow!*" He tried to duck and weave away from the assault of rapid-fire stones and finally yelled out, "Stop that, you renegade! Stop!" Both of his ears were bleeding, and there was a deep gash above the bridge of his nose.

"I quit!" stammered Fleebit. "Let's talk this over! Stop throwing those damned rocks!"

Clyde said, "That's good enough for me. It's getting dark, and we don't know where we are! I'm heading back through the trees to that fresh springwater and make camp for the night. If you want to try to keep up with a guy who has a bleeding foot, I might not finish you off with a much bigger rock after we get there!"

The small natural spring gurgled out between two large, moss-covered boulders. A wind began to stir in the tops of the dark pines, bringing a night chill to the high country. A faint *thump, thump, thump* sound echoed up out of the distant forest. Clyde began picking up fist-sized rocks and asked, "Can you build a fire without burning everything down around us?"

Fleebit had a worried expression on his face. "Yes, I can build a fire, but what are you going to do with those rocks? Are you still pissed off?"

Clyde said, "Yes, I'm still pissed off, but I'm more hungry right now. That thumping sound is a flock of pine grouse getting ready to roost for the night. I'm going hunting!"

Clyde came out of the darkness a short time later to the glow of a small campfire, carrying two plump pine hens. Without a word, he set about to the task of field dressing the birds. He washed them thoroughly in the springwater and skewered them with green pine sticks. Then he propped them over the flickering flames and prepared his bed. He braced his saddle on the ground for a backrest and rolled out his green wool army blanket in front of it.

Fleebit said, "You are pretty handy! Where did you learn how to throw rocks like that?"

Clyde stretched out on his bed within arm's reach of the birds. "My name is Clyde Deerhide, and I came from Pine Ridge, South Dakota. My mother is a full-blooded Lakota Indian. She taught me how to hunt small game with stones and a curved throwing stick. Do you have a problem with that?"

Fleebit added some dry sticks to the fire and seemed uncomfortable with the question. "Well, no, I don't! I've never known any Indians before now, but I sure wouldn't want to get your mother pissed off near a pile of rocks. My ears are swelled up so big that my hat won't sit on my head. My name is Fleebit Shepherd, and I came from Big Scratch, Montana. You've probably never heard of it."

Clyde held up a piece of pine bark and studied it. "You are wrong about that. My mother's family owned the trading post there. My grandmother was a Lakota woman named She Walks Lightly. She married a man named Philippe Dobbs. He was a Frenchman with roots that went back to the British fur trade company. I spent a summer with them when I was a kid and helped them build some hitching rails for tying up big teams of horses. I haven't been back, but my mother still owns some land there."

A big smile replaced the forlorn look on Fleebit's swollen face. "Well, boy, howdy! There's a café there now where the trading post once stood. Those old hitching posts are still there. How about that!"

A long pause of silence seemed to make Fleebit uncomfortable. He had to break the silence. "Do you mind if I ask how you got the name of Clyde Deerhide?"

Clyde reached over the crackling fire and spun the birds on the sticks. "I'll tell you how I got my name after you tell me how you got yours."

Fleebit used his dampened handkerchief to wipe the blood from his nose. "Okay, that's fair enough. My dad was a good-looking gambler named Starkey Shepherd. He won a big pot of gold in a poker game in Big Scratch, met my ma there, and she fell in love with him. When Starkey found out that she was with foal, he hung around just long enough to name the colt and then ran off to another game in another town like a coyote that smells fresh scent on the wind.

"Starkey told the nurses at the hospital to write the name of Fleebit Shepherd on my birth certificate, because he was leaving town, and his kid would have to either grow up tough or die. Then he took off, and I've never seen him. My mom didn't change my name, because she thought Fleebit sounded Hungarian, and there were a lot of Germans and Swiss around Big Scratch, working in the gold mines. She called me Flea when I was little.

1

"But when I started school, I started getting into fights. Some girl would giggle, and I'd turn red. Some guy would laugh, and I'd bust his head. Life wasn't easy for a boy named Flea-bit Shepherd from Big Scratch, Montana. I ducked out of school and never finished. I went to work early and never learned to read or write."

Clyde scraped away some of the fire until there was a small bed of coals resting beneath the roasting birds. He gave each of them a short half turn. Melted fat dripped from the golden flesh and crackled in the fire, sending the scent of roasted meat up into the still, pine-laden night air.

Clyde gazed up above the small fire toward the night sky and saw a crescent moon lying on her back with both tips pointing upward. A droplet of fat plopped down into a red, burning coal. It exploded, sending small sparks of red embers skyward.

Clyde lamented, "I grew up without a father too. My dad was a white man and a cowboy named Jess Morgan. He married the prettiest girl on the reservation. My mother's family name is Many Deerskins.

"The truth is, at the time, it was very unacceptable for whites and Indians to intermarry. The families from both sides of the union either objected or strongly cautioned against the marriage. My father and mother both had deaf ears to their families' pleas and followed the young passion of their hearts.

"Soon, the sad reality of much advice became evident; the full-blood Indians wouldn't accept my dad living on their reservation, and the white ranchers my father worked for wouldn't accept my mother. My mother and father split up after I was born, and then my dad was killed.

"I was raised by my mother and grandfather as a full-blood Indian, and I took my mother's last name of Many Deerskins. I went to school with whites and Indians.

"I found out that if you had an Indian name, the white kids made fun of you until you learned how to fight or get whipped. I felt sorry for my cousin, Two Dogs. I know on some days, he wished he'd never been born. But he turned out to be a real good boxer!

"The big jokes about my name were, how Many Deerskins does it take to make an outhouse tent or a jacket to cover up a half-breed Indian? How Many Deerskins get chewed up by the town dogs? How Many Deerskins end up in the town dump?

"I changed my last name to Deerhide. I found out that any sorry-ass idiot could think he was a poet by saying Clyde Deerhide! By changing my name, it made me popular in school, and I didn't have to fight very often. I guess it's hard to fight with somebody who makes you laugh all the time. Just by mentioning my name, bullies could somehow feel good about themselves. It made me popular with the sorry-ass idiot poets at school. I had to learn how to fight, but it was a lot easier for me to become a clown than a fighter. I didn't get kicked out of school and disappoint my mother. She thought that an education was very important for me.

"At first, I liked going to school. Reading and writing were easy for me. Those two things became a source of freedom. When I learned how to construct my first sentence, I felt like it might be possible for me to write my own dreams of escape, away from reservation life. I liked reading the early history of the Indians and the cowboys. I really liked the story about a white rancher who married an Indian woman and built a cattle empire over the old buffalo range. I could clearly see how two cultures could adapt to modern changes. I felt encouraged that I could do that too. I wanted to ride a lot of different horses and blend in. Here I am!"

Clyde stood up and stretched. He crouched down and grasped the green pine sapling handles. "Only one last quarter turn this time!" With a wide bark shovel, he scooped up fresh coals from Fleebit's adjacent bonfire and placed them in a circle around the golden birds.

Fleebit fed the larger fire for heat and light, while Clyde managed the slow-cooking fire.

Clyde continued, "I liked school and didn't have to fight with the cowboys any longer. Then some of the full-blooded Lakota boys started treating me like a second-class citizen. They thought that I'd gone over to the white man's side, and they started calling me bad names.

"It seemed like I had to choose one side or the other. Then a big, stout Indian named George Mountain Lion Jr. started giving me a hard time. I did everything to stay out of his way. When his girlfriend took a shine to me, that became impossible. Everything fell apart. George told everyone that he was going to kill me, and he started following me around the reservation. I knew that he was going to get me any day, and I had to do something quick!"

Fleebit leaned forward over the fire with his mouth hung wide open in suspense. Two large, brawny hands covered his cauliflower ears.

He gasped, "Did you kill him with a big, sharp rock?"

Clyde glanced toward the fire. "That is another story. It's time to eat!"

Clyde pulled out a new Swiss Army knife that his mother gave him and opened up a sharp saw blade. He used it to saw through a large section of dead pine bark and fashioned two large, hollow, wooden plates that were open at both ends. He washed them off in the small spring and began filling each of them with a nest of watercress and wild garlic from the natural, flowing garden. Clyde lifted one of the golden birds away from the fire and sawed off both ends of the long pine skewers, leaving just enough length left for two handholds. He placed it midcenter of the wild salad and handed it to Fleebit, who took it with silent appreciation and astonishment.

Clyde said, "One more thing!" He reached inside his saddle pocket, pulled out a Hostess Twinkie, and broke it in half.

They both ate in the silence of a flickering firelight under a new moon of future possibilities.

The next morning, Fleebit awoke disoriented. He'd been forced to sleep on his back all night over protruding tree roots. Each time he'd tried to roll over and rest on his side, the rough ground rubbed against his ears. They were more swollen and inflamed than before. He quickly glanced over toward Clyde and was alarmed to see that he was missing. He panicked. *That kid took off in the night and is already at the Bar-V Ranch ahead of me!*

Then he relaxed when he saw Clyde resting far away from the dying ashes of the campfire in the shadow of a giant ponderosa pine. His bed had been moved under the old tree and on top of a thick mattress of pine needles. He was sitting on his bed, washing his foot with mud and green leaves.

Clyde noticed the movement. Without looking into a panic-stricken face he said, "These serviceberry leaves and cold mud will take that swelling down. You look like a baby elephant!"

Fleebit said, "Thanks. I'll take you up on that! Hey, I have an extra pair of boots. I don't need them. They'll be too big for you, but my mom bought me several pairs of new socks. She told me to think about her every time I put my new socks on. She left me several reminders, bless her heart! I don't think she would mind if you put on two or three pairs. She will worry about me, but she'd feel real good about me having a companion who could use them."

Fleebit rummaged around through his duffel bag and brought out a shiny, new pair of handmade Paul Bond high-heeled cowboy boots with fancy stitching. The tall tops with mule ears were stuffed full of white, fluffy socks.

"Put these on, and we can hike over to the Bar-V spread. I don't think it's much farther! I laid awake last night thinking. I decided that if they won't give you a job because you are a kid or because you're an Indian, I won't take one neither. I'm not going back to Montana, though! The way I see it, there will be another cowboy job somewhere on up the road!"

Clyde said, "Thanks. I will take you up on that offer, because I'm lame. I will put on those new socks and try on those new boots. But you need to know this right now! If they don't hire you because you are a dress-up, look-alike Tex Ritter who can't ride a horse, I'll feel sorry for you, but I'll probably take the job, anyway."

2

NEITHER CLYDE NOR FLEEBIT COULD REMEMBER WHO THREW
the first punch on that night after all these years. Clyde shifted in
his saddle and laughed. "That old truck of yours nearly burned me
to death. I figured that the junk dealer you bought it from started it
all. After we both got jobs as horse wranglers on one of the biggest
ranches in Wyoming, it didn't matter. It was my dream come true."

Fleebit patted his big gelding's neck and said, "Yeah, it was my
dream come true too. Ben Gables was a good, fair man to work for.
He was hard on us at first until he realized we were there to stay.
When all the other hands left him for high-paying oil field and
construction jobs, he took a look around, and it was just you and me
beside him. When Ben found out that both of us grew up without
fathers, he softened up and taught us a lot. He took his time to tell us
everything he knew about ranching, horses, and the cattle business."

Clyde laughed. "Ben told me one time, he said, 'When I hired on
you two boys, I felt like I was taking a chance on a couple of misfits.'
He got tears in his eyes and said, 'You two boys were the best gamble
I ever made!'"

Clyde tilted his hat back and looked at Fleebit. "Ben told me that
you were a natural-born cattleman. He said that most cowboys could
look at a big herd of look-alike cows of the same breed and couldn't

tell one from another. He said that you could tell each one apart, and you were the only hand he ever had on his ranch who could always match the cows with their calves after they were separated during a long drive or a roundup."

Fleebit said, "Ben always told me that you were a natural-born horseman. He said that you could get the best out of an unridden young horse by using patience and kind hands. He said you could read a horse like a book, and you knew when to work them and when to rest them. Ben was real proud of you, and I could see a glint in his eyes when he watched you take on the wild, young ones."

The smell of pine upon the north wind abruptly stopped. A calm stillness gave up the rich smell beneath the men of heated horse and oiled leather.

Clyde breathed in deeply and exhaled. "That is my favorite smell in the whole world!"

Fleebit replied, "It used to be mine too, but now I'm getting more partial toward French perfume and the smell of fresh apple pie. I used to love the smell of cows too, but now I prefer the smell of a clean house with flowers in a vase on the center-room table."

Clyde said, "I think some jealous husband hit you over the head with his wife's flowerpot somewhere back down our trail, and you are having daymares while you're still awake. So quit dreaming, because we still have a lot of things to do before we get home. You would rust up and die if I didn't keep your engine and parts moving around!"

The skyline became streaked with red and pink and then a pale white. Suddenly, a solitary spot of brilliant gold shone like the striking of a match over the dark horizon. The gold spark spread up and outward, raising the bright circle of brilliant, golden light to a full dimension. As the sun lifted on top of the ridge, the advancing light moved quickly toward the opposite ridge to the west, unveiling golden aspen leaves atop glistening, white trunks that shone like silver. As the sun moved higher, the shadows of a darkened stage revealed elk grazing on the mountainside. The light moved lower, and the shadows moved away quickly now, exposing a herd of mule deer leaving the creek bed below and a herd of Red Angus cattle spread out down through the lush meadows.

Then the sun lifted up high above it all as it began its rotation around and toward the south, exposing the many earthmovers, bulldozers, trackhoes, and construction sites.

"Old friend," said Clyde, "the country would still be the same if the people hadn't all changed. When we first rode up here in the dark in 1968, we were hired to bring three hundred horses in out of that meadow down below. Back then, this country hadn't changed all that much since the buffalo disappeared.

"Some of my Lakota family probably camped down by that spring and hunted here. All the years I worked here, I tried to imagine what it was like back then and feel what the Indians felt when they were forced to move off and see the white man's cows replace their buffalo. When we first came here, it was easy to imagine those distant times. There were a few fences then, but the land was still the same. It was open, and it wasn't dug and chopped up like today. Now I know how the Indians felt when they lost this land."

Fleebit looked across the wide, green valley below and said, "Old Ben would be mad as hell to see his ranch all dug up and his livestock replaced with 150 developed, miniranch sites, an eighteen-hole golf course, health spa, indoor swimming pool, and a stable of ATVs and golf carts to take people around to see it all. But they do keep a pet farm of fifty cows to make it look like a ranch, and they hired us to brand and vaccinate them. I guess that makes it a ranch in their eyes."

Clyde said, "I don't know about you, but I just came back here to see my old home range again. I knew it wouldn't be the homecoming I'd hoped for. I knew that things wouldn't be just as they were in the old days. When these new owners wrote to us and asked if we would help them work their cows, show them where to move them, and how to manage their grasslands, I wanted to come. Are you sorry that you came with me?"

"Clyde, you and I have ridden the range together for all these years now, and I haven't regretted anything until yesterday."

Clyde turned his horse facing Fleebit and pulled his hat down low. "Okay. Tell me what happened yesterday."

Fleebit hesitated and stammered, "The owner's wife caught me when you were out somewhere, and she told me that it didn't take all day to watch a few cows eating grass. She wanted you and me to come up to their big house and do some gardening and work on their big swimming pool. She took me around and showed me lots of things that she wanted done. She gave me a big, long list of things she expected done, and you can't do any of them from the back of a horse. I was afraid to tell you!"

Clyde slapped his chaps with open palms and frightened Fleebit's horse, causing him to shy sideways. Clyde exclaimed, "Well, that really don't surprise me much! All we are to them are some token cowboys that they can show off to their rich friends when it's convenient for them to do so. If they can show their rich friends and these miniranchers that this is still the Old West, they'll all feel good about ripping up all of this good open country. They can look out their windows or look up from their golf carts and believe that they've done very well. They can convince themselves that they are a part of its history."

Clyde gritted his teeth and glared toward the excavation sites, the torn earth, and giant, yellow machines. "I'm real thankful that you didn't tell me all of that until now, because I wanted to see the sun come up today over Wild Horse Ridge, and I wanted you to be here with me. I think it's time to quit this chickenshit outfit right now and blow out of here!"

The two men had long faces as they were preparing to load up their saddle horses inside their big-rig trailer and leave. There were still six horses tied to the side of the trailer when Fleebit glanced toward the big lodge and exclaimed, "Oh no! Here she comes!"

A richly dressed woman was running straight toward them and their horses, shrieking and frantically waving her arms in the air. The horses had their ears pointed, and their eyes were large and filled with terror. As she neared the horses, they were braced and ready to hang back on their ropes. When Clyde saw what was happening, he ran toward the woman, yelling, "Whoa there!" He stopped her just in time. It was the land developer's wife who had given Fleebit the work list yesterday.

"You can't be leaving!" the woman pleaded. "We are having a large reception tonight and tomorrow for potential buyers, and we told them that there would be real cows and real cowboys at our event. And I have so many things for you both to do. All of our guests will just adore seeing you!"

Clyde said, "Oh, we'll be back. We are just going to pick up our wardrobe and the Indians."

"What is this about your wardrobe and some Indians?" she asked.

Clyde casually turned around to his horses at the trailer. "Well, since you expected us to put on a show, we are going to put on our cavalry uniforms and chase Indians on horseback down through that big meadow in front of your lodge this afternoon. We're going to practice our reenactment of the Little Bighorn. We are going into Fanbelt to meet the Indians and pick up the costumes."

She said, "Oh my, I can't wait to tell everybody!" She turned and ran back toward the lodge, paddling the air with her arms as frantically as when she'd first appeared.

Fleebit started choking on a suppressed laugh until the lady disappeared inside the building, and then he cut loose in a baritone "Haw-haw-haw!" After he finally got his breath, he asked, "Why did you tell that lady all of that?"

Clyde tilted his hat back and looked Fleebit seriously in the eyes. "I just couldn't stand to see that woman cry over me leaving. I think she was falling in love with me! She told me that I was the most handsome man she'd ever seen."

"Seriously, Clyde, why did you tell her all of that baloney?"

"Okay, seriously! I wouldn't ride down in that meadow again for that woman if she gave me all fifty of those cows! Now let's get out of here quick before she comes running back here waving her arms and scaring my horses again. If my horses are scared of her, then we should be terrified, because she is probably crazy! Maybe we can find some Shoshone Indians in Fanbelt, get them drunk, and talk them into burning out these homesteaders!"

Fleebit took the wheel of their super truck and drove them away from the sadness of their boyhood dreams.

Clyde looked out the window at all of the new vacation homes that dotted the far-off landscape and said, "Before we fuel up for the long drive home, I need to stop at the post office in town and check my mail."

Fleebit asked, "Why don't you quit paying for this post office box here in Fanbelt, Wyoming! Heck's sake, you live half of the year in Big Scratch, Montana, and the other half on the road."

Clyde retorted, "Well, my inquiring friend who seems to know a hell of a lot about a post office but never reads or writes a letter, I have personal reasons for not wanting some people to know where I live. It's kind of like owning a fake camp where you might get shot at and sleeping elsewhere."

Fleebit asked, "What do you mean? Who might want to shoot at you? Is it that Mountain Lion family?"

"My paleface friend, you don't know what it's like to have so many distant relatives who show up at your door with a hard-luck story. I only paid for this post office box so I could receive letters from my aging mother in South Dakota while we worked around here. I found out that by using my white father's name of Morgan on the PO box, it was a lot easier to deal with white ranchers who wanted to find us and hire us. My Native American extended family could come looking for a relative who earned a regular paycheck but not have a key to where I lived.

"My mother passed on a long time ago, but I felt like I should keep this mailbox. I still get news from the reservation, and I like to know what's going on. There's some good news about my cousins and nephews who are doing great things for the earth and for our people.

"It's only a minority of people who I used to hang out with who would take me for my money or kill me. This post office forwards my mail to our Montana PO box at the end of each month. It might be money thrown away, but I'm a cowboy who likes to throw some dirt over his back trail. Pull over!"

Clyde came walking back to the truck from the post office grasping a torn envelope and reading a letter. He slid into the passenger seat and exclaimed, "Wow! John Baxter died and left me that quarter section of his ranch with the original homestead cabin attached to it! Let's fuel up and head home!"

Fleebit said, "Well, that's real good about John leaving you that eighty acres. It's the only ground that he didn't leave to the national forest. I was told that he made a deal with the government many years ago. All of his five-thousand-acre spread would go back to the Lolo National Forest. He could live on the ranch until he died, but he wouldn't have to pay any taxes on that big spread, and they could buy it from his sons at fair market value after he died. When his two sons left him and didn't come back to help run this big ranch, he worried a lot over what might become of it. When you started seeing after John's cows and checking up on his affairs, I guess he figured that he owed you something. I can't believe it! He left you the best part of the ranch!"

"No," said Clyde. "He left it to both of us!"

Fleebit replied, "Yeah, I worked for John Baxter some, but it was you who looked out for his affairs after he was all alone and too old to ride the range any longer."

As Fleebit pulled away from the post office, Clyde's mind was racing. "Now I own a place where I can settle down with roots, some land surrounded by national forest where I won't have any neighbors, and a place where I can retire in peace with my horses."

The idea pleased him greatly and made him feel more hopeful about the future.

Fleebit had seemed reluctant to come with Clyde this season. Since his mother in Big Scratch, Montana, passed away and left him her old home place outside the city limits, it was getting harder to get him out of town. He had his own place too!

He and Clyde remained best friends and worked together as top hands all over the West, working, sorting, and shipping cattle over great distances. Their two names traveled over a word-of-mouth telegraph wherever someone needed an important cowboy job done. These days, it seemed like the West had drastically changed, and the job was not all that important. A lot of the people who now owned a few cows acted self-important and demanding, and some of them didn't know the difference between a cow and a llama. Clyde just wasn't ready to give it up yet and take to the rocking chair, so Fleebit had endured some adventures back to their old home ranges that were well financed but often very disappointing in the long run.

3

IT WAS SO HARD TO REMEMBER EVERYTHING AND PUT things in place. Like one of the large jigsaw puzzles that her grandparents gave her when she was a little girl, it was a nature scene with hundreds of pieces. The mountain, the waterfall, the aspens, and the elk were strewn about on the table and difficult to put together in one large picture. There were five hundred pieces in this one, and it would take some time. They were scattered everywhere.

This nature puzzle and the coloring books of wildlife and landscapes were Christmas and birthday presents from her grandparents. They brought her to this place, but everything seemed out of place. *Sense of a home place takes me back to the ocean and Monterey Bay, not the Rocky Mountains.* Perhaps there was a mistake and the two puzzles became mixed up together in one box. That was it! She would have to sort out all of the pieces before she could begin to complete either picture.

It should be easy, because her whole life revolved around nature in wildlife and landscape settings. She would start with Monterey Bay. It was a regular outing for the Colter family. Her father spent most of his time at the law firm, but he reserved Sundays to take the family walking the footpaths or renting a boat so little Katie could watch the seals, otters, dolphins, and whales. The coloring books and puzzles were fun gifts from family members. But they eventually became dead things. You couldn't hear the wind, the crashing surf, or the bark of a seal. You couldn't smell the salt water, the kelp, or seaweed in crayons after you colored between the lines on paper.

You couldn't smell the earth, a scented wind, or the water in the television set, either. But Jack Hanna and Steve Irwin took her around the world with them while she was growing up and enriched her with a visual scope and vitality for wild animals and nature. She dearly loved Steve! He was her childhood hero, and he gave his life so that she could experience a ride on the back of a giant manta ray.

Katie cried out, "I don't want to tour the bay on Sundays anymore without Steve!"

For several days, she refused to eat until her father took her to a nice man who was a specialist. He seemed to be her only friend who understood how deeply she felt about Steve.

Then there was high school. Her friends liked surfing and beach parties, but none of them shared a common passion for the earth and its natural wonders. Only her best friend, Jess, liked to hike on the shoreline and ride mountain bikes with her in the foothills. Oftentimes, even she became bored from sitting with her for hours on end with binoculars, trying to spot an occasional whale breaking the surface.

She said, "KC, if you had a boyfriend, whale watching wouldn't take up so much of your time!"

High school seems to drag on forever, and I can't wait to enter college. Daddy wants me to become an attorney like him. That could be my second or third choice, and then it would have to be environmental law. I want to do something in life that will make a difference for the natural world. Perhaps I'll become a wildlife biologist or a botanist, or maybe I'll get a forestry management degree.

I can go to any school with a scholarship ride, but before I can choose, I need to know a lot more. I need to read everything on the Internet about climate change.

Katie cried out, "I'm about done on the computer. I'll be in to eat soon. I promise!" She continued reading.

The world's leading scientists are announcing today that the arctic ice is melting ten times faster than formally predicted. The greenhouse gases in our atmosphere have accelerated a warming trend that could reach a tipping point, possibly a point of no return! Freshwater glaciers around the world that produce drinking water for millions of people are vanishing in some of the most populated countries of the world.

"Daddy, I already ate today, and I'm not hungry! I'm about finished with this program."

In Alaska, Eskimo villages are being relocated because of melting permafrost and rising water. Their culture of survival with dogsled teams is being replaced by motorboats. Their traditional hunting grounds are becoming barren of fish, seals, and walrus.

The polar bears are being threatened by starvation and drowning by miles and miles of open water. The cubs are most in danger!

The rain forests are rapidly disappearing from burning off many square miles for timbering and commercial farming. Thousands of acres of old-growth trees that clean our air and cool our planet are being shipped to China. Plants and animals, many rare and yet undocumented, are facing extinction.

The Great Plains throughout much of the United States heartland once supported millions of bison on native prairie grasses. They were replaced with modern agriculture and cattle. Today, deep aquifers are being pumped dry to support thriving local economies. Professional hydrologists claim that deep underground rivers that took thousands of years to fill may never come back.

"Okay, Mom! I heard you. I'll be there in a minute!"

Oil companies are using hydrofracking to release pockets of oil and natural gas. Protected by US patent laws, they are not required to divulge the types of chemicals they pump into the earth. In areas with much drilling, water wells and natural springs are becoming unfit to drink.

"Katie, dear! Please come and eat. Your dinner is getting cold!"

"It don't matter what college I attend. This is too much for one person to change. It's all so depressing! What kind of future is there beyond the tipping point? Why would I ever want to have children? What future would they have? Steve is dead. At least he won't have to see all of the animals die!"

Katie stirred in her sleep and tried to sort out the pieces of the other puzzle—the picture of the Rocky Mountains. *The pieces are still mixed up. I've got to finish with the ocean scene first ... I don't want to go to college. There isn't time! Can't you just get it? By the time that I finish four, six, or seven years of college, there won't be anything left to save ... I don't want to ride my bike, and I don't feel like going to the beach. Why would I go to a party with people who don't understand?*

"Mom, I already told you, I'm not hungry!"

"But, Katie, your father and I remember when you behaved this way after Steve Irwin's death."

Katie cried out, "Why can't you just leave me alone!"

"Katie, wake up! This is your dad, and you've been sleeping for days. You need to eat something. I called an old friend in Vermont, and his son is very active in the environmental movement. This young man initiated a grassroots campaign that influenced Vermont state legislators to ban hydrofracking in their state. He's an active member of the Sierra Club and a hometown, local hero. Besides that, your mother thinks he's handsome! Now wake up, because he's coming to visit tonight. He wants to talk with you about working with their group."

"Daddy! Is that you?"

The mountains! The waterfall! The aspen forest! And, oh yes, the elk! The pieces of the puzzle were fitting together now, becoming one clear picture. Katie awoke in a daze and was gasping for breath. She pushed her face away from the inflated air bag and breathed in deeply. She sucked in the fragrant scent of aspens and cool mountain air.

Okay, her head was clearing now. She could remember returning from East Park, where she found her grandmother's keepsake. She'd lost it during the protest against the clear-cutting operation. Their group was attacked by some men after sundown. The hospital treated the guys for minor injuries. The sheriff interviewed them and told them to get out of town. Their group was splitting up at a gas station and preparing to return home when she noticed that her prized possession was missing.

Instead of heading directly toward the interstate highway like everyone else, she headed back up the mountain to search for her grandmother's ivory elephant, encased in a golden locket.

When she returned, the trees had all been cut down and hauled away. Out of the corner of her eye, a flicker of gold in the fading sunlight revealed the broken chain that lay embedded in a deep bulldozer track. It was buried in the dirt where she had been chained to a machine. She quickly grabbed it out of the dirt and ran back to her car. She raced away, heading back down the mountain toward the interstate highway. She was driving around the curve when the elk jumped out in front of her car.

Katie opened the door and stood up. She stretched her arms wide. She picked up her legs one at a time and wiggled her toes. She looked around her and said, "Boy, are you lucky!" She suddenly realized that her car had skidded through a narrow opening in a long alley between majestic, tall aspens with wide, white trunks. "Just hitting any of one of them would have killed me!"

Her car came to rest inside a small, green meadow. It was a short distance from the main road, and her car was probably hidden from view. "Now what about the car?" She walked around it. It appeared that all she had to do was change the flat tire and drive back into Big Scratch to repair the flat and replace the window for the drive back home to California.

"No, forget repairing the flat and replacing the window!" Instinct told her that she should get far away from here to fix those things. The car seemed to be intact except for a dented bumper and a cracked windshield. "Now, will it start?" She deflated the air bag with her Swiss Army knife and started the engine. "Everything is good!" She could see well enough through the windshield to get beyond Big Scratch, Montana.

She'd been doing these kind of protest demonstrations for three years now and had never run into a vigilante, redneck town like this before. Now that she had her locket, she was getting out of this area. She felt bad about hitting the elk. It was her fault for driving too fast and not paying enough attention.

She had the car jacked up and was preparing to mount her spare tire when she became very dizzy. She staggered backward and came to rest with her back braced against a large, old-growth aspen.

She thought, *Okay, I passed a big ranch gate just before I came around that curve and hit the elk. I can't lift the tire, and I'm not fit to drive right now. A friendly person will find me here. I just need to rest a minute, and I'll be able to mount that tire and leave.*

Katie thought about the other trips she'd been on, doing similar things to stop the carnage. When Josh rescued her from her depression and got her involved in the movement, she felt alive again. Her appetite returned, and she gained some weight. She could camp out with people who had a common cause, and it was fun. They were a mobile army, defending the earth from companies and big corporations that polluted and destroyed the earth.

They'd been arrested several times in the past and used private donation money for bail. Josh always made sure that they had adequate funds for food, gas, and bail before they set out on one of their cross-country missions. Katie's father pulled some strings more than once and got them released without charges. He knew some people who could turn the wheels of justice over minor offenses.

It gave the group confidence that her father was an attorney who was sympathetic to their cause. But he regularly cautioned her and them against causing personal injury or getting caught destroying private property. Josh insisted that their mission should be peaceful. Their mission was to slow down the destruction and let the public news media inform the world. Public pressure would force the politicians to shut it down.

Her father and mother worried about her each time she left home, but they could see a light in her eyes, and she looked healthy again. Her secretive, random exploits were the trade-off between her depression and anorexia. Before she became active with this group, they knew she was dying. They hadn't had much hope for her recovery three years ago.

Katie looked up at the sky. Puffy, gray clouds were sinking down low over the forest canopy, and it smelled like rain. She could hear the deep rumble of an engine coming slowly up the road. She picked up a stick, unfolded her sharp pocketknife, and began slicing away at the end, creating a short, sharp-pointed spear. She felt weak and lightheaded, and she couldn't sit in this posture any longer. She grasped her locket in her left hand and lay down beside the stick on her left side, facing the large, white aspen trunk.

Katie focused upon the soft, white bark and thought, *How amazing! An aspen can tell its life history from the slightest scratch upon its surface.*

She thought about Steve.

4

CLYDE JUMPED INTO THE DRIVER'S SEAT OF THE F-350 KING

Ranch pickup truck while Fleebit was checking the oil underneath the hood. He slid the seat forward and adjusted the large wing mirrors.

Fleebit shut the hood and saw Clyde with his hands resting on the steering wheel. *He never drives! What in the hell is he up to? And why is he staring a hole through me with that bird-of-prey look in his eyes? Why is Clyde giving me the evil eye? What did I do wrong now?* Fleebit thought. *I can't deal with this now. I need to sit down and think things out.* Fleebit shut the hood and walked away toward the Quick Mart.

Clyde yelled, "Where are you going?"

Fleebit mumbled, "I have a pressing matter to attend to."

Clyde responded, "I thought you just did that, not four miles from here!"

Fleebit ignored Clyde's menacing look and shuffled away in short steps. Upon entering the busy store, he paused to smile just inside the door and tip his hat at the pretty checkout girl at the counter. She ignored him and directed an irritated reply into the face of a tourist. "All I know is this: if those goddamned environmentalists come to Wyoming and mess with our jobs, they might all become missing persons!"

Fleebit quickly brushed past the small, startled man and was relieved to find that the communal restroom door was unlocked. He locked the door behind him and looked into the mirror. "You handsome devil, you! Six foot six inches tall and three feet wide across the shoulders—every rodeo queen's best dream and every steer's worse nightmare!"

This big, private, handicapped restroom was a place where a big man like him could relax for a minute and sort things out. He hadn't been going regular lately. The stress from living out in the wild country with a primitive bathroom environment had caused him to lock up. He couldn't get a chance to relax for long, because Clyde was always yelling, "Hurry up! Let's get down the road! We have a contract to get to!"

Fleebit thought, *Clyde can wait a spell. Indians are real good about waiting. They can let time pass slowly without getting upset.* Then he reckoned, *Well, Clyde is only half-Indian, and his patience might not last too long!*

When they were trapping wild cattle down in southern Utah for the Ute Indian tribe, he'd been forced to sit over a log. It was hard for him to find any big trees that could support his heavy frame, and one morning, he was running out of time. His horse was in full-running stride chasing some cows when nature screamed at him. He pulled the steel bridle bit back into the corners of his horse's mouth and yelled, "Whoa!" Sliding his horse to a stop, he leaped off his running mount and quickly wrapped his reins around the limb of a dead aspen lying horizontally across the trail. Fleebit pulled his pants down and perched himself over the rotten log. Then, just as he relaxed and everything started to flow, his horse walked forward with reins tied to his perch and began pulling on the tree. Then he snorted, hung back, and broke off the limb. He trotted away after the fleeing cattle. The dead tree popped and cracked, dropping him to the ground, while his stream shot wildly over his right leg and soaked his boot. His horse ran off without him, headed toward Clyde and the cow trap, dragging a broken tree limb down the mountain in a cloud of dust.

And then they stayed in that isolated cow camp down in New Mexico where they were hired to clear the range of cattle for a bank that held the mortgage on them. That old outhouse roof had leaked for a hundred years, and the wooden seat was warped and splintered. He hunted around until he found a sandstone rock and then used it to grind off the splinters before he could sit down. Smooth and seated, he suddenly remembered a terrifying caution and jumped high off of the seat! He'd forgotten to look down the hole for rattlesnakes and under the seat for black widow spiders.

Fleebit thought, *Yeah, it sure would be good to sit here and relax, think about some things, and work everything out in a safe, stress-free environment.*

There was a knock on the restroom door. A squeaky, high-pitched man's voice exclaimed, "Hey, I have to go! Is anybody in there?"

Fleebit yelled in his deepest baritone voice, "Occupied!"

Fleebit thought, *Why did Clyde take over the driver's seat and stare me in the eye like that? What did I do wrong now? Maybe one of the horses has a scratch on him, and I didn't see it. That could really piss him off! Maybe Clyde is still mad at me for letting that bunch of wild cows get away.*

Those Indian eyes! Those same eyes that Clyde could make piercing and terrifying were also the same soft eyes that drove the ladies insane. Everywhere they traveled, some woman would flirt with Clyde and tell him that he had the most beautiful eyes. "Oh!" they would say. "A girl would just kill to have those big, hazel eyes and long lashes!"

Fleebit was getting real tired of having good-looking women approach him only to make inquiries and small talk about Clyde. Fleebit considered himself to be a downright handsome man, and he had his own following of admirers back home. His girls liked to brag about his Clint Eastwood looks. May thought he was a sexy

Rowdy Yates. Helga thought he was a Dirty Harry. Ellen called him the Enforcer! They all thought he was hot!

Clyde knew that this could take a while. He was patient, but not when it came to stupidity. He decided to kill the time by washing all of the windows on the big crew-cab truck and the side windows on the six-horse trailer. The big truck and long horse trailer blocked both gas pumps in one lane beneath the large, steel canopy. The other lane was empty, so he took his time. Clyde was standing on his tiptoes with a long-handled squeegee sponge that was soaking wet. He leaned over the hood to reach the center of the windshield when something bumped hard against the horse trailer from behind. It jolted the six slant-tied animals forward with a banging and scuffling of many unbalanced feet. The six horses became afraid and whinnied loudly.

In a flash, Clyde was at the back of the horse trailer, where he discovered a chrome-infested, orange-and-black tiger-striped Hummer with a rack of big lights that could light up an indoor stadium. It was parked an inch away from the back of his rig.

The fat, soft face of the driver was turned inward and midway between the passenger seat and the occupants in the backseat. He and the occupants around him were roaring shouts of victory and laughing loudly together. The left-side driver window was down when Clyde appeared suddenly from out of nowhere.

Clyde reached through the open side window with the long-handled, thick foam brush, soaked with dirty, soapy water and thickened by untold miles of yellow bug guts. He jammed a full pint of the stinking mixture into the man's left ear and cheek. It soaked him and ran down the front of his shirt. When the surprised man gasped from the sudden shock and spun around, Clyde pushed the soggy foam brush into his open mouth and held it there, filling his open mouth with gore and pinning him against the safari-print seat cover.

The terrified driver began choking. Clyde pulled it out of the window and took a step backward. He swapped ends with the soap brush, revealing a menacing, long wooden stick pointed directly into the man's frightened face. Clyde could see two of the passengers inside the Hummer frantically trying to call out on their cell phones.

Clyde shouted into the open window, "You dumb ass! So you think it's funny, huh? You just made a priceless load of horses step all over each other in that trailer! I think you need to be taught a lesson! Step out of that machine so I can ram you from behind with this long handle!"

The driver quickly started his machine while trying to roll up his window and throw it in reverse. Clyde poked him in the ear just as the window snapped shut tightly around the wooden handle. It jerked out of Clyde's hands and dangled sideways out the window as the Hummer burned rubber backward and roared away from the Quick Mart.

There came a *boom! boom! boom!* against the hollow, fireproof, steel-framed door of the restroom. The same desperate, shrill voice shouted against the door, "Are you about done in there? This is the only restroom, and I need to get in there soon!"

Fleebit bellowed out in his deepest, earth-shattering voice, "Get away from that door, you pip-squeak, or I'll stick your head in this hole when I'm done with it!"

He reflected on how Clyde had kept him away from home where he had girlfriends. When he was with Clyde, he had to play second fiddle. When there was a buffet of pretty girls at a rodeo, he always got to pick through the leftovers. It was always Clyde they went after first. Young girls fresh out of high school flirted with Clyde and mentioned his eyes, his midlength, jet-black hair, and his perfect tan. Clyde either reminded them of Elvis or a picture of Jesus. *It is sickening, for Christ's sake!* he fumed.

He'd only recently overheard two ladies over in the next aisle at a grocery store comment about Clyde's wide shoulders, slim waist, and tight ass.

Fleebit thought, *I can't believe how times have changed. Nowadays, young women are so bold about saying things and going after a man they want, even if it's a much older man! Clyde knows he looks thirty-five instead of fifty-eight, and he thinks these younger women don't know what they're getting into.*

But Fleebit knew better. When he opened up the door of their horse trailer at a rodeo and found a twenty-one-year-old barrel racer lying naked and waiting for Clyde, he quickly ran her off and later confronted Clyde. "These younger women know what they want when they see it, all right. They just don't care!"

Fleebit had seen a lot of women throw themselves in front of Clyde, especially after the pair of them won the team roping event at a big jackpot or rodeo with a five- to ten-thousand-dollar split. But the amazing thing about Clyde was that he never let it go to his head. He even had a line for brushing women off that most men wish they could use to get with them. He could accept a compliment and then tell a girl good-bye while making her think that she had the privilege of royalty.

Then there was Clyde's code of cowboy ethics: "Don't mess with another man's woman!" Fleebit saw women sneak away from their husbands and boyfriends during a rodeo. They would slip away between rows and rows of parked horse trailers to find Clyde, unsaddling and grooming his horses in the darkness after an event.

Fleebit thought, *Clyde is always too particular or has a good excuse for riding away from a relationship. It wasn't always that way! He used to be a lot of fun at rodeo dances and social activities. Then he fell in love with that schoolteacher from back east. He let her slip away and has regretted it ever since. Now he drives both of us hard from spring to fall between roundups and rodeos. It's always "Hurry up! Daylight's burning! Let's get down the road!"*

Fleebit thought, *The only thing that will slow him down and get him off my ass is a new woman!*

Boom-boom-boom! Boom-boom-boom! A gruff voice yelled, "Hey, you in there! This is the manager, and you've been in there much too long! My customers are complaining about your rude behavior, and I've called the cops. A week ago, a man committed suicide on that toilet seat and splattered blood and brains everywhere. It cost me a lot of money to clean up that mess. Those wet brains peeled off all of the paint, and it was very expensive to replace this steel door after the cops busted it down!"

Fleebit threw open the door with a loud bang and lunged into a chunky, gruff-looking attendant in a red-and-blue uniform. Hunkered down behind him was a short man wetting his pants. Fleebit bumped them both against a vanity and bolted through the store, racing toward the parking lot. He was still trying to tuck in his shirt and fasten his big championship belt buckle as he ran out of the store.

"Damn! Clyde is nowhere in sight!" He quickly concluded that Clyde was angry with him over something and had driven off without him. With no alternatives left, he sprinted around the corner and took off down the street. He glanced over his right shoulder and noticed their rig parked around in back of the store.

He ran around the building just as two cop cars roared up to the front of the store with red and blue lights flashing. Four men ran inside the store with hands reaching for the guns at their hips.

Clyde demanded, "What in the hell took you so long in there? Why are those cops here? Did you rob that place?"

Fleebit stammered, "No, but they robbed me from having a peaceful bowel movement. Move over so we can get out of here quick! Hey, why are you in the driver's seat? You never drive on these long runs unless I can't stay awake or I've been drinking with the boys. I'm not a bit sleepy!"

Clyde growled, "Get in!"

Clyde pulled out of the Quick Mart in Fanbelt, Wyoming, leaving the Wind River Range behind. He accelerated down State Highway 287, heading northwest toward their home range in Montana. The golden aspen canopy and tall ponderosa pines flew past the windows quickly as Fleebit stared out the passenger-side window.

The northwest traffic was light, with occasional family campers heading home before their kids started school, traveling much too slowly for homeward-bound cowboys with a big, fast horse. Pickup trucks with out-of-state plates pulling small, two-wheel trailers met them coming from the opposite direction—hunters arriving for the Wyoming elk hunt. The country changed with the drop in elevation. Scrub pine and sagebrush now covered a broad expanse as far as both eyes could see. A gentle rain fell softly in the night, and the pungent fragrance of damp sage came in through the open vent in the top of the cab.

"Fleebit, you are staring at that window like a blind man and not saying a word because you know! And I know you know why I'm driving this truck instead of you!"

Fleebit remained silent and frozen toward the passenger-side window.

"I am driving this truck so that we can talk about something, and if you were driving, you would probably drive off of the road and kill us all when you hear what I have to say. That woman back there got to you, didn't she? When she waved that list in your face and told you that it didn't take all day for you to watch some cows eat grass and told you to work on her swimming pool, you froze up! Didn't you? You got lockjaw and nearly had a stroke because of that. I've seen you do that a couple of times, and it scared the hell out of me both times.

"Now it's one thing for those people to kill all of that wide-open country back there, but it's quite another when they almost kill my best friend. And I know you wanted to tell that woman off, but you couldn't. You wanted to tell her that you had pride and that she was insulting you, but you didn't. I understand you couldn't tell her off, but you don't have to be afraid to tell me right away when something like this happens. Now you don't need to act like you're in trouble anymore. I'm going to pull over up here now and let you drive. You are braver than me at passing those big Winnebagos!"

Clyde thought about the fancy, rich, married woman they were leaving behind in the dust. She had been really hot for him the night before! She wanted to play miniranch cattle queen or cowboys and

Indians after sundown. When nobody was around, she found him alone with his horses and pushed her breasts into him. She shoved him against the corral poles and invitingly suggested that the two of them share the hot tub together at the stroke of midnight.

She probably gave Fleebit that work list just to get rid of him so that she could get Clyde alone in the hot tub. Clyde laughed silently and thought, *I received an invitation to go skinny-dipping, and Fleebit got a work order to clean the pool! That work list scared him almost to death. I could never tell him. Well, maybe someday.*

As Fleebit took the wheel, Clyde took over the radio and scanned back and forth on the dial, searching for a particular station: static ... Spanish ... hard rock ... revival Spanish polka ... static.

Fleebit said, "I know what station you're trying to find, and you can't get that one until we circle around under the Madison Range. And it's that damned environmental talk show that gets your Indian blood a-boiling, and we always get into an argument. Besides that, they play that screechy electric-guitar music that hurts my ears. Just find us a country station!"

Clyde said, "I've heard that they put up a new radio tower on this side, and I'll pick it up in a minute."

Fleebit asked, "Where did you hear that news while we've been chasing cows out in the middle of nowhere all summer?"

Clyde turned the radio dial back and forth, back and forth. "A coyote told me one morning out in the Book Cliff Mountains while you were sleeping in."

"You are full of it," said Fleebit. "If you are Indian enough to talk to animals, tell me how a coyote in Utah knew about a new radio transmitter way up here in Montana?"

"He told me that a sandhill crane was passing through, and it told a crow that told him. He said that the sandhills were real pissed off because that new transmission tower interrupted their migrational flight pattern."

Fleebit said, "I call bullshit with a capital *B*!"

"Hey, quiet now! Here it is."

In a few minutes, we are going to have an interview between timber-logging interests and representatives of the Sierra Club over clear-cutting our national forests and public lands. This heated debate comes on the heels of the national news story about Katie Colter, the twenty-three-year-old California girl last seen in Big Scratch, Montana, four months ago after her group of Sierra Club members attempted a peaceful protest by chaining themselves to logging equipment in a national forest clear-cut near East Park.

Local officials arrived on the scene to find the group beaten by unknown assailants. They were treated at the local hospital and released without charges. The four-month-long investigation still continues for information or leads about the missing woman.

Clyde said, "I hope that girl is still alive and that some of our local hotheads haven't gone too far with this environmental war."

Fleebit yelled, "Will you turn down that loud rock-and-roll crap so I can hear myself think?"

Clyde turned the radio off. "There now, what is it?"

Fleebit shook his head from side to side. "I feel bad for that missing girl, but she shouldn't have come here in the first place. Those California people shouldn't be telling local Montana people how to live and what to do. Heck, they brought us those damned wolves that are eating up all of our elk in Wyoming, Idaho, and Montana!"

Clyde became defensive. "This talk show and news story about a missing girl is related to clear-cutting on the national forest. The radio didn't tell us that Katie Colter had some wolves tucked away in her suitcase when she came to our hometown. But since you always bring up the topic of wolves, let's talk about wolves! I agree that the wolf experiment went bad, and they got overpopulated, but you can buy a license to kill four-legged wolves now. When they get thinned out, the elk will come back, and I believe that the elk herds will be stronger. We'll have to see. But the worse kind of wolf has two legs, and they are killing more elk than the four-legged kind ever will! They kill herds of elk for generations to come, and you can't do anything about it."

"What do you mean?" asked Fleebit.

"What I'm saying is, these real-estate developers are eating up these big ranches that are critical elk winter and summer range. They are the alpha wolves! After they swallow up thousands of acres of elk habitat, they regurgitate it up into small pieces to feed the wolf pups."

Fleebit blurted, "That is nonsense! Feed what pups? I think that screechy music has wrecked your mind!"

"My friend, every year, millions of people throughout the world visit our national parks up here, spending a week or so in paradise with nature at its best—a perfect world! And when they are heading back to their cities with their noise, pollution, and social problems, they see a billboard sign advertising ranchettes for sale just outside the borders of paradise. And they want to buy into it. Those are the innocent wolf pups that migrate out of our national parks and gobble down the small pieces of future elk herds. They fence and cross fence the land until it's a death trap of wire to big moving herds. They build new roads to everywhere, and the elk get killed by the traffic. Plastic shopping bags tagged on barb wire flap in the wind and flag them howdy from a different world. You cannot kill a two-legged wolf. They are protected for life. But there is one thing a concerned citizen can do about this predation. Stop the truck after you get to this straight section up here."

"What for? Why? What's wrong?" stammered Fleebit.

"Just like last time!"

"Oh no! You scared the hell out of me that last time, and Clyde, we are going to get caught and arrested!"

"But we didn't get caught, did we? And what are you afraid of anyway? Heights?"

Fleebit shouted, "Well, yeah! I tried to be your lookout while you ran off into the brush with that chain saw running. I surely do realize that the open west is getting torn up by these developers, but I don't want to see us get thrown in jail and have our rig impounded."

Clyde said, "Just pull over! It will be just like last time. I'll rest good this winter in the company of the Big Scratch head-up-their-asses political monopoly. I'll have the personal satisfaction of trying to save a rare piece of Wyoming."

Fleebit started pushing a little harder on the gas pedal while explaining, "I really tried to help you cut down that real-estate billboard sign. But, Clyde! My balance isn't as good as it once was! I got the nervous shakes up there when I saw that white car come speeding around that curve. I thought it was the highway patrol. I was waving my big hat back and forth at you, and you wouldn't look at me. I was yelling at you, and you couldn't hear me over that loud saw. I almost fell off the top of the horse trailer!"

Clyde said, "Yeah, I looked around. I see a lot more than you think I do. When that white car full of Chinese tourists came past us, you looked like you were posing for a portrait. They were all waving at you with big smiles and shiny teeth. They slowed way down and took your picture too. That is why I send you up on top and tell you to stand up tall. You are the attraction distraction! Those tourists saw a big cowboy waving his hat at them like the picture on the Welcome to Wyoming sign. They thought you were the real, authentic, cowboy image saying, 'Thanks for coming! Y'all come back!' What those people didn't see was me making firewood out of a Miniranches and Ranchettes for Sale sign.

"*Ranchettes!* That really sounds like something wolf pups would love to eat, kinda like chicken nuggets or tender steak briquettes. Ranchette briquettes. Tasty! The tourists keep coming to our country every year and gobble them down."

"We saved some elk from the wolves that last time. Those Chinese tourists might have gobbled down that whole ranch and ate those elk herds with chopsticks! So pull over here, and we'll do it just like last time. There are a lot of wolf pups heading through here from Jellystone right now, so it's the best time to get rid of wolves!"

"No, Clyde, I just want to go home!"

Clyde asked, "If I give in and don't cut down this sign, will you do me a favor?"

Fleebit blurted out, "I'm not going to let you drive! You might pull down across the ditch and try to push over all of the real-estate signs between here and home. Besides, half of this rig belongs to me, and I don't want any scratches on it."

Clyde glanced out his window at the open landscape and sniffed in the smell of damp sage. "I don't want to drive. I want to stop at the John Baxter cabin on the way home and make a tobacco offering to John's spirit. I think I owe him that. You can sit in the truck and wait or go off and leave me—either way."

Fleebit shuffled in his seat and adjusted a mirror. "We can't get this big rig very close. We'll have to unload and ride two miles, but we have a lot of daylight left, and it might be the last chance we get before winter sets in. I'm with you, Captain!"

Clyde thought, *He can't wait to get into town and strut his stuff with those old women and stuffy churchgoers. The West has gone to shit! Fleebit goes to shit and loses $5,000 worth of cattle.*

Clyde wanted to hear that talk show about the national forest clear-cutting debate, but he knew that Fleebit would get upset. He didn't seem to understand the difference between a debate and an argument when it came to environmental issues. He was easily influenced by the hometown crowd who was looking for a fight instead of a compromise. It was a cowboys-against-the-Indians mentality that Clyde took personally.

Being a cowboy and an Indian, he could weigh both sides of an issue and fight for the underdog on either side if their cause was just. It was his half-breed mentality!

Clyde turned off the radio and closed his eyes. As they accelerated down the highway toward home, he tried to picture the young girl and her life growing up in California. He thought, *She came all the way out here and risked her life to save the trees and Mother Earth because of global warming. Whatever happened to poor little Katie Colter?*

5

A BRILLIANT, GOLDEN CARPET OF ASPEN LEAVES SURROUNDED
and covered the roof of the small, hand-hewn cabin, cast down from tall, white, shining trunks rising up like pillars supporting heaven above the earth. A supernatural architecture connected the known with the unknown.

A silent, vertical highway to heaven revealed those who went before and made the ascent—countless black scratches embedded in thick, white aspen bark revealed a road map of bears climbing up and disappearing into a crystal-blue sky.

Clyde looked up the tall trees toward the sky and then walked a silent, private circle around the small, hand-hewn log cabin. He sprinkled some loose-leaf tobacco into the golden leaves until his full circle of steps was completed. He walked over to Fleebit, who was holding his horse by the reins.

"Let's unsaddle and stay here all night. It's going to get dark soon. There's a lot of grass in that big corral, and the horses are leg weary from the long drive."

Fleebit was irritated. "You said we would come up here and then go home. You promised!"

Clyde said, "Go ahead and leave. Just leave all of those horses here and walk back to the truck and trailer on foot. When you get back to town, you are going to forget all about your horses, anyway, and pursue something that you can do with your two big feet. This morning, you told me that you preferred the smell of French perfume over horse sweat.

"Why are you in such a hurry to get back to town? You'll have all winter to bellow, fart, and shake your horns down the backstreets of Big Scratch. Yeah, you can tell when old cowboys have given up and are ready to die!"

"What do you mean by that snide remark?" growled Fleebit.

Clyde turned away and began unsaddling his horse. "An old cowboy is like an old bull that bellows loud, paws the ground, and shakes his horns from side to side. He wants the old cows to think he still has it, but he puts on the biggest show because he's more concerned about a younger bull thinking he's a cow."

Fleebit became upset. "Now I take offense to that! I'm not washed up yet! I'm like a finely groomed prize bull at the fairgrounds when I get home, not some stringy range bull that's worth half the price of beef on the open market. And I'm not afraid of some younger bull neither. When I shake my horns, somebody had better get the hell out of my way!"

Clyde laughed and shook his head. "Let's turn these horses loose, and I'll get the woodstove going inside the cabin so you'll be warm and safe inside tonight, sleeping on a real bed. It might get cool tonight, and I don't want you to catch a chill. I don't want you to have a cough or a sniffle when you slobber in the faces of your cow herd when you get home. I'll rustle us up some food. If you're going to stay here, build us an outside campfire without torching my cabin and burning down my barn. Forty years ago, you almost burned me to death in your truck!"

Fleebit said, "Yeah, your daddy was probably a pistol, and you became a rock-chuckin' son of a gun. You almost killed me that night! I guess it won't hurt to stay up here one night, but promise me that we'll leave first thing in the morning. I sure wouldn't mind feasting on one of those slow-roasted pine birds for dinner."

Clyde pulled his saddle off and scratched his horse's back with his fingers. "I doubt there are any pine hens around this big aspen grove, but there's canned goods inside, and I hid some canned peaches in the wood box where nobody would find them."

Darkness came quickly, and the flickering firelight cast a golden glow outward between the log barn and cabin. The horses moved about in silent shadows, cropping tall grasses inside the pole corral. Clyde came out of the cabin carrying two tin graniteware plates heaping full of steaming pork and beans on a bed of white rice. He went back inside and brought out two large cans of peaches. "No meat on the menu tonight! You can fill up on that tomorrow and call it dessert."

Fleebit rinsed off their plates in the gurgling spring and refilled their tin cups with the cold, pure water. He pulled a pint of whiskey out of his saddlebag. "Let's have a drink to John Baxter!"

Clyde threw a chunk of wood on the fire. "It sure was good of John to leave us this place where we can wait out old age ... although there won't be any cows on this range to tend, and there won't be any golf courses or miniranches, either. I stayed up here many times when I worked for John, but it sure looks different since my name is on the deed to this land."

"Do you have a last will and testament?" asked Fleebit.

Clyde bluntly inquired, "If I had a will made out, why do you want to know? If you knew you were the heir to my silver bits and spur collection, you might drop a rattlesnake down the outhouse hole on your way out and my way in. If a poisonous snake bit me on the ass and I ran back to the cabin and asked you to suck out the poison, you'd say, 'Oh man, you're going to die!' And that would be it! Next day, you would be riding my fancy bay gelding down to the widow Jorgenstein's place, and there would be a fancy silver bit in my horse's mouth and some fancy silver spurs strapped to your big feet. Knowing you, you'd hire a bulldozer and just bury me in that poop pit over there!"

Fleebit laughed. "Clyde, you are so full of it. Anyway, you would blend in fine with a funeral arrangement like that. I only asked you about a will because my daughter recently asked me, and I thought maybe you could help me decipher it some, and I could understand it a little better myself."

Clyde's eyes began to glaze over, and he looked upward toward the sky. "How did you answer your daughter's hard question?"

"I told her that I'd thought it out on what I wanted done with my remains. I told her that I'd spent my whole life outdoors on the back of a good horse in big, wide-open country and that I've lived off the land by eating the wild game from the forests and prairies and wild trout from the lakes and streams. I said, 'I want my remains given back to all of that which gave to me.'

"My daughter asked, 'So you want to be cremated, then, and have your ashes spread at a little spot on some ranch in the Rocky Mountains?'

"I said, 'Heck, no! It's a little bit more complicated than that. I want my body spread out over every ranch I worked for in five different states. I want my remains frozen after I die—and I don't want chemicals put inside my body to preserve it. I've drunk enough good whiskey in my lifetime to take care of all of that. Anyway, I want to be fresh meat. I want you to take my frozen body to Delmer's Wild Game Processing and have him saw me up into small chunks and pieces. Then I want you to take these pieces of my flesh to different places and feed the wild animals, the fish, trees, flowers and grasses that fed me and my horses for all these long years.'

'I want my pieces of flesh and bone to be scattered over the earth. I want one of my hind quarters ground up into burger and I want you to spread my hamburger down every river and creek so that all of the little fishes can get a bite.'

'I will make a list of all the places where I want my body to go, and there will be a detailed map of how to get to each place. I've saved up a little money over the years to pay for the meat processing, all of the Coleman coolers, dry ice, and gasoline to get me there.'"

Clyde asked, "What did your daughter say to all of that?"

Fleebit hesitated, stammered, and replied, "She got plumb ornery and said, 'Dad, you've been watching too many *Lonesome Dove* reruns. You are not Augustus McCrae, and I am *not* or ever will be Captain Call!'"

Clyde asked, "What in the hell were you thinking? That would be a gruesome task for a daughter. Can't you imagine? And don't expect me to do it, either. *N-o, no!* Don't even think about it! It's probably against the law, anyway. Don't be so weird! And don't you ever call me 'Captain' again!"

6

AS SENIOR BIOLOGIST ON THE BEAR CAPTURE AND
relocation project, Tim addressed a group of journalists out in
the field. "You've all seen the video of the biologist who released
a captured adult male grizzly bear from a culvert trap and how
suddenly everything went wrong! We now make sure that everyone
is a safe distance away when we open the trapdoor. The public
should be inside a vehicle with windows shut tight and doors firmly
locked when we release a tranquilized bear. We very seldom invite
untrained people to join us during a release.

"I know that some of you who are with us today documenting
this release for the news media might have sympathetic views about
what we're doing in our organization and about the future of this
bear. Our hard line is this: three strikes, and a bear is out! We will
relocate it twice. If it comes back a third time and we can't donate it
to a zoo, it's basically a dead bear!

"From private video, we know that the bear in our culvert trap
has broken into a cabin. But there is an unknown factor here, as
well. This bear could be taking the blame for other incidents around
this area that other undocumented bears are committing. That is
why our research is so important! Our priority is to keep the public
safe, to try to document numbers of bears, and try to keep innocent

bears from facing the death penalty. Now that our captured bear is wearing a radio collar, we will be able to monitor his movements."

Tim continued, "Very often, bears do come back to where they remember finding an easy meal. We are using a new preventive measure to try to stop this. Since our funds are limited, just one problem bear who is a repeat offender can exhaust our funding and resources. Our new release method is proving very effective. Instead of a quiet, tame release, we now give the bear a frightening experience that he can associate with bad bear behavior."

Tim said, "Okay, our bear is fully awake now. Everybody cab up!" When Tim was sure that the news reporters were safely locked in their truck, he asked his crew, "Are you all ready?"

Jenny's two trained Karelian bear dogs had been bred in Russia to pursue giant Kodiak bears. They were fearless and excited over the anticipation of another release.

Jenny replied, "Anytime, boss!"

Collin said, "Just say when!"

Maggie said, "Ready!"

Tim began backing the 4×4 pickup truck in reverse. The front bumper guard was attached to a long steel cable that extended to the culvert trap. It stretched tightly over the pulley on top of the steel trapdoor. The truck rolled far back, and the door lifted up and open. Tim's crew was braced and ready, standing beside open truck doors on both sides.

"Now!"

The bear lunged out of the culvert trap to freedom amid loud shouts of "Hey, bear!" "Go, bear!" "Bad bear!" Barking dogs loudly shrieked with adrenaline, expressing their desire for the chase. Tim fired firecracker shells behind the bear. M-80 explosions erupted behind his galloping back feet. Collin hit him in the ass with two or three rubber bullets from a semiautomatic rifle.

Jenny ran after the bear a short ways, with the dogs pulling and howling on a leash. Collin was right beside her with the kill gun. The last shells, yet unfired, were high-velocity lead slugs.

The video was shown to the news media to remind them of how unpredictable a bear could be. Tim and his crew all knew about the danger they faced every day catching and releasing bears, but it humored them when they witnessed the reaction of a sympathetic, teddy bear group of writers and photographers.

The old video was a reminder of how an angry, sedated grizzly bear could suddenly turn back against his captors. The video portrayed a male grizzly bear walking out through the open door of the culvert trap, turning around, and looking up. He climbed on top of the trap and attacked the man behind the lifted gate. The short film made a lasting impression on today's bystanders.

The bear study group headed back down the rough back road through narrow gaps of encroaching pine trees. The lightweight culvert trap and trailer bounced, bumped, and rattled through potholes and over protruding rocks. The hollow, galvanized tube scraped and screeched loudly against close brush and leaning trees along the narrow logging road.

Finally hitting a county road and heading off of the mountain, Tim said, "We probably won't have many good-weather pickup-truck days left. When you see those pumpkins on front porches and Halloween decorations in the storefront windows, our season is about finished. We might have to make a tent camp this season and bring out the skis until they all hibernate for the winter.

"I think we had a great day today. It was the best of timing all around. You guys did a great job! We didn't stress the bear because you each moved fast with the tranquilizing and collar. And bottom line—neither man nor beast got injured. Jenny, your dogs worked great today. You were smart not to turn them loose. They scared that bear enough for the first time. If he comes back, maybe you can let them off their leashes and rip some fur out of his ass!

"Collin, you were right on with your aim. I saw you hit him at least two times with those rubber bullets. I don't think he'll break into that cabin again. At least I hope not!"

Collin replied, "Tim, you sure are right about the timing! During a bear's release, it all happens so fast. Sometimes they hang back after the door is open, and sometimes they bolt out and hit their backs on the bottom of the door before it's even half-open. I'm learning to get my aim centered more on instinct, rather than with posture and open sights. I'll bet that we get a lot of good PR out of this media thing today, and maybe it will boost private contributions."

Tim shifted gears in the Montana state truck as they hit blacktop and said, "I hope so! The state will try to match the funds of private donations toward our bear recovery program, but our flow of money could dry up anytime. We never know from year to year if we can keep this thing going."

Maggie was the newest member of the bear study group and the most recent wildlife biologist graduate to join them out in the field. It was very exciting for her to get out of a stuffy classroom and finally get out where she could hear and smell knowledge not found in books.

She waited until everyone else on the team had finished with their insights and evaluations. When everyone became quiet unto themselves, making mental observations about the day, she said, "I think we got a lot of PR out of the media today too! Tim, you were real good at explaining all of the science behind what we do, but you also addressed the teddy bear aspect of things. You pointed out how emotional ties can sometimes hinder the bears' survival. A fed bear becomes a dead bear! The emotional side of the bears' survival sends contributions that can keep us working, but it doesn't override the real-life issues that occur between the public and bears."

Collin said, "You can never tell how someone from the media feels about all of this, but their written version of the story often reflects how they personally feel. Tim, when you showed them that video of the big grizzly bear pulling that man off of the culvert trap and biting and clawing him, I saw the looks on their faces. And later, when you yelled, 'Cab up!' those people took off and sprinted off toward their Jeep Cherokee like running sticks of jerky."

Everybody laughed.

Leaving the national forest behind them, the country opened up with sprawling ranches and large, flat, bottomland meadows dotted with grazing cattle and open hay fields. Thick pine forests and wild country bordered western agriculture on all sides. They passed a large iron-gate entrance with elk antlers stacked on both sides and No Trespassing signs.

Jenny sighed. "I hope our bear makes it and doesn't get shot. I hope he doesn't come down this far. A bear doesn't have to be guilty of killing cattle when he passes through here. Even the media can't change someone who hates bears!"

Tim said, "It's time to check on the wolf study group. They should be heading into town." He called out on his radio phone. "Hi, Fred! We are on our way toward town. Yes, we are all starving! I thought I could hear a bear, but it's Collin's stomach growling. Okay Fred, we'll meet up with you at the hardware store. Over and out!"

The two Montana Fish, Wildlife and Parks nongame management teams left the hardware store and headed over to the only food-eating game in town. They tried to time it right, but being ever cautious, they surveyed the scene before they entered the Grab and Growl Café.

If there were semitrailers that hauled livestock parked out in front and down every side street around, it was a really bad choice for an evening meal.

If there were several trucks parked there with the doors' side panels advertising "Simple Log Homes and Lumber Co.," the local grocery store and some bread and peanut butter sounded pretty good.

If there were some hopped-up, jacked-up, chrome-infested monster trucks out in front with rifle racks in the back windows, a half-empty bag of jerky with mold on it sounded good enough for dinner.

Three boys and one girl worked on the wolf study group, and two boys and two girls worked with the bear study group. They all came from different states, but they had all attended the University of Montana in Missoula. None of them were radical extremists; they just wanted to work as wildlife biologists for state wildlife management agencies. In fact, they all ate red meat! You could say that their most radical affiliation was a subscription to *National Geographic*, but it seemed that many of the local townsfolk treated them as the enemy.

If the coast was clear and there were no rednecks who thought they were animal rights activists; tree-spiking, antilogging terrorists; or simple, tree-hugging communist vegetarians; they still had to go inside and face the owner, Lefty Meyers. At least Lefty was honest in a bad sort of way; he didn't try to hide the fact that he disliked them, but he wasn't abusive. Lefty didn't go out of his way to make them feel welcome, either. He made them wait for service until they'd get up and leave. The wildlife biologists all learned that if they got their own menus, came to his kitchen where he was hiding, and ordered from him face-to-face, he would reluctantly cook them up some food.

Perhaps they had all been observing the habits of wolves and bears much too long, for they found themselves smelling the food before it reached their lips. None of them could cook very well, and they were always hungry from living and working up at high altitudes, often hiking, snowshoeing, or skiing several miles each day. The Grab and Growl was a headliner that described their hunger mode and most adequately described their present occupation.

When the acclamation of "All violence clear!" was unanimously voted on, they just went in and took their chances with Lefty. After regular visits of placing their own orders and waiting on themselves, they had all reached some kind of an understanding with Lefty. But he was weird. He always seemed to be hiding from them.

They came in at the slow hour when they knew that nobody else was parked out front. As they pulled their two pickups up in front of the café, they were all astonished when they witnessed Lefty run out the back door of his kitchen, jump in his pickup truck, and race away.

Fred, the senior biologist, said, "The front door is unlocked. The Open for Business sign is still in the front window. That means that we can legally go in and see what's on the menu today."

There was nobody around when they carefully walked inside. The only sound was coming from a Merle Haggard song about prison on the kitchen radio.

They all filed back into the kitchen. Jessica reached up to a high shelf and turned the dial on the radio until it caught an Eagles song. Everyone joined in with the chorus of "Take It Easy" while the boys began washing all of the dishes that were stacked up high in two big sinks. Maggie and Jenny cooked up pasta that was garnished with every fresh-looking item they could find. They made giant salads from everything that was green and wasn't wilted. They broiled up steaks and appropriated some prepared dessert items and then sat down to the best meal they'd ever received inside the establishment.

When Lefty finally drove around in the back alley and came inside, they were all gone. When he came back inside his kitchen, a mountain of dishes were washed, the floor was mopped, and there was a wad of money lying there next to his toaster.

The note said:

> The door was unlocked, and we were hungry, so we helped ourselves. If we owe you more money, we'll be back tomorrow.
>
> Signed,
> Maggie

When Lefty counted it all up, there was $150! He felt sort of dazzled about what just happened. He thought they would leave if he wasn't there for them to personally confront and demand some food from. He had headed out the back door as soon as he saw them pull up and took off in his pickup. He figured they would leave his place, but he couldn't seem to get rid of those people. Now they'd hit his weak spot; they washed his dishes and paid him more than he was worth. He questioned his earlier remorse about forgetting to lock the front door.

What really upset Lefty was something that happened last spring. He was out driving down Route 6 early one morning and became stuck in the snow, down off a steep embankment. His truck was heavily loaded with a valuable cargo, and nobody came along for a long time to help pull him out. Finally, a truckload of tree huggers came along and offered to give him a hand. They saw something sticking out from beneath his tarp, and they became very interested in the cargo that was inside the back of his truck. It seemed that they were a group out hunting for big-game roadkill to use for baiting wolves and bears.

They asked why he was picking up dead animals off Highway 6. He lied and told them how a little girl was killed because somebody ran over a moose and left it lying in the middle of the road. The little girl's family came along, hit it again, and wrecked their car. Lefty tried to convince them that he was a good, concerned citizen and was very grateful that someone else could perform this valuable service now. That was last spring, and it was very dark outside on that early morning, but he recognized one of the guys from the wolf study group. He feared that someone might recognize him as the owner of the Grab and Growl Café.

That was the reason why he hid from them and tried to keep them from looking directly into his face.

One night, the two groups came into town when it was their favorite time for dining. Lefty seemed to be happy with the new arrangement of them cleaning his kitchen and paying him generously. There were no visible threats outside, and there were no occupants inside. Lefty was rapidly driving away.

The eight biologists were starving, and they voted unanimously, "All clear!"

They unloaded from both vehicles and were walking toward the front door when two guys wearing cowboy hats walked around from the back of the building and blocked their entrance. The men started calling them tree huggers and goddamned environmentalists. One of the cowboys tried to pick a fight and take on all six of the guys by himself. The biologists were thinking about obliging him until a crew-cab, super truck whipped up to the front door, and out stepped a giant with two smaller giants on each side of him.

Tim yelled, "It's a setup! Let's get out of here! Run for the trucks!"

It was a setup by the Strickler gang. It was a devised plan to beat them up and run them all out of town.

The big, seven-foot giant began shoving each of the guys around until he had them all backed up toward their trucks. He grabbed Maggie and pushed her into his group of friends, who circled around her and blocked her exit. They began pushing her back and forth into each other's arms and laughing.

Suddenly, there was a siren, and Sheriff Tolliber pulled up. He stepped out of his car and told the group of troublemakers to get out of town pronto.

He asked each of the girls if she was injured, and then he unsympathetically left them standing there, got into his car, and sped away.

7

THE DAYS WERE BECOMING SHORTER, AND WINTER WOULD
soon clench its grip on the high country. The last of the aspen
leaves gave up the ghost with the slightest breeze and gently floated
downward. There was a crispness in the air and a shortness of
breath as Clyde breathed in deeply the strong scent of aspen, fresh
mint from the spring, and the pungent, fresh smell of horse manure.
He exhaled and could see his breath in the early, frost-laden morning
light.

Clyde became acutely aware that it was on rare occasion when
Fleebit had his horse saddled first, especially on a cold, frosty
morning like this.

Clyde pulled his cinch snug and turned to Fleebit, who was
preparing to catch and halter the other four horses inside the pole
corral. "Just leave those horses there until we come back later."

Fleebit halted in his tracks. "What do you mean?"

Clyde said, "Let's go ride the boundary of the Old Baxter Ranch
like we did in the old days. We can ride up on the north end next
to the Strickler Ranch and see what kind of damage they've done."

"But, Clyde, you promised! You said that if I came up here with
you, you could thank John in the Indian way, and I respected that.
Then after we got here, you talked me into staying up here all night.

Now you want to ride around five thousand acres, and that will take most of the day. I want to get home and check on my property. Besides that, those Stricklers don't like anybody on or near their property. And they have those spy cameras set up at their gates. You've seen that big gang of tough men who walk around their property line, carrying military weapons!"

Clyde kicked a pile of horse shit sideways with the toe of his boot and scattered it across the golden leaves. "I will keep my promise about going home today, but this might be the last time that we can get up here this fall before winter sets in. It's a beautiful, clear day, and my horses like it here too. They remember this country, and they love this rich, high-altitude grass. You are getting soft and mushy. I can't believe that you are afraid of that Strickler gang! I can remember the day when you would have taken them all of them on by yourself. Come on! Cowboy up! We'll be back by noon!"

"No!"

It was very hard for Clyde to accept the fact that winter was almost here, and he couldn't remain at his summer cabin, but Fleebit was anxious to go home, and the unimproved dirt road up to the cabin would soon be closed by the forest service. It was time to load up the horses in the stock trailer and head down the mountain.

The past few winters had been mild and warmer than normal, but it would be foolish to risk staying up this high and become trapped by unpredictable Montana weather. A man could stay up here and get around on snowshoes, but horses could become trapped until spring and starve to death if you ran out of hay. It was a hard process to bring feed up here.

Wintertime in Big Scratch could seem never ending. He would feel lost were it not for his seven young horses to ride and train all winter. Clyde had turned them out on summer pasture when they'd left last spring, and a neighbor had watched them and the place while they were gone. It was time to bring them all in and get them enrolled in school. It was something that he could look forward to.

Some winter days, it was so windy and cold that you had to

remain indoors and read or write letters to friends and family that you seldom visited.

Fleebit seemed enthusiastic about going back to his mother's old house in town and waiting out the long winter months. Several German and Swedish widows in town sparked his interest, and they kept him busy and involved with church social activities. It was becoming more obvious to Clyde that his friend was about ready to give up the wild life of living and working all summer from the back of a horse. He was beginning to show his age after completing a long roundup over rough country. He did fine on the short jobs, and he loved to travel to a roping or rodeo, but he was getting longer in the tooth and slower on the big circle.

Clyde thought, *At least I have the mountain property to look forward to if we both decide to quit working so hard all summer.*

Fleebit's house, referred to as the town house, was a simple and comfortable place for them and their animals. They'd spent the past few winters there, and if you had to live in town, it was the perfect place. The old house and twenty acres was located on the outside edge of town, and it joined up against several thousand acres of open federal lands to the north. You could look out the back door upon undisturbed open backcountry for as far as the eye could see. If you had to share space in a valley with two thousand people, it couldn't get any better than this.

They'd made a lot of improvements on the old place since Fleebit's mother passed away, and they'd customized it to fit their needs and make them feel more comfortable. The only thing they'd changed on the old house was the bathroom, but they changed everything behind it. For two cowboys who spent most of their lives outdoors, a house was just a shelter from the wind, rain, and winter cold. The important changes they made to the place were foremost priorities and offered them more comfort.

Their first priority required the completion of a large network of corrals where they could keep all of their horses, Fleebit's pet longhorn steer named Cheyenne, and his riding mule named Blue.

Their second priority was the construction of a log barn with stalls, hay storage, and open facing sheds where their animals could get inside out of the cold wind and snow.

The last project was a work in progress. They were building and adding on to an Old West town between the house and the corrals. This was where they spent most of their time, and it reminded them of their youth and a colorful past. The project started out small with a pickup truck loaded with rough-cut pine boards and a few simple hand tools. The construction of the feed store encouraged them to build the blacksmith shop and then the livery stable.

The town was growing.

The Pink Garter Saloon was a triumph and a masterpiece. It was a place where you could hang out with cow shit on your boots and spit into the sawdust on the floor. It was a place where you could have a drink from the original, old cow-town bar that was full of bullet holes. You could line up shot glasses on the bar and shoot them into pieces with your Colt pistol, and nobody would throw you out. You could shoot at the mice as they ran across the floor, and nobody would complain. You could clean and oil your saddle in the bar and spill saddle oil on the floor, and it wouldn't matter. The large, overstuffed chairs were very comfortable. Some old guys probably cried when their wives made them haul them off to the dump, because they were old and threadbare. The potbellied woodstove was a chrome-covered antique that kept the room fairly warm on cold winter days and spilled wood ashes onto the floor.

Fleebit made sure that the old house was maintained as very neat and orderly. It was where they ate, slept, and cleaned up. The saloon was where they liked to hang out.

Fleebit exhaled a long sigh of relief as he turned the big rig onto Main Street.

"We are finally on the last homestretch!"

Suddenly, there was the burst of a siren and flashing red and blue lights behind them. The sheriff car quickly passed them with *whoop! whoop!* and gave escort with flashers through town.

Clyde nervously looked in the rearview mirror, expecting other lights coming from behind.

Fleebit winced. "It's all my fault! I was mad when I left that store in Fanbelt and shoved into some people. That pissy little man cracked his head on a sink. I picked up a bag of peanuts on my way to the restroom and forgot to pay for them. They will take me back to Wyoming. I'll have to go back and straighten things out. I'm sorry, Clyde!"

Clyde focused on the flashing lights up ahead. "No, the cops are after me! While you were in that store farting around and shoving into people, I rinsed some dude's tonsils with a soap brush and tried to poke his brains out with the handle. He looked like a rich politician. I'll bet he was a senator on vacation. He probably owned one of those lots back at the Bar-V."

Fleebit glanced nervously into his rearview mirror. "I just knew you were going to get us in serious trouble!"

The sheriff car cut the lights upon entering the gravel driveway leading up to the homestead and pulled out of the way. Fleebit parked near the barn, and Clyde jumped out, glaring toward the officer.

He whispered, "What do you think he wants?"

Sheriff Tolliber walked over to their truck. "It's good to see you guys back home. Howdy, Fleebit!"

"Howdy, Tolly! That was some escort you gave us through town."

The sheriff said, "I couldn't pass that up. I've been following you since you pulled off the interstate. I wanted to catch you and give you the real news before you heard it in town. I could have used you guys this past summer. Everything went to hell around here after you left last spring. Have you guys even heard about the missing girl?"

"Yeah," said Clyde. "We heard about it yesterday morning when we were leaving the Wind Rivers. Any clues?"

Tolly kicked at a rock in the driveway. "None! There's a lot of pressure on me too, since she was last seen in this town. I still can't believe that a bunch of kids with the Sierra Club came here from different states and chained themselves to that logging equipment up at East Park! The timber company called me up there at daylight, and I found a bunch of kids chained to loaders and skidders without keys to unlock themselves. The loggers said that somebody else got to them before they arrived for work. The men had been beaten with pine clubs, and the girls were terrorized and partly stripped of their clothing. Two girls were candidates for hypothermia, and one boy needed some stitches.

"I had to radio the ambulance and notify them to bring blankets and heavy-duty bolt cutters with them. The group said they were beaten and tormented by a gang of masked men, and two of the assailants were very big men. Some of the men on the logging crew were very big, but they were all eating breakfast at Lefty's when the kids were attacked.

"Those kids sure didn't protest when I cut them loose and brought them to town. I got them checked out at the hospital and made my report. Those girls were scared to death, but they said they weren't sexually violated. I couldn't charge them for trespassing on public land, and they didn't destroy any equipment, so I turned them loose. I figured that they all learned a hard lesson, went home, and that would be the end of it.

"But I started getting calls from California two days later. Katie Colter was the only member of the group who was from California, and she never made it home. The others had all traveled together from the east in a van, with drop-offs in Illinois, Ohio, Vermont, and New York.

"Right after the incident, the summer drought was broken by a torrential downpour. It poured down rain up on the mountain for two days. It was a gully washer! I went back up there after I got the call, and I searched every back road, campground, and piss-path byway surrounding this area. No tire tracks, nothing!"

Clyde asked, "What about that Strickler gang?"

Tolly said, "I got to thinking about a gang of big men, so I checked them out as best I could. They all had alibis. I tried to get a search posse together on horseback to hunt for clues, but I didn't get much cooperation from the local cowboys. You guys know the deck I had to draw from. The attitude around here is ugly and hateful toward outsiders. California and New York license plates in town are like neon advertisements of fresh liver to a pack of wolves. You guys know how it is! Everybody around here is related to somebody who feels threatened by the environmentalists. Hell, my job is related to all of the interests around here too. I'm just a small county sheriff that was elected by these people, but I'm being hit hard by the national news media to do something and to find that girl at all costs. I look for the FBI to show up at anytime."

Clyde said, "If there are any clues out there, they'll soon be covered up with snow. If you need us to help search on horseback, you can count on me."

The sheriff asked, "What about you, Fleebit?"

Fleebit responded, "Me too, Tolly!"

Clyde said, "Help us turn these horses loose, and we'll all go inside and make some coffee."

"No, thanks! You guys just arrived home and have stock to tend. I'll try to come back and visit the Pink Garter and have a shot when things die down some. Clyde, I've been practicing my fast draw, and I think I can win my money back."

Clyde opened up the wide alley gates and turned the horses out into the big, open pasture while Fleebit dug their bedrolls and duffel out of the tack room. After years spent together on the same work routine, words were never wasted conveying who did what chores. Clyde was head horse wrangler because he was so particular and fussy about the care for his personal rope horses. He would become enraged if Fleebit left a gate halfway open, didn't latch the feed room door, or missed seeing a scratch or blemish on one of the animals.

Fleebit was head of household because he didn't think Clyde was neat and tidy enough with bedding, laundry, and domestic organization. A little bit of dirt didn't bother him, but it irritated the hell out of Fleebit, and he didn't trust Clyde to use the washing machine or to get the dirty dishes clean enough.

Fleebit usually held things inside and thought about them in private, preferring to listen to Clyde because he was better educated. Anything that he might personally say about a topic other than horses, cattle, and team roping might sound misinformed and stupid. He was self-conscious about it. He'd always depended upon Clyde and his mother to read his personal mail and to pay his bills. He greatly respected Clyde for his ability to communicate and often encouraged him to recite. But he sometimes thought that Clyde got carried away. Since his mother died a few years ago, he had become more reliant on Clyde to help manage his business affairs. He also had become more vocal, revealing sudden new and shocking pieces of information. It seemed that anything might set him off into a tide of unexposed revelations.

They returned to the town house and were settled in after taking care of their horses and unloading their tack. They didn't have a television set inside the old house, but there was a very old, arch-style cabinet radio that was occasionally turned on, and it was set on a Great Falls "silver oldies" country music station. Johnny Cash was Fleebit's favorite. The country music station finished up its afternoon program with "Folsom Prison Blues" by Johnny Cash.

When the song ended, Fleebit got up, turned off the old antique, and announced, "Clyde, did I ever tell you that I was famous but that nobody ever found out because I don't like publicity?"

Clyde's eyes glazed over when he thought about having to hear a repeat story about Fleebit's love life. He braced back in his favorite recliner chair and tilted his legs upward.

"Yeah, right! Is this about the time when you saved all of those nurses from a wrecked bus that skidded off into the ditch? Those women were all so grateful for Clint Eastwood saving them that they each took your picture and wanted to marry you. Yeah, I've heard that one many times!"

"Take down your long rope," drawled Fleebit. "This is a far reach from anything that you've ever snagged before, and it's a true story. I never told you about my half brother before. I was afraid that you would make jokes about it.

"Just before my mother died, she told me about him. I told you how my dad told the nurses to write the name Flea-bit Shepherd on the birth certificate because his kid would have to grow up tough or die. Well, he did the same cold shit down in Tennessee, when he fathered a boy down there. He named him Sue Shepherd. He's the boy that Johnny Cash sings that song 'A Boy Named Sue' about!

"My mom helped me find him, and he seemed real happy to know that he had a brother who was a cowboy. He told me the whole story of how he found our pa at a poker game down in Louisiana and how they fought it out. He said that they nearly killed each other, but they both came away with a different point of view.

"Clyde, Johnny Cash sang a song about my family, and it makes me feel kinda proud like! There are a lot of folks out there who are blue bloods, but they never had somebody famous ever sing a song about 'em.

"After I talked to my half brother about it, I started thinking about all of the men that I fought and busted up for laughing at my name. I started feeling bad about being so mean and hateful all through life. I went to church and told God that I would never get mad and fight no more over my name! Clyde, we've ridden a lot of range together all these years, and you never once laughed at my name. You are my pard! Whaddya think?"

Clyde sat quietly thinking for some time, contemplating Fleebit's story. *Wow! This is too good to be a coincidence! How many boys could have been named Sue Shepherd and have a Flea-bit brother? And how many Shepherd pups might be out there running around from Montana to Louisiana?* Clyde thought, *Wouldn't that would be some kind of family reunion!*

"Fleebit, I always thought that you gave yourself that name to truthfully describe the cur dog that you are! You've always been the big dog that breaks his chain where good-looking females abound, and you eat out of several bowls at once when you get the chance. You've knocked over several trash cans since I've known you, and I've tried hard to keep you out of the pound. I can just visualize you and your brother, Sue, making cats a favorite family sport and the two of you going on the same date! Ha-ha-ha! Yeah, I'm very happy that you found religion and buried all of that anger over your name. You are going to feel much better now! Ha-ha-ha! Ho-ho-ho! Hee-hee-hee!"

Fleebit looked at the floor and said, "Boy, that was real funny! It almost seems like you had all of that stored up for a long, long time. That was a lot of dog jokes all at once! Yep, it sure is a good thing that I made that promise to God that I wouldn't break any more arms and legs, beat anyone into a pulp, or try to ruin some guy's manhood again over laughing at my name."

Clyde became silent and thought that perhaps he'd gone too far this time with his stupid jokes and offended his best friend. Fleebit seemed ready to quit the wild cowboy life at any time, and all during their last several contract jobs, he'd been moping around over something. The last thing he wanted to do was drive him away or hurt his feelings.

Horse training had taught him a lot about the use of spurs. They were useful in moving a reluctant horse forward, but if you jabbed them in hard and held them there too long, your animal would try to throw you to the ground. He was wondering if maybe he'd dug Fleebit too hard in the guts this time.

"Hey, partner," drawled Fleebit. "I'm just funning with you! It's okay! I knew a long time ago that you slam-punched a few miners, truckers, and cowboys for making fun of me. You never told me, but word gets around and back around. And I always noticed how you protected my name and never introduced me to anyone in public by my full name. When you pronounce Fleebit fast-like, it sounds Hungarian and not like a flea-bit dog. You've always treated me with respect around other people. Even when you give me a hard time to my face, I'll always know that you have my back. I know that I'm big and dumb, but I sure am good looking! Haw-haw-haw!"

Clyde looked out the window at the fading sunlight against the Pink Garter Saloon and said, "I think I'll go back to the corrals and fix that broken gate before it gets dark. A two-dollar job might save a priceless horse. What are you going to do with the rest of the daylight?"

Fleebit knew exactly what he was going to do, but he wasn't going to tell Clyde. He'd been looking forward to seeing his lady friends for several weeks. He really liked Ellen, but he thought that Helga, May, and Selma were hot too. They would be waiting for him, because everybody in town knew that he was back after their big-rig truck and trailer came rolling back down Main Street. News traveled fast in this small town! For Fleebit, coming back into town and parading their big-rig truck and trailer back down Main Street was like coming back home as a war hero. He was extremely excited about the homecoming.

Fleebit finally came back to Clyde's question and replied, "Oh, I have a lot of errands to do. I need to go to the feed store and see if they sold some of my rawhide quirts while I've been gone. Then I'll go to the bank and get some cash. If I can locate the guy, I need to talk to him about braiding some hobbles. Then I might go have a cup of coffee with Lefty, and then I'll be back later. Don't wait supper on me, though!"

Clyde heard the back door slam, and he thought, *I know just where he is going! But I rode him pretty hard today, so I took off my spurs and didn't say anything. But tomorrow is another day, and I will have my spurs strapped back on!*

8

THE WINTER SUN WAS COMING UP OVER THE FLAT HILLTOP
above Big Scratch, Montana, and horse school was in session. Clyde
had already ridden and relayed two of his seven young horses on
a one-hour circle in the hills surrounding the small town. The
winter remained mild with above average temperatures, making
it easier for a horse trainer with an early schedule and a strict
routine.

As the sun broke over the ridge to the east, Clyde was changing
saddles and dressing his third young gelding of the day. It didn't
matter if it was rain or shine, snow and cold. When Clyde started
his winter training, he didn't stop or break his routine unless there
was sickness, lameness, or a howling blizzard blowing down from
the northern mountains.

Sheriff Tolliber stood him up at the last minute. Clyde planned
on riding with him in search of the missing girl. Tolly said that he
had other business to attend and didn't think they had a chance of
finding someone who could be anywhere between Montana and
California. Clyde liked to ride alone, anyway, so he took each young
horse out in a different direction and made a sweeping circle while
watching the ground and the air for a sign. He didn't know what
he might find out of the ordinary, but it was from habit that he

could notice a broken tree limb, a disturbed rock, or a cluster of carnivorous magpies.

The magpies were short-sighted, visual hunters that told you where the remains of a poached deer or elk lay hidden, and they were smart and tricky. If they saw you riding near their food source, they would abandon it quickly and scatter to steer you away. They would stay away until you left the area.

The buzzards could be seen miles away, circling wider and wider until the smell of decaying flesh could be located. Their amazing sense of smell brought them closer and closer until they could zero in on their target.

After four months and a heavy rain, tracks would be erased or indistinguishable. A missing car could be turned over in a gully or slid off of a steep embankment in the dark forest. There were many miles of that terrain surrounding the general area. Sometimes missing hunters and Boy Scouts wouldn't be located in the mountains for several years. Their bleached bones became a statistic and a mystery if there were no dental records of someone who could be tied to the place of discovery.

It didn't appear to Clyde that the townsfolk were overeager to search extensively for Katie Colter, and there were thousands of acres that could require an exhaustive search. Like the sheriff, anyone who was concerned could have given up, because there was no proof that she hadn't driven away from the area.

But Clyde had a gut feeling about her last being seen in Big Scratch, and he would continue to search for clues. He wanted to ride near the Strickler Ranch. The road from East Park came down the winding mountain road and past their back-gate entrance to the property. They had surveillance cameras mounted at the gate and pointed at the entranceway from the main road. Their cameras might have shown her car driving past their gate. Clyde wondered if the sheriff had asked for those tapes after her disappearance. Probably not. The local people and law enforcement seemed to give the Stricklers a wide berth. Tolly said that he checked out Bobby and his gang, but there were several of them, and new faces frequently joined his crowd in town.

It was as though George Strickler owned the town.

Clyde thought, *Even Fleebit seems wary of riding onto their land. A few short years ago, he would have taken on the Strickler gang all by himself. He would have encouraged both of us to ride onto their property and have a look around. And yesterday, he pouted, became angry, and refused to go on the ride with me. He wanted to go home! What a sorry-ass deal!*

Clyde spoke to his young horse beneath him. "I'm not giving up, and I'm not afraid to ride over onto the Strickler property to look around. I know every inch of that ranch, and I know it better than a bunch of dress-up cowboys will ever know it."

Fleebit slipped in early that morning without waking up Clyde. He didn't get much sleep the night before, so he'd slept in late. He was thankful that Clyde was gone early and would stay busy riding his horses all day every day as long as the weather stayed mild. He hoped that the weather would stay this way, because he had a lot of catching up to do, and as long as Clyde was busy, he wouldn't have to be confined with him indoors and answer hard questions.

Fleebit strode into the kitchen and felt the graniteware coffeepot. It was still hot. That was the good thing about a wood cookstove. He took his cup of coffee into the living room and turned on the old cabinet radio.

You are listening to silver oldies 92.9 Great Falls. And now the weather.

The weather in Great Falls and surrounding area will remain fair until Sunday, and then look out, folks! A huge cold front coming down from Canada is going to blast into warm tropical air coming up from the southwest, creating a slow-moving storm of gigantic proportions. Meteorologists are calling this the perfect storm. This storm could produce several feet of snow with extremely cold temperatures and high winds. This is an advance winter storm warning, folks, so prepare for blizzard conditions for the surrounding area.

Fleebit thought, *This just isn't fair!*

It was difficult to make all of his rounds. His past experience taught him where to start, where to finish, and how to get to each stop without being detected as he drove through town.

Helga was very excited to see him and wanted to talk about her social activities at church. She forced him to eat a huge piece of cake and told him how handsome he was with his hair longer. She also liked his new sideburns that made him look so sexy. It had been hard to get away from her, but he got away with the same excuses that Clyde seemed to believe. He had to come back the next day, because she needed a strong man to move some furniture around, and she scolded him for not having a phone. She would have his favorite lunch prepared.

Selma shrieked with joy, and she smelled so good when they embraced. She had to show him her new knitting and pictures of her new grandchild, and she had to tell him all about her social activities at church while he ate a giant piece of fresh apple pie. She told him that he was getting better looking with age, but she didn't think he looked good with sideburns. It was hard for him to leave there, but he convinced her that he had to get to the veterinary clinic before it closed. She said that she wanted him to come back the next day to fix her garage door and that it was too bad that she couldn't call him.

May was wearing a new dress with a plunging neckline, and when she pushed into him and embraced, he thought that he would burst with joy. She had to show him her new bedroom carpet and new fabric for a dress that required his personal opinion. She told him all about her social activities at the church and women's lodge. May insisted that he try her new carrot cake that she'd made just for him as she shoveled a very large piece onto a plate. She told him that he was still handsome, but she wanted to cut his hair because she liked it short. She offered to buy him a new cell phone in trade if he would check out her plumbing. May wanted him to haul away some big stacks of magazines as soon as he could find the time. He explained to her that he had several errands to finish since he had just arrived in town but that he would be back real soon.

It was getting late by the time he arrived at Ellen's house, but her porch light was still on.

The local weather forecast had Fleebit worried. He knew that he only had two more days before the big winter storm hit. He had some unfinished business in town to complete that didn't include his four girlfriends. He would get back to them as soon as he wrapped up a few other things, but none of these current obligations smelled as fragrant or looked as appealing. Although Clyde paid the bills and taxes and took care of other business that required literary skills, there were some things that Clyde couldn't do for him. His driver's license was expired, and that required a personal visit to the small municipal building.

The old stone building sat on top of a steep hill, with a winding road that came up and around three curves to access the handicap parking lot and unloading zone. The larger parking lot was below at the bottom of the steep hill, with access to the building by four flights of narrow, concrete steps that were bordered by steel handrails.

A city work crew had the easier access temporarily blocked as Fleebit drove by in the old green pickup, so he entered the parking lot at the bottom of the hill. He didn't mind climbing all of the stairs, because he felt like he needed to lose some weight, anyway. He parked the truck, and as he reached the first concourse of steps, a young boy with a skateboard in his hands stood looking up at the top of the steep hill and exclaimed,

"Here he comes!"

Fleebit looked up and focused on another young man at the top of the first flight of steps. He watched in amazement as the boy jumped up with skateboard in hands and mounted the iron handrail, standing upright on the board. With arms spread wide for balance, he began sliding down the steep railing and gained speed. When he reached the end of the first concourse, he leaped over the wide gap between railings and expertly caught the second handrail and gained more speed. He made the jump a third time, his board making contact with the narrow pipe rail with a resounding *whack*. Sliding now and gaining tremendous speed, he leaped over the last opening and hit the last stair railing heading for the parking lot. A small car came around the corner, the driver unaware of the advancing daredevil heading toward her. The young man reached the end of the last railing just as the car came past. The boy reached down, grabbed the board with both hands, and leaped high in the air, flipping over sideways and over the top of the passing car, going straight between two parked cars, landing on the asphalt, and speeding away without incident. The young man standing next to Fleebit yelled, *"Awesome!"*

A bug flew inside Fleebit's open mouth, and he spat it out. He asked the boy next to him, "What does *awesome* mean?"

The boy looked up at the big cowboy with incredible disbelief. He answered, "Awesome is the opposite of awful!" He then jumped on his board and skated out of sight with his friend.

As Fleebit drove away from the courthouse, he thought about his new word and pondered the profound meaning and implications of it. The difference between awesome and awful, he reckoned, was like the difference between this nice, seemingly warm spring day and the oncoming blizzard.

It was the difference between May's, Selma's, Helga's, and Ellen's cooking and eating tough jerky and cold beans out of a can when he rode the wild country with Clyde. It was the difference between the nice clean houses that his girls lived in and the rat traps that he and Clyde camped out in that were full of rodents, rattlesnakes, and black widow spiders that frightened him and made it awful. It was the difference between sleeping in a soft bed and getting a hot shower at Motel 6 that Clyde would roll on past after a dirty week of living in a rat trap and taking a bath in a cold lake and sleeping on the hard ground, which Clyde expected them to do.

Now that his awful town errands throughout the town were completed, he was heading to Helga's awesome house to have an awesome lunch with her.

As he drove through town, he thought about living an awesome retirement with a lovely woman, good food, a graceful touch, central heating, her own money, clean, a graceful touch, loving ... but he dreaded the awful task of having to tell Clyde that he didn't want to live that old life anymore.

Clyde knew that the weather was going to change before he heard it announced on the cabinet radio. He could feel the power of nature churning. The smell of it in the warm moist air coming up from the southwest and a foreboding stillness in the north felt like two advancing armies in the sky that were about to wage war on the inhabitants of earth. From living outdoors for most of his life, he could sense these changes several days in advance. It was important that he get all of his horses ridden every day before the big storm arrived, and he was scurrying to saddle his fourth student of the day.

The winter started out mild and warmer than usual. Canadian geese hadn't migrated to the south and were still swimming on open water in neighboring ponds. Prairie dogs still denied winter hibernation and remained vigilant at their large town, where they scolded him as he rode past on his horses every day. His horses hadn't grown heavy winter coats this season and were now shedding off. Clyde was a man who had every instinct and reason for being concerned.

The local people at the coffee shop and feed store scoffed at the term "global warming." It was just more environmental, tree-hugger rhetoric! It was part of their political agenda to influence elections, make more trouble, and stop world progress! Clyde wasn't so sure about that. He'd lived here a long time and knew that Montana was experiencing warmer winters with less snow in the mountains.

This change in the seasons was becoming a pattern, and it had him worried. A big mountain spring dried up last summer where he and Fleebit had watered cattle all of their lives. The pine forests were dying, and there were a lot more forest fires in the state every year.

That morning, all of the horses were running around the corrals and down through the pasture bucking, rearing, and kicking high into the air. The slightest noise or movement made them snort and run. Each one of the young horses he was riding today seemed anxious and filled with a nervous energy that he realized he had to pay attention to. There was a risk for a blowup when they might spook and try to jump out from under him.

He wondered if the residents of Big Scratch and people elsewhere in the big world were not paying enough attention to the changes occurring on their mother planet.

9

AT THE MIDNIGHT HOUR, AN ARCTIC BLAST CAME HEADING
south off of the high mountain peaks with sixty-mile-per-hour
winds. A much warmer wind gust of forty miles per hour came
boiling up out of the southwest, and the two opposing wind currents
slammed into each other over the town of Big Scratch.

A four-by-eight-foot sheet of pink Styrofoam insulation was
caught up in the whirlwind of battle. It tore away from an improvised
shelter constructed by a teenage girl who cared about a stray dog
that her parents rejected.

A strong wind gust from the southeast picked up the large
pink object and hurled it across the vacant street. An opposing
blast of frigid wind from the northwest held it there, pinning it
against a neighbor's front-yard fence where it shuddered with
a drumming sound that no one heard. Another mighty blast of
accelerated wind hit it from the opposite side of the fence and
sent it cartwheeling end over end into a mailbox, breaking off
one pink corner. And then another mighty, whirling gust picked
it up and brought it back to life, spiraling it up, up, and away into
the night.

The strong storm continued to rage into the daylight hours
with blasting cold wind and snow. All across town, chimneys

puffed white wood smoke up into the swirling snow, and residents huddled inside or ran quickly from shelter to shelter.

Wood smoke billowed out of the chimney at the Pink Garter Saloon.

Clyde slipped on a denim jacket and went out at first light to check on the livestock. He hadn't rested well because of worrying about his horses. The wind tore loose a corner of metal roofing on the blacksmith shop, and it had banged loudly all night.

Clyde reached the big longhorn steer's corral behind the town house and immediately noticed something different. There were chunks of pink Styrofoam all over Cheyenne's corral, and one large piece was impaled on one of his long, massive horns.

"Cheyenne, it looks like you had quite a party last night!"

Cheyenne shook his head and waved the pink trophy high in the air.

"What a mess! You've torn that thing to pieces, and now I have to clean it up before it blows everywhere! I try to keep things clean around here, and you kids leave your toys scattered all over the place!"

Clyde found an empty sack inside the feed store and was running after the pink pieces and trying to catch them as the gusting wind tried to take them away. He noticed that there were holes or gashes in most of the pieces as he placed them inside the sack. Clyde looked at Cheyenne and laughed. "I wish I had a movie camera set up out here so I could watch a rerun of you tearing up that sheet of insulation."

Cheyenne shook the horn with the pink attachment one more time.

"Okay, I'm not going to take it away. You can keep that one toy!"

Clyde was walking into the fierce wind with his head down and on his way toward the saloon when Fleebit came out the back door of the house on the run.

Clyde yelled into the strong wind, "Where are you headed?"

"I've got to check out May's plumbing," stammered Fleebit.

Clyde laughed and yelled into the wind, "I've heard it called a lot of things!"

Fleebit halted in his tracks and said, "Doggone it, Clyde!"

"Did you just say a dog got on it last night? No? I'm sorry! I can't hear in this wind!" Clyde started laughing and slapping the sack full of Styrofoam against his leg.

Fleebit shook his head from side to side in exasperation and ran for the old green pickup truck to get out of the cold.

Clyde took his sack to the saloon and stoked up the fire in the large, antique woodstove. A mouse darted out from a hole in one corner and ran across the open room and into a hole on the other side. Clyde strapped on his old navy Colt revolver, took out his pocketknife, and sat down next to the stove. He emptied out the sack onto the floor and sorted through the chunks of pink Styrofoam pieces, choosing different sizes and making mental observations. He then selected six of them. Using his razor-sharp knife, he began carving the soft foam into the figure of a man. He took his time and thought about things as the time passed. Finally, he held it up and approved of the completion. He set it aside and started on another one.

As he carved, he thought about his friend of many years and worried that Fleebit would be shoveling heavy snow away from three or four houses and garages today. He knew that heart attacks and strokes were common among men Fleebit's age when doing snow removal in frigid air. Fleebit was sixty-four years old now. He was like an old workhorse with a big heart and could easily be worked to death by an inconsiderate master. He was putting on weight too, from eating too much pie, cake, and other rich feed from several sources of female persuasion. But he was his own man, and Clyde had never told him what to do. Clyde could caution him and tease him, but he couldn't hold him back. He thought that Fleebit had special feelings for Ellen, but he wouldn't let on that he cared that much about her. He was secretive. He was like outhouse drunks or sneak-and-hide smokers that say they've quit but run around the corner to do something they like to do and don't want anyone else to know about.

It was sometimes humorous to hear his white lies and excuses for leaving the house and then visualize an old cur dog that gets off his chain, jumps the fence, and runs panting down the street, going door to door to get sugar treats and to be petted. He'd been caught running away this morning and surprised when Clyde asked him where he was going. He was probably going to fix a leaky faucet for May this morning.

Clyde said out loud, "He said he was going to check out May's plumbing! Ha-ha-ha! That guy sure can make me laugh!" Clyde talked out loud a lot when he was alone, and he often recited poems that he'd written on paper bags and old feed-store calendars. He would save them for a day or two and read them aloud to himself and then start a fire with them in the woodstove.

The last of the six pink men of different sizes was finished. He picked them up and walked over to the bar. Clyde looked at the first one and said, "Marty, pink is your color!" He stood the pink little man on the old bar and said, "Let me buy you a round!"

He stood a second man figure upon the bar and said, "General George Armstrong Custer, welcome to the Pink Garter Saloon. Have a shot! Let me buy you a round!"

He placed a tall man figure next to a smaller one on the worn bar top and said, "Well, look who showed up at my establishment today! It's George Strickler and his son Bobby Ray! Go belly up, men. Ha-ha-ha! And let me buy you both a round!"

He looked at the next one and said, "Colonel Chivington, you are a long ways from Sand Creek. Let me buy you a round!"

Clyde studied the last pink man for a moment and said, "Stranger, you look like you could use a drink. You have a hole in your belly! Don't start any trouble in here, and I'll buy you a round." He poured a shot of Wild Turkey and sat it on the bar next to the last pink man.

He turned around and was walking back to the woodstove when a mouse came scurrying across the floor and abruptly stopped in front of him. It looked up at him, emitted a shrill squeak, and went speeding back from where it came.

Clyde reached the stove at the other side of the room, spun around, pulled his gun, hammered down, and rapid-fired his Colt pistol at the six pink figures across the top of the bar.

When the thick, acrid, black-powder smoke finally cleared, Clyde casually walked back to the Old West bar, walked down it, and asked aloud, "Where did everybody go? I was going to buy you all another round!" He then tossed down the undisturbed shot of whiskey at the end of the bar.

Fleebit came home after dark, cold and exhausted. The temperature had dropped below zero degrees, and May's plumbing froze beneath her house. She showed him the diagram of the plumbing structure, but he couldn't read it and mistakenly shut off a secondary valve instead of the main water valve. With a thirty-six-inch pipe wrench, he used his brute strength against a frozen union and stripped the threads. Water gushed all over him and under the substructure of the house. It took him several trips of crawling out beneath the small space into the cold wind before he fixed the problem.

His coat, shirt, and pants became stiff and frozen. He warmed up some by shoveling the snowdrifts away from May's front porch, back porch, and garage. Selma called May and said that she needed Fleebit to help her as soon as he was finished there. May handed him a new cell phone and told him, "Now don't lose this one! Call me later!"

When he arrived at Selma's house, Marty was there and needed him to help unload a new snowblower from his pickup. After they unloaded it, Marty showed him how to run it and watched out Selma's picture window while he cleaned the snow away from her sidewalks and driveway. Selma gave him a big piece of frosted cake and sent him with Marty for a few minutes. Marty needed a big, strong man to help unload a new shipment of snowblowers at the hardware store. Selma waved good-bye and said, "Call me!"

By the time he reached Ellen's house, he was exhausted and frozen. She cut off his frozen clothes with a set of pruning shears and forced him to get inside a tub of hot water. She brought him a hot toddy and said, "You big brute! What did those people do to you today? Do you want to have a heart attack?"

Ellen brought him a bathrobe that had belonged to her deceased husband. The sleeve length came to his elbows, and its bottom length came above his knobby knees. They sat at her kitchen table, where she fed him the Crock-Pot meal of German design she'd prepared for their lunch date six hours earlier.

"Fleebit dear, you are cold and tired. You should stay here tonight."

"Now, Ellen, we've talked about this before. It just won't look right when the neighbors and the preacher see Clyde's old truck parked here in the morning. People will talk, and I don't want you to go through that."

"Yah-yah-yah!" She jumped up, brought him a shirt and a pair of purple plaid trousers, and slapped them down. "I wish you had a telephone in your house so you could call me when you make it home safely."

Fleebit answered, "Clyde don't want a telephone in the house."

Ellen shouted, "Clyde, Clyde, Clyde! It is always what Clyde wants! It is your house, and you need to stand up to that man!"

When Fleebit arrived home, he reached inside his coat, and the new cell phone that May gave him was missing. He tried to sneak inside the house and make it to his bedroom, but Clyde was waiting in a dark corner beside the washing machine and flipped on the lights.

"Where did you get those tiny, funny-looking clothes? You look like a big, silly jackrabbit stuffed inside a cottontail skin! This is one of the funniest sights I've ever witnessed. Ha-ha-ha! Hee-hee-hee! Is a woman making you do some kind of kinky sex thing in her dead husband's clothes? I hope I can laugh myself to sleep!"

In a firm, angry voice, Fleebit said, "I want to put a telephone inside the house."

"Now wait," said Clyde. "We've been through this before. If we had a phone in your house, half of the women in this town would be driving both of us nuts because it would never stop ringing. Old buddy, I am only looking out for your health. If those women could call you, they would work you to death. How many cell phones have you had and lost? I found one in the bottom of the horse tank when I cleaned it and another one smashed in Cheyenne's corral. Did your girlfriends give you those phones in trade for working over their plumbing?"

Fleebit scratched the top of his head. "Yeah, they gave me those phones, but I never could figure out how to use the complicated computer sons of bitches, and I lost them before I had time to learn how. But we need a phone to take care of contract jobs and rodeo entries."

"No, we don't," said Clyde. "The US mail takes good care of everything. Besides, a telephone call is not a binding contract between people. People can tell you something on the phone and do something entirely different. But when you have a hand-signed letter with a government stamp on it, you have something personal that you can take to the bank or to a court of law. People write to us and ask for our help. I write them back and give them a cost. They write back and sign a US mail contract without some expensive attorney getting involved. That's the way we've always taken care of business, and I mail in our rodeo entries with a check months before we get there.

"Since you can't handle a cell phone, why don't you use the pony express? If you rode your horses as much as you drive my old truck back and forth through town, you could deliver the news and keep good horses in condition. You can't expect me to ride them for you. If you don't want your horses any longer, just give them back to me. Maybe you should tell your girlfriends to spend your telephone money allowance on building a hitching post or a corral behind their houses."

Fleebit added up all of Clyde's abusive comments and finally reached a boiling point. Like an old steam engine, he huffed and puffed internally until he'd built up too much steam and was about ready to blow. The embarrassing comment about sleeping with Ellen in her dead husband's clothing finally came up to the surface and blew off the pressure gauge. It triggered an explosion!

Fleebit shouted, "At least I know how to love a woman, and if she takes off my clothes, I don't care about what I have to put back on. Maybe you would be happier living in the saloon or the barn, where you can tell the mice what to do! Maybe you need to go to a whorehouse so you can remember what a woman feels like! If you don't want me to drive your old truck, just say so! I'll sell my half of our big truck back to you and buy me a new one. And I'm not giving my horses away to you or anybody. They can live out in my pasture until they die of old age."

After Fleebit finished shouting, Clyde turned away and went inside his bedroom. He didn't laugh himself to sleep. There was no rest when he thought about his friend's hurtful words.

Clyde thought, *Yeah, I jabbed him pretty hard with my spurs, but he needed to wake up. He'll be over it tomorrow. At least he's not ready to give up his horses. That's something! I got him to stand up for himself tonight, and that's good. Now, if he can just find the guts to stand up for himself with a woman. It was Ellen who got him riled up like that! She's never liked me from the start!*

It continued to blast down wet, heavy snow. Frigid arctic wind blew ferociously all that night and into the next day. The horses were huddled together as a windbreak, all animosities forgotten, standing closely, nose to tail beneath their sheds and surrounded by three-foot snowdrifts. The thermometer hanging outside the back door of the house registered twenty below zero.

It became too cold to inhabit the uninsulated saloon any longer. With the giant potbellied stove glowing red hot, the buckets of soaking rawhide that Fleebit placed in front of it were freezing rock solid. The mice that contaminated his horse's grain and chewed up his tack often scurried across the sawdust-covered floor and offered target practice. Now, even they had abandoned the saloon for warmer habitation elsewhere.

Clyde was baking sourdough bread in the town house kitchen and glancing out the window at the swirling, wind-driven snow and bleak winter landscape. He said to himself, "If you can't ride a good horse on a cold day, bake a good bread in a hot oven."

Fleebit took a long time to pour himself a cup of coffee and fumble around Clyde in the kitchen, pretending to search for the sugar that Clyde placed next to the flour on the kitchen counter. He tried to sing the Kenny Rogers song "Lucille." "It took a long time to leave me, Lucille, four hungry children and a crop in the field. I've had some sad times ..."

Clyde was smiling at the silly, off-key version of the song, and without turning around from the window, he said, "I want to apologize for last night. I'm sorry for telling you what to do in your own house. I'll go to the telephone office and fill out the paperwork for you if you really want one. And you can drive my old truck anytime you want to. It saves us miles and fuel by not using our big truck."

Fleebit stopped singing and dipped into the sugar canister. "That's okay. You're probably right about the telephone. I had a tough day yesterday, and the only reason I was dressed like that is because several women had a telephone. You are just looking out for me, and I shouldn't have yelled at you like that."

He took his cup of coffee into the living room and turned on the old cabinet radio.

You are listening to 92.9 Great Falls, your favorite silver oldies station.

Power is out through parts of the county, and the utility company is hindered by high winds and drifting snow. County road crews are assisting them with snow removal while trying to maintain open main roads.

County commissioners announced yesterday that they will oppose a new wilderness bill that includes five thousand acres of new national forest property. The transfer of the Baxter Ranch to the federal government and its proposed wilderness designation has become a heated controversy among local groups and residents.

Local law enforcement officials have ended their search for Katie Colter. The California resident was last seen near Big Scratch after a logging protest near East Park last spring. Her family has announced that they will continue the search and are offering a reward for any leads or new information.

Fleebit shut off the radio and sat down in front of the coffee table, sorting magazines. "I can't find anything interesting to look at in any of these magazines!" yelled Fleebit.

Clyde yelled back, "That's because most of them are magazines that a woman buys and reads. Why do you let your girlfriends talk you into hauling all of their junk back here for me to trip over? Hey, I did read a good article in one of those ladies' magazines, and it was about a scientific study they did on German women between the ages of fifty and sixty-five."

"Clyde, is this one of those articles that are stored up in your head and you spill out just so you can get to me?"

"No, no," insisted Clyde. "I read it right here, sitting at this table!"

"Let me see it," demanded Fleebit.

"Why? You can't read!" Clyde began sorting through a stack of *Ladies' Home Journal*, *Better Homes and Gardens*, and *Today's Woman Now*, searching convincingly for a certain magazine and a certain article. "Here it is. 'Older German women's brains become more active with age, and they are actually growing more brain cells. They scored them on aptitude tests, and the results show that German women became smarter over the course of fifteen years.' Cowboy, Ellen Jorgenstein is getting smarter. Can you keep up with her? They did other tests as well, and they discovered some other things about their hormones. It seems that the increase in brain activity really affects their sex drive too!" Clyde slapped his leg. "That must be why they discovered that male enhancement drug over there in Germany!"

He continued, "'In this long research study, it is found that German women become widows or get divorced because their husbands are worn out. A multitude of older German women move to the United States each year because the American men their age are not worn out yet.'"

Clyde pretended to continue reading. "'They also did a study on German men between the ages of fifty and sixty-five and found that they were worn out from carrying heavy buckets full of soapy water and standing on ladders washing ceilings; from moving heavy furniture around and from being on their knees a lot scrubbing floors; from digging up acres of dirt with shovels to plant flowers, trees, and garden crops; and from shopping and from running errands all over the countryside.'"

"Well, I know I can't read and I'm not too smart," chuckled Fleebit, "but I get more handsome every day! Haw-haw-haw! Clyde, I don't think you read it in that magazine. I think you wrote it in your head!"

Clyde said, "You are the one who makes things up, telling the whole world how handsome you are. You need to turn on the exhaust fan in the bathroom when you shower, and wipe that fog off the mirror! Maybe you need to fix that broken wing mirror on the driver's side of my old truck!"

Clyde complained a lot about those stacks of women's magazines just to goad Fleebit, but when his friend was gone, he scanned through them, read the articles, and copied baking recipes. After spending most of his life in lonely cow camps out on the range with nothing to read except soup-can labels, he found that there was some rich stuff to learn from the female world.

So after he'd worn the covers thin on *Western Horseman*, *SuperLooper Magazine*, and *Pro Rodeo Sports News*, and when Fleebit was absent, he homeschooled himself. He always knew that women freely shared information with each other, but it was a secret society, and men like Fleebit and other old cowboys could only guess at what they were thinking. He felt like it was his duty to be informed.

By reading their magazines, Clyde learned a lot about what women want and what they think and say to each other. He learned about their food, their fashions, their cosmetics, their diets, and their desires. In the articles he read, he found that women could be lewd, rude, vulgar, snippy, mean, bitchy, whiney, depressed, optimistic, builders of faith, and builders of architectural design. Women could be nurturing, caring, and loving, and they liked to tell each other about their sexual desires, shortcomings, and deprivations.

In some of the articles, women considered themselves to be experts on how to handle men and generously offered their advice to others of their gender on male psychology. It was while reading these male training tips for other women that he realized that his big, slow cowboy partner could be in a lot of trouble. After all, these magazines had already been studied by Helga, May, Selma, and Ellen.

By reading about how women could train men, Clyde realized that women used hidden techniques in their training to achieve their male behavior goals. It was a lot like horse training!

He figured that May had already thrown a hard twist rope around Fleebit's long neck, and she was just letting him run with it loose while he stepped on it and tripped over it until his neck got good and sore. When the time got right, she would dally it up around her bedpost and yell, "Whoa!"

Helga had another approach. She was baiting her wild horse with lots of sweet feed and trying to curry him every chance she got, trying to earn his trust and get him to hold still while she slipped the hobbles on his feet without him noticing it.

He wasn't worried too much about Selma. Clyde figured that she wasn't smart enough to catch a dumb old lame horse or a lame man. She was attractive, but she was tricky and manipulative, and she would work his best friend to death like a desperate man who rode his only horse until its heart gave out. She was also one of the worst town gossips and a close confidante to Marty at the hardware store.

Ellen was using the extreme training device called a "Running W." It appeared that she had a hobble on each of Fleebit's ankles with a light rope that was tied off to the left hobble, threaded up through a D ring in the crotch of his Wranglers, and back down through a ring on his right hobble. While she watched behind him with this continuous rope in her grip, if he decided to make a wild run to get away and was in full stride, all she had to do was stay behind him and pull on the rope, and both of his feet would stay suspended while he crashed on his face. Clyde had personally used this extreme, last-measure device on big, runaway workhorse teams at Benny Benion's ranch.

Fleebit's four girlfriends think they have it all figured out. Since Big Scratch is such a small pasture, and there's just one old, slow horse to catch, it shouldn't take that long to outwit him, shut the gate behind him, and slap their burning brand on his hide.

Clyde knew that he still had a lot to learn about women. He could read about them, but that wasn't like being with them or living with them. The only true love experience that he could personally relate to was a long time ago, and her name was Mary. He began thinking about the beautiful young woman he had fallen in love with many years ago.

Fleebit left for Nevada to help trap wild horses for the Bureau of Land Management while he went to work feeding six hundred horses for the Benion Ranch, north of Jordan, Montana. Jordan was a tiny little town with three saloons, a two-pump gas station, a general store, a one-room school and dormitory.

Mary was from Chicago and was hired to live and teach at the isolated school that was surrounded by big ranches from many miles in all directions. Many of the kids traveled long distances from home to get an education. During wintertime, blizzards across the open plains often made travel a dangerous undertaking. The dormitory was built for the students and the teacher to live in.

Mary was a girl fresh out of school herself, and this was her first teaching job. There were not many pretty, single women around the area, and she was a big attraction that didn't go unnoticed by all of the single cowboys who came into town. Clyde quickly caught her attention at a dance one night, and he became her favorite suitor. They spent all of their free time together. If she could get to the ranch on weekends, she helped him feed the herd from teams of big horses and long bobsleighs filled with hay and grain. He dressed her up warmly with mittens, covered her face, and held her close to his side, protecting her from frostbite under the blast of biting north winds.

When Clyde could get into town, they met at the old schoolhouse, where she helped him perfect his English. When Mary witnessed the short stories and poems he'd written while living in isolated cow camps, she encouraged him to write and perfect his hidden talent. She said that in his writing, she could smell the sage and feel the horses beneath her. She gave him an old English grammar book and a Webster dictionary. She encouraged him to become self-educated in his free time.

Clyde got out of his chair and walked over to the window. He stood there, trying to imagine what she looked like today. It was like trying to remember what the top of the mountain looked like in this blinding storm.

It was his twenty-second birthday. Winter had ended its fury, and new grasses were beginning to green at the borders of melting snowdrifts. Clyde was about ready to move back to Wyoming for the summer.

All of the kids caught a bus home that afternoon when the weather cleared, and they were all alone in the schoolhouse for the first time. She locked the doors to the school and quickly led him to her private room. They made passionate love.

Mary told Clyde that she'd decided to return back east when school ended. Confessing her love for him, she encouraged him to marry her and return to Chicago, where her father would find him a job working for the railroad. After one estranged winter in northeastern Montana, she was not prepared to spend the rest of her life in the vast, unpopulated West.

Clyde thought about his grandfather's last words to him: "Grandson, each person is like two people inside one body. When two people decide to marry, it is very important for each of them to find their own oneness in the Middle Ground. If they have not found it or cannot find it, then it is like four people bumping around in different directions. This is why it is much easier for a single person to find the Middle Ground first."

Marrying a homesick girl and giving up a cowboy's way of life didn't sound like something that would last for very long. There were too many people and not enough wide-open spaces. Horses were his whole life. How could he give them up for her and a job with the railroad? One side of him said, "Yes, go with her." The other side of him could see the railroad tracks that split open the plains, the buffalo herds, and the hearts of the Indian people.

Though he loved her very much and it split his heart wide open, he put her on the train in Miles City and said good-bye.

10

CLYDE WAS RESTLESS. HE PLOPPED DOWN ANOTHER
magazine and strode over to look out the window again for the fourth time. Fleebit was keeping the count and casually said, "You can't make this weather go away by watching it every ten minutes. I know you want to ride your horses, but you would freeze to death out there in that cold wind and snow. Springtime is just around the corner, so just rest up and relax. You don't know it, but you work too hard for a man your age. Not many younger men can put an hour ride on seven young horses every day."

Clyde said, "If I didn't keep going like I do, I would give up and get old."

He wasn't brooding about not being able to ride his horses on a day like this. He was actually thinking about the missing girl, Katie Colter, lost and alone out in a blizzard. The local news had finally abandoned the tragic story, but Clyde knew that her family in California was probably watching this big storm front move in where their child was last seen alive. He somehow felt like she was still in the area, and there was one place far from town where he wanted to search for clues. It was irritating and made him restless that the high-country location couldn't be reached by horseback until late spring or summer.

Clyde announced, "Katie Colter was about the same age as Mary. She had her whole life ahead of her when she came to Montana. I can understand how Katie must have felt about protecting the trees. The national forest belongs to everyone, and it's held in the public trust. Anyone and everyone can have a voice that determines its fate."

Fleebit became irritated. "Those tree huggers want to shut down everything, and if you start sticking up for those people, you're not going to have any friends left around here!"

Clyde slammed his empty coffee cup down. "The whole earth is being chopped up, ground up, and sold off. If there weren't people like Katie out there, there wouldn't be anything left. The earth would be as bare as the moon! Maybe I'll join the Friends of the Earth if I don't have any friends left around here. Hell, man, you've got grandkids! Don't you want them and their kids to have clean air and clean water, wild places left that they can experience outside of a zoo?"

Clyde stared out the small frame window at the raging storm and thought, *Fleebit is sixty-four years old, and he has family in sunny, warm California. But he is sitting here counting my steps as I watch a blizzard in Montana.*

Clyde thought about the shocking news when they found out that he had a daughter about ten years ago. Clyde took him to the post office in Big Scratch to sign for a registered letter addressed to Fleo Shepherd. Clyde had to read the letter to him, and that was when his friend first had a terrible seizure.

The lady said that she was Les Slater's granddaughter, and her grandfather told her who her real dad was just before he died. She said that she was six months old when her mother was killed in an accident while having a horse race with a cowboy. Her grandfather said that her mother's saddle turned and her foot caught in a stirrup. She was dragged to death.

The lady told her story of being married to a businessman in Santa Barbara and having two small children. She had tried many times to find Fleo Shepherd, but there were no existing phone records. Her grandfather told her to look in the Great Falls area for her biological father. She hoped that she had finally found the right person and wanted to make contact with him if possible.

Clyde and Fleebit both hired on for Les Slater's Slash Bar Seven brand, and they stayed there about six months before moving on. It wasn't a great outfit to work for, and top hands didn't stay long. Mr. Slater didn't want his daughter to have anything to do with the working cowboys, because he watched them come and go. He saw most of them as saddle tramps who only owned a saddle and bedroll, who showed up in a flash and then suddenly tramped on.

Mr. Slater's daughter was a wild-child cowgirl, and Fleebit caught her attention. She made it obvious to the other hands but not to her dad. Pretty soon, another hand caught her attention, and then another new hand. Pretty soon, there were fistfights in the bunkhouse every night. It was Clyde who pulled Fleebit away from there before he killed all of the other cowhands. When they pulled up stakes at the Slater ranch, they were just like other top hands of their time. When boundaries and fence lines of a big spread became too familiar, when the fresh horses became boring and lazy, when the cook would quit, when the pretty girls were all taken, or when there was a high-stakes rodeo up the road, they left a casual romance behind in the dust of other traveled back roads.

Clyde sat down across from Fleebit with a pen and writing tablet. "You haven't mentioned your grandkids for quite some time. I'll help you write them a letter."

Fleebit finished his cup of coffee and belched loudly. "I haven't mentioned them none because that's a sore spot with me. I'm afraid that my grandkids are on their way toward the cull pen. All them kids do is look at a computer or text on their cell phones. When I went out to visit them in California last year, I was looking forward to talking with them about their friends, what they do in school, how they play at the beach, and so on, but they didn't have anything to say about anything. I was hoping that I could tell them some stories about the good old days when we were breaking wild horses to ride, catching and branding wild cows out in the brush, and living off the land in the big, Wild West. But, Clyde, those pups never even asked their old grandpa one question. They didn't seem too interested in the history of what used to be. It seemed like I was just an interruption on their computer screen and something they couldn't punch a button to get rid of.

"Those kids talk to their friends and people they never even met on the computer.

"They play games on it with other kids in other states and even across the big pond. They do all their schoolwork on the computer, and they even do their shopping on it. What they don't do is go out and play like normal kids ought to. I never did see them go outside in the yard and get some sunshine. It doesn't seem right!

"My grandkids don't know how to talk to people at all. It was like my big head was a TV screen that they could stare at, but there weren't any buttons to push so they could communicate with it. It used to be that you were born an idiot, you were born to be a little bit slow, or you were born normal, but you had a long run at life to change things for the better by learning and socializing with other people. It scares the heck out of me when I think about what their future might be."

"Oh, don't worry over it too much," assured Clyde. "They aren't any different from other kids of their generation. They have new technology that wasn't even dreamed of when we were their age. We were so poor when we were kids that all we could afford were our imaginations. It's a different world that kids live in today."

Clyde came back from the corrals after sundown. He stomped and shook off the wet snow from his coat before he stepped inside the back door of the town house. Fleebit met him at the door with a broom. "Now sweep yourself off so I don't have to mop this floor again!"

Clyde took the broom and began sweeping off his pant legs. "There's a real Montana blizzard out there! I could barely find my way back here from the corrals. When I threw hay out to the horses, they wouldn't come out of their windbreak to eat. They just stood there in a corner of the shed and shivered. They must have thought that winter would never come. I guess we all did! They didn't grow the heavy winter hair that Mother Nature usually gives them to keep warm. Now without a warm coat, they are freezing. We don't own enough horse blankets to put on all of them. I'll feed them extra rations of oats with some molasses mixed in and try to make them warm from the inside. It hurts me to see them act so cold. Without their protective coats, it would be like us standing out there in our underwear. Our horses probably think this is a dirty trick. Horses didn't cause this to happen to other horses. This sudden change of weather is going to be hard on the wild animals, as well. People around here think that global warming and climate change is all bullshit, but something is wrong. Our seasons seem all messed up, and these sudden changes are affecting everything."

Fleebit said, "Yeah, I didn't think that winter would ever come. We've been fooled by the past few winters that were warm and mild." He handed a steaming tin cup to Clyde. "I fixed us up a hot toddy. You look like you need to warm up from the inside too!"

Fleebit plopped down in his big chair next to Clyde. "While you were checking on the animals, I listened to the news and weather report on the radio. It looks like this storm is going to last for a few days. The news talked more about that teenage boy who committed suicide because he was bullied at school. I can't understand why a kid would do something like that. I probably had it as bad at school as any kid, but I never thought about hanging myself. Kids sure can be cruel, though!"

Clyde took a sip and then a longer one. "Yeah, we both had it rough in school, but we fought back. We also quit school and ran away. We were both lucky the way things turned out. There have always been bullies, and you can't protect your kids from facing that while they grow up. They've got to face cruel, ruthless people in the adult world too! When you bunch people up together in a school or in a workplace, they are like a pen full of horses. The older horses become the bullies. Put a new horse in with them, and they chase him, bite him on the ass, and drive him away from feed and water. Put another new horse in the pen, and he will be the meanest one to bully the newest horse. It's something you can't change when you turn a new horse or a new kid loose in the pen and walk away." Clyde took another sip of the hot, spiced rum. "This is real good! I wish I could give some of it to my horses on a cold night like this."

Fleebit gazed off into space. His sheepskin slippers hung over the end of his recliner. "When we first met up that night in the Wind River Range and sat around that campfire, I didn't think there was any kid like me who had the same problems growing up. When you told me your story, I knew I wasn't alone. You told me that the full-blood Indian kids got mean when you quit fighting with the white kids. You told me about some kid named Mountain Lion, but you said it was another story, and wouldn't talk about it. I always figured that you killed him with a rock, then run off to Wyoming!"

Clyde finished his drink. "Mix me up another one of these, and I'll finish the story.

"George Mountain Lion Jr. was the biggest, meanest kid at school. He never liked me, but when his girlfriend got the hots for me, he told everyone that I was a dead half-breed. He was not only big and mean but his family had political connections with tribal affairs, and I knew if I killed him, it would go hard for my mother and her clan.

"The Bloods were highly traditional, and they believed in sacred ceremonies and spirits that are out there that could mess with you. So I made them think I was crazy!"

Fleebit laughed. "What did you do to make them think you were crazy?"

"Hand me that drink! I just happened to be standing outside an open window and overheard my second aunt tell my third cousin something that made my ears perk up. My aunt told my cousin that the big liquor drop was going to take place that night, but that George Mountain Lion Sr. was in jail and wouldn't be able to pick it up. Booze was illegal on the reservation because the government thought that if all of the Indians got drunk at the same time, they might remember their victory with Custer and put on their war paint. George Mountain Lion Sr. took up a collection from the other families, and he was the only one trusted to hold the money, make the connection with the illegal bootlegger, and make it back with all of the hooch. The time and the location were a big secret.

"My cousin told my aunt, 'Go find George Mountain Lion Jr., and tell him that he must make the meeting tonight on top of Knob Hill because his dad is in jail. Give him this sack of money, and tell him to be on top of Knob Hill at exactly 6:00 p.m. to make the pickup. Also tell him that if he doesn't bring it all back, he'll be one dead Indian!'

"I slipped away without anybody seeing me or knowing that I had this information. Knob Hill was a couple of miles out of town, and I knew the exact route that George Jr. would take, so I got there at 5:00 p.m. to get set up for my theatrical performance. I got there and made my stand below the top of the hill a ways and off the path to one side. I knew that when George Jr. came up the path and around this big rock, he would have a clear view of me, so I took off all my clothes and put them behind a bush. Then I rubbed black soot all over my face and neck. I took a little bit of water, some baking soda, and a big, ugly-looking stick, and I sat down and waited.

"I could hear George huffing and puffing as he hiked up the long, winding trail, so I put some water inside my mouth and a big handful of baking soda. I started sloshing it around inside my mouth until white, bubbly foam started coming through my lips. I spewed it out of my mouth until it was all over my black face and running down my black chin and neck.

"When I knew the time was right, and George was coming around the big rock and into view, it became showtime. I started throwing a fit. I spewed out white foam like a wild animal with rabies, and I shook all over. I growled like a bear and bit at the wind. I jumped up and flew around where he could get a good look at me from another angle, and I started shouting at invisible people all around me. I picked up my club, spewed out some more foam and started swinging my club wildly at hidden foes.

"I looked away from the direction where George was hiding because I didn't want him to think I knew he was there. I looked up toward Knob Hill and yelled at another invisible person. I acted like I was mad and didn't like their answer, so I threw a fit and started up the hill a few paces. I stopped, turned around toward George's direction, and I stuck my head up high and sniffed the air like a wild bear seeking out the enemy. I started looking around toward his direction with eyes that would kill. I heard a clatter of rolling rocks and saw George jump out from behind that big rock and run for his life down off Knob Hill."

Fleebit asked, "What happened when you ran into George again?"

"I always acted like nothing ever happened. That's what made people wonder. It was like that saying, 'Speak softly and carry a big stick.' I never had to worry about George after that. He worried about staying out of my path."

11

THE NEXT MORNING, CLYDE WAS TAKING A DUTCH OVEN
full of sourdough biscuits out of the antique wood cookstove when
Fleebit walked into the kitchen and reached around him for the large
graniteware coffeepot.

"What's for breakfast this morning, cookie?" asked Fleebit.

"How does scrambled eggs and beefsteak sound, with some of
these biscuits topped with butter and chokecherry jam?"

Fleebit yawned and looked at the food. "That sure sounds fine.
We always eat well at your chuck wagon and always have. If it was a
fair day outside, you would already have two horses ridden by now
and might have a third one tired and tied up out back of the Grab
and Growl. You're a lot better cook than Lefty.

"I've been thinking 'bout that story you told me last night
when you made that Mountain Lion feller think you was crazy.
That was a good un! That was the funniest story I've ever heard!
Haw-haw-haw!"

Clyde poured himself another cup of strong cowboy coffee
and sat down at the table across from Fleebit. "I regret that I told
you that story because I didn't tell you the whole story. It was
something that I've tried to forget. You fixed me a couple of drinks,
and I told you something that made you laugh, but the story was

a lot more serious than you know, and I'm afraid that you might not understand."

"You know that you can tell me anything," insisted Fleebit.

Clyde hesitated and thought for a moment. He got up and stared out the kitchen window. "Okay. If I tell you the rest of that story, will you promise me that you'll never mention it again?"

"Sure, Clyde!"

"Well, then, I feel like I have to tell you this even though you might not understand it all. When I painted myself up and waited for George Mountain Lion Jr. to stumble upon me that day, I knew that he was going to shoot me or knife me as soon as he got the chance. I thought that I was pulling a good one on him if I could scare him and make him crap his pants from seeing me act like a crazy person up on the hillside that afternoon.

"But something strange happened to me while I was growling, biting at the wind, and shouting at unseen foes all around me. When I turned around, lifted my chin up and sniffed the wind like a mad bear seeking out the enemy, I was ready to charge my enemy with a fierceness and killing power that I'd never felt before. Something I can't explain came over me, and then I became very weak after George ran out of sight. My legs were like rubber, and my head felt strange. I had to curl up under that big rock and sleep there all night.

"After that incident, there were several people who stayed away from me. I didn't know the whole story until my grandfather invited me over to his house to smoke his pipe and have a little talk. I always knew I was in trouble when grandfather brought out his pipe and wanted to have a little talk.

"He said, 'Grandson, George Mountain Lion Jr. is telling the people that he saw you turn into a bear with rabies. Would you like to tell me about this?'

"I said, 'No, Grandfather, because I don't understand it myself.'

"He tried to explain some things to me that I didn't take seriously at the time. He told me that I had a special gift that nobody had shown for several generations. Grandfather said that in the old days, there was a time when the people had lost all hope. A deep sadness and despair came over our people after their defeat by the cavalry. They were forced to give up their old hunting grounds, abandon their family graves, and give up their freedom for life on a reservation. For many, it seemed impossible to go on living. Many of the old people who carried our wisdom and our life history wanted to give up and die.

"Grandfather said there was a Lakota man who was a clown and a trickster like me. He tried to explain how the clown used a special power and magic by using jokes and tricks to distract the people from their sadness. He would tell them funny stories and jokes and do many silly and ridiculous things to divert their attention. While they were distracted by his strange behavior, he transferred his medicine to them without them ever knowing it.

"He told me that the clown kept the spirits of the people alive, and that is why the Lakota people didn't give up when it seemed that all was lost. When their spirits were elevated, they became open to accept a deeper message of importance. That message was to preserve our knowledge and our history for future generations so that the human beings could carry on through hard times until the buffalo returned.

"Grandfather said that food nourishes the body, but laughter and happiness fuels the spirit of people. He told me that I could use my wit and my joking around to do good things for the people, or I could just remain a smart-ass who nobody would ever take seriously. Then came the big one: he told me that the same blood from the clown was in my family tree and flowed through my veins. He said the same power that does good things can also become a killing power, as well. He also said, 'Grandson, this is something that I hope you consider and never take lightly!'

"I didn't try to understand a lot of things back then. There's a lot that I don't understand now about life's mysteries. Sometimes I wish that I could ask my grandfather about some things."

"Thanks for telling me the rest of that story," said Fleebit. "I've lived with you for a long time, and I understand a lot more than you think I do!"

Another strong wind gust blasted down from the north ridge and shook the square house with a thunderous vibration. Clyde put down his magazine and strode over to the window. He heard Fleebit's baritone voice softly say, "Sixteen!"

Clyde asked, "What did you say?"

"Oh, I didn't think you could hear me," mumbled Fleebit.

"Well, I did hear you, and I don't know why it bothers you so much every time that I get out of my chair to look out the window. You said sixteen the last time that I walked over here, but it's seventeen times now, and if you don't know how to count numbers, I recommend that you count silently so that it doesn't bother anyone! Have you talked to your brother, Sue, lately, down in Tennessee?"

"Clyde, dammit! You know that he don't go by that name! He tolerated it some before the gay jokes came along, and that was when he put his foot down. He put his foot down on a bunch of bikers in a bar and wiped out six big men all by himself.

"My brother, Sue—uh, I mean Leonard—he's kinda queer, but he ain't gay.

"Clyde, you should better practice on bulldogging your tongue, because he's going to come here and visit us pretty soon. And you better not be cracking no more dog jokes, neither! My brother, Leonard Shepherd, is as big as a mountain and tougher than bobcat jerky. Really, Clyde, you don't want to upset him none, 'cause he don't tolerate smart alecks."

Clyde became irritated. "So you think I'm a smart aleck, huh? I want you to tell me and define to me what the word 'aleck' means."

Fleebit remained silent and thought, and then he said, "I can't describe it for you. It's just a word that folks use, but I can't tell you what it is exactly!"

"So tell me who these other folks are who are calling me a smart aleck," demanded Clyde. "Is it the preacher's sister or some of those German women that you help out?"

Fleebit scratched underneath his arm and remained silent.

"Old buddy, I've told you not to try to use words that you don't know the meaning of. That always gets you into trouble! The word 'aleck,' sounds like a German word for elk. It sounds like something your German girlfriend would say. I can hear her now: 'Oh, *Fleebit*! Are you going to chute an aleck diss fawl?' I think you called me a smart elk. Hey, I really like that! That's a great Indian name! Thanks, Fleebit! You gave me a new Indian name, and I like it a lot. That makes us related in Indian terms and kinda like brothers. If I make a fool out of myself in front of some important people over in Missoula, I'll tell everybody that my name is Smart Elk Shepherd. Everybody needs an alias sometimes, and I think I'll use my new name when I travel away from here to a bigger city. If I should get into any kind of trouble at all, I'll say that my name is Smart Elk Shepherd. If I get wild and shoot out the streetlights in Dodge City, Kansas, my name is Smart Elk Shepherd. If I meet some old gal over in the next county and I want to brush some dirt over my trail, I'll say that my name is Smart Elk Shepherd. If she asks me if I am Fleebit, I'll say no, I haven't had that problem since I shaved off my beard.

"Why did you invite your brother, Sue—sorry, I mean *Leonard*— over here in the dead of winter? There isn't anything to do around here this time of year. You should have invited him over here in the summertime when we are at the cabin on our summer range. That way, you Shepherds could run wild all over that big, open country and not get into any trouble.

"When you Shepherd brothers get together in this town and stay penned up, you are both going to jump the fence, duck under the police, and knock something over. Somebody will get upset, and pretty soon, everybody will be talking about those two Shepherds running loose and going wild on the town. I'm afraid that I'll have to bail you both out of the pound!

"Here's something to think about: you should think about your brother following you wherever you go. The Jorgenstein woman that you say you don't date but has you fetching and carrying for all the time is going to have twice as much help with things. She'll have to fix up a heaping batch of sauerkraut and sausage. You and Leonard can sit by her piano and howl like wild coyotes. You Shepherd pups can go out and dig up all of her flower beds for next year. You can both volunteer to take out her garbage.

"Since your brother is a strapping, big single man who isn't gay, maybe he'll want to go on the same date with you! I hope the two of you don't get into a bad fight over a bone!"

Fleebit suddenly came back to reality and stammered, "You are right! I should tell Leonard to wait until summer! Then we can get out of town and look over a big country, because there isn't anything to do around here this time of year."

Sometime during the early morning hours, a deafening silence magnified the endless roar of winter's fury. The residents of Big Scratch all jolted awake in the same instant, fearful that they were now deaf and misplaced, lost in an uncertain and quiet void. However, once fully awake, life became a joyous celebration. Like the sleeping prairie dogs that burrowed deep in the hill above their town, they too peeked out of doors and made plans to venture outside.

When Clyde heard the roar against the house and the banging of metal roofing stop, he smiled awake. "I can ride my young horses tomorrow out of the wind!"

But everything started out wrong. It all began early in the morning when he noticed a hole in one of his best wool saddle blankets. Upon further inspection, he discovered that mice had eaten a tunnel down through three others in the same stack. Cheyenne opened his gate again and tore open several bales of hay with his horns, scattering everything down the alley.

The young gray gelding that he was saddling up threw a fit and hung back on the lead rope, tossing his best training saddle into a pile of fresh steer shit. It was one of three yearlings that he'd bought at a sale in Thermopolis, Wyoming. You could never tell how any of them might turn out, but this one's flashy color had caught his eye. This student was at the back of Clyde's class of seven, and it was the only reason why he was trying to get him ridden on a day when the temperature was extremely cold and his mood was sour.

When Clyde first started this three-year-old, the horse had tried to buck. When he realized that he couldn't get Clyde off his back, he threw himself down and sulked. He finally got him going on the routine, but his no-name gray gelding continued to be lazy and awkward.

Clyde took him on a long ride and was two miles from town when he threw a fit. Clyde gripped with his spurs and tried to hold on, but the gelding tripped and fell going down a hill. Clyde jumped away to keep from falling beneath his mount, and he lost his reins. The young horse jumped up and ran back toward the barn like he was a front-runner in the Kentucky Derby. This forced Clyde to walk back home in a foot of snow, wearing high-heeled cowboy boots. He was pissed!

When he got home, he found that his fancy gray gelding had stopped at the barn and reached around and chewed on both fenders of his nice saddle. Both of his long reins were missing. Clyde put everything away and decided to quit for the day. When he reached the back door of the town house, it was wide open, because Fleebit didn't latch it when he ran panting down the street to his girlfriend's house. The fire was out, and the house was cold.

Fleebit came in late that evening, plopped down in his big chair next to Clyde, and asked, "Would you tell me one of those old Indian stories before I go to bed?"

Clyde abruptly said, "I don't feel like talking tonight!"

Fleebit drawled, "If you're not feeling too good, I can mix you up some of my white man medicine that always seems to perk you up some."

Clyde sat there brooding. "Is that the same drink you mixed

up and gave me a couple of nights ago that's a remedy, cure-all medicine?"

Fleebit said, "Yeah, that's the one!"

Clyde asked, "Are you suggesting that I become a motormouth or something? Do you think that I tell the whole world everything I know after I have a drink? Is this an Indian thing? Do you want to see me do a war dance?"

"Heck, Clyde, I didn't mean to tick you off! I'll just drink it myself, and then you can listen to me rattle my jaw. You know how after a few drinks, I'll tell you everything I know and a lotta stuff you wouldn't know, shouldn't know, and probably wouldn't want to know. I'll spill my guts to you about all of the women that did me wrong and didn't appreciate the jewel that they had in their grip and let go, but now they're real sorry about it and would like to have another chance, but it's too late now."

"Yeah," moaned Clyde. "They all opened up their soft, delicate hands and dropped their jewel into a cow pie and said, 'Adios!' Can I still have that special health remedy? I'm starting to feel a lot worse all of a sudden.

"Okay, so you want to hear an Indian story. A big thing happened in our town before I was born. Several young Indian men all came home at once after the Korean War. They were strong and as tough as any seasoned fighting men could be, but they were also Indian warriors now! The problem was, there were not any jobs for them on the reservation. They all wanted to prove how tough they were to everyone, but there was nothing for them to do except copulate with the opposite sex. That meant that in a few months, several Indian girls were all pregnant, and they were all going to give birth about the same time.

"The other big news was about a circus train that was coming across the prairie from the east. The moccasin telegraph that preceded the train told wild tales of exotic animals and two-headed serpents that would eat small babies and children. The parents all told their kids to behave or the train might stop at our town to feed their animals.

"Sometime in the middle of the night, there was a loud crash and a long, low rumble. The shock waves knocked cups off shelves and vibrated the glass windows. Everybody thought that it was an earthquake. Not long afterward, women started screaming and wailing, young men were shouting, and old men were singing their death songs. There were wild animals running everywhere through our town.

"Everyone still rode horses back then, and there was a big corral where several families kept them. There was a big stack of hay there, and a big elephant showed up at that haystack and spooked all of those horses. They snorted, busted down the corral, and took off down the road. When they got to the main street in town, some zebras and a big giraffe intercepted them and scattered them down every alley and backyard.

"Those horses were so terrified that they stampeded over and through everything, tearing down clotheslines, smashing old parked cars and trucks, and tromping everything. Some of them had clothes attached to them as they sped past.

"A bunch of monkeys and a big gorilla showed up in the center of town, and they grabbed people's clothes and swung them around, screaming, 'Eeeeee! Eeeeh-eeeeh!'

"Those horses went crazy! They would run through town in one direction and see that giraffe or some monkeys, and then they would blow snot and run the other direction until they would get to that big elephant. Then back they would come with some zebras running with them. Someone yelled that there was an African lion loose in town.

"The circus owner showed up with a loudspeaker called a megaphone and started shouting in a big, loud, deep baritone voice. Nobody from our small town had ever heard a megaphone before, so everyone thought that it was the Great Spirit telling them that he wanted help rounding up his animals and that he would give everybody a hundred bucks to help with the gather. Some of our people who were Christianized thought that Noah was asking them to help load up the ark and get a reward.

"All of those young Indian men back from the war wanted to prove how brave they were and earn some eagle feathers by counting coup. They all went out and tried to catch one of those panic-stricken horses. Many of them were tromped on and injured.

"It seemed like all of the wild commotion and excitement started several Indian girls into labor. One girl was giving birth in a bedroom when that big gorilla swung in through the open window of the parlor where the father and grandfather waited. He knocked over some things, screamed, '*Ohh-ooh-eeeeh*!' and sprung back out through the window.

"After things calmed down the next day, there were some new additions to our tribal family, and everybody was trying to sort it all out. When it came time to name these new babies, there was a lot of discussion among the elders and a few disagreements. Some of the new names were Many Horses Afraid, Giraffe Wears Red Shirt, Zebra Drags Hurt Man, Monkey Jumps Fence, Lion Kills Monkey, Little Elephant Man.

"There was one family who had a big disagreement over which name to give the infant. This was the family where the gorilla jumped into their parlor during the childbirth. The grandfather was insistent on naming the child from what the father's reaction was on that night. He chose the name of Man Afraid of Big Monkey.

"The father was insistent on naming the child from the grandfather's reaction to that incident, and he wanted the name of Man Afraid Punpun Pants. It was a standoff, and neither side would give in, but they were running out of time. They all believed that the Great Spirit had caused all of this for a reason and that the baby and the family would be blessed by the right name. They only had so much time before the power left.

"The first sound the baby ever made was a high-pitched,

"*Eeh-eeh-eeh*," and that scared the old grandpa so bad that he brought in a medicine man.

"Well, with the help of the medicine man, they finally reached a compromise and named the child Man Afraid of Big Monkey Punpun Pants. That gave the dad and grandpa both some credit. The problem was, everybody got lockjaw from trying to say this long name. That boy acted like he was part monkey, and he was into everything. They were always yelling at him, and by the time they would get his long name out, he would already have something destroyed and be long gone and into something else. They finally had to shorten up his name to make it easy on everybody in the family."

Clyde finished his drink and said, "End of story! I'm going to bed now. Good night!"

"Hey, wait," said Fleebit. "When they shortened up that kid's name, what did they call him?"

"They called him Monkey See Monkey Doo—that's Doo as in *doo-doo.* That kid was always the talk of the town. His folks just couldn't control him or make him keep his pants on. When he got about fifteen years old, he ran away and joined up with a circus back east. He became one of those flying acrobats that soar through the air and swing from those little chairs they call a trapeze. Today, everybody refers to him as the Flying Lakota." Clyde stood up out of his chair and said, "The end! Good night!"

Fleebit was on the edge of his seat with his long jaw gaped open. "Is that a true story?"

Clyde's eyes changed from a fun, inventive, thoughtful look to his Indian, bird-of-prey, dark eyes. "Why do you ask?"

"Well," said Fleebit, "I don't recall any train tracks going through that Pine Ridge country."

Clyde pointed his finger at Fleebit. "You didn't ask for anything other than an Indian story, and I am an Indian, so if you have grown particular, I will just go to bed when I am tired at night, and I will refuse to tell you any more bedtime stories!"

"But here is the thing," stammered Fleebit. "You told me an Indian story one time, and I believed that story. I repeated it at the coffee shop and was told that it was a bunch of baloney and wasn't but about half-truthful. When I asked you about it, you got mad at me! You also told me that you were one of the few people who could tell a story like that and get away with it. You also told me that I didn't have a proper license to repeat those stories. You said that since you were one-half Indian, you could tell a story that was the rich, dark truth. You also said that since you were one-half white man, you could tell a poor white lie to go along with the story. That is the only reason why I'm asking about that dammed train!"

Clyde heaved an exhausted sigh and said, "Okay, I will tell you this: if you ever decide to ride your mule from Big Scratch, Montana, to Pine Ridge, South Dakota, during a blizzard in the dead of winter to catch the train, I will tell you if this is a true story. Now good night!"

12

THE GRAB AND GROWL CAFÉ WAS A LANDMARK IN THE
small town of Big Scratch, Montana, but nobody really knew
why, except that it was possibly the only café in town. It was a
meeting place for farmers, ranchers, loggers, truckers, miners, and
occasional housewives who were about to die from kitchen fever and
dishwashing blues. The food was only fair, but there were no other
public restaurants or cafés to compare it to for many miles.

Many of the local residents referred to it as the Last Resort Café.

Two of the most regular long-term patrons of Lefty's café were
Fleebit Shepherd and Clyde Deerhide, who spent the winters in
Big Scratch and rode their horses to and from the café for meals
and coffee. Two older cowboys with big reputations around this
area, they were more of a landmark than the café was itself. It was
told that Clyde helped a previous owner build the hitching rails
out in the back, where they tied up their riding animals. Nobody
remembered how long ago it was when he did it, but old-timers from
around the area commented that it was long, long ago when the
previous building had been a trading post and a feed store.

Lefty was upset because Clyde and Fleebit acted like they owned
the real estate all around there and he was just a tenant, using the
building only with their permission. They came into town wearing

cowboy boots, hats, chaps, and spurs and looking like remnants from the Goodnight-Loving Trail drives and a far, distant past. He got along fine with Fleebit and usually Clyde, but their horses were a constant cause of filth, maintenance, and emotional irritation. Those damned horses just shit, shit, and shit!

Everyone was welcome at the Grab and Growl by the owner and cook, Lefty Meyers, and a very diverse element of folks got along just fine until the environmentalists started coming into Big Scratch every summer. Lefty had a particular dislike for the wolf and grizzly study people, and he had a secret and particular reason for disliking them. As long as they wore a shirt and shoes, he had to let them into his café and serve them, but he didn't have to try to please them.

Lefty was not sure when his reputation for fine cuisine became blemished. He had a good idea that Clyde Deerhide had something to do with it, and he took out his spite on Clyde and the wolf and bear people. Somehow, it got around town that Lefty had been serving up road-killed deer, elk, and moose meat for many years. People were now referring to his establishment as the Roadkill Café. Since this new name became public, the old name of the Grab and Growl even sounded like something incriminating. Clyde was a connoisseur of good meat and always appreciated a good cut of meat that was fresh and taken care of properly. He'd eaten every kind of wild game imaginable, but his preference was for perfectly aged beef. He noticed that some of the meat on the daily lunch special tasted questionable, and there was no question left when he found a deer hair mixed in with his beef stroganoff.

Clyde noticed that Lefty left town in his pickup truck in the early hours just after daylight and headed west on Route 6 past the Lolo National Forest. He might not have noticed Lefty's routine at all had it not been for his early-morning horseback rides above the town. He also noticed that Lefty's routine altered some by the changing of the seasons. Lefty made his early morning drive down Route 6 only during the wintertime. When it became warmer, he stopped his routine. That was the same time when the wolf and bear biologists showed up in town, and it was well known that they drove down Route 6 to pick up dead elk, deer, and moose carcasses. They used dead animals hit during the night by long-haul truckers to bait their snares and culvert traps during the day.

The pieces of the puzzle all came together one morning when Clyde tied up his horse to the hitching rail behind the Grab and Growl and noticed that some town dogs had tipped over a trash barrel. Lying on the ground at his feet was a leg bone from a young elk calf with the hoof still on it. Clyde looked inside another barrel and found parts of a moose and more hoofs and bones from a deer.

Lefty saw Clyde out the back window of the café as he tied up his horse, and he was ready for him. Lefty ran out the back door and yelled, "When are you cowboys going to come back here and clean up some of this horse shit? I'm tired of cleaning this mess up every day behind a respectable restaurant! I try to keep things sanitized around here and serve clean food, but you cowboys just draw flies to my kitchen!"

"Lefty, I might question your respectability right now." Clyde kicked the elk leg toward him and asked, "What's the lunch special today?"

Lefty huffed up, slapped his dish towel against his leg, and marched back into the kitchen. From then on, it seemed like folks would only come into the café to drink coffee and fill space. He was starting to throw away a lot of good food, and his customers were dwindling down every day.

Clyde thought about his beef stroganoff with the deer hair in it, how nasty and decayed the dead elk calf carcass looked, and how Lefty yelled at him like a second-class citizen. He decided that it was his civic duty to inform the town.

Clyde was not a gossip, and he didn't care for people who eagerly circulated other people's personal information. He didn't believe in it, but he knew how to spread the word like wind on a raging prairie fire. He just happened to stop by the hardware store to loaf around just before lunchtime. Marty not only owned the hardware store but he was also the town's dogcatcher and the arsonist that started prairie fires of gossip all throughout the town.

It was seldom that Clyde came into this store, and Marty was hungry for anything that he could spread throughout town about his most unfavorable cowboy named Clyde Deerhide. Marty detested Clyde's reputation of being bigger than John Wayne. Clyde was always secretive about where he went and what he did. He wouldn't tell you where anyone else went or what they did, either. His rude manner of hiding information that other folks were entitled to made Marty and his circle of friends distrustful of him.

So what if he was reputed to be a famous all-around cowboy. He was still only a half- breed Indian!

Marty knew that he couldn't pry any information out of Clyde, so he asked, "Are you about to go over to the café to get lunch? It's lunchtime, and I am getting hungry."

"No, Marty, I must have eaten a bad piece of meat yesterday, and I feel kind of sick today." Clyde began sorting through a discount bin of cheap Chinese tools near the checkout counter. "Marty, have you ever noticed how Lefty always serves ground or chopped meat for lunch and dinner?"

Marty walked toward the front door with his keys in his hands, impatient to leave the store. He turned around with a puzzled expression on his face. "Well, I never really thought about it, but you're right!"

"Yeah," said Clyde, "and it's always hamburger steak, Sloppy Joes, meatloaf, or stroganoff with lots of spices and heavy sauces of some kind. I think I'll just go home and cook up a solid piece of beefsteak with just some salt and pepper on it. I'm getting tired of the same old menu at the Grab and Growl. Well, I have to go now. Hey, wait a minute! Since you are the town's dogcatcher, I think it's your duty to get a handle on all of these town dogs around here that are getting into everybody's trash and causing a ruckus all over town."

"I haven't heard about any trouble with stray dogs until now," responded Marty.

Clyde insisted, "Well, just go and look behind the Grab and Growl Café! Some dogs tipped over some trash barrels and scattered trash and bones everywhere. You might want to look inside some of those barrels out back to see if you can come up with some lids or containers that will keep those town dogs from getting into them. It just isn't sanitary."

13

FRANKY MEYERS HIT A SMALL GOLD STRIKE IN THE ISOLATED
Nevada desert. It was just a thin vein that wasn't very long, very
wide, or very deep. In fact, the description of his lucky find was a
mirror-view image of Franky's personality and of his character.

Franky had tried several things to make it big, and gambling
was his longest run at any one occupation; however, it was the run
where he always finished in last place.

Franky had been married four times, and his multiple wives had
experienced multiple and varied types of adventures. Franky's life
resembled migrating flocks of blackbirds that arrive somewhere in
the fall and swoop, duck, and dive without any serious intent to stay
in any one tree for very long or commit to a straight and continuous
flight to any specific destination.

Most of Franky's brainchild get-rich schemes had involved
someone else doing the work while he watched and waited with
his hands out. This last adventure was a solo act, and the work of
using a pick and shovel had almost killed him. He realized that
he was getting too old, and this might be his last chance toward a
peaceful retirement.

Franky dug and dug until he knew there was no more gold left
in that claim. He also realized that if he stayed in Nevada very long,

his addiction would pull him back to the casinos and that he'd be right back where he started several times before. Broke!

His brother in Montana told him how cheap a small business was and how there was a big opportunity for everything to grow. He knew that he had enough gold to buy some land and start up a small business of his own. By being a bachelor for many years, he had become a pretty fair cook, and he thought that perhaps he could make a go with a small restaurant somewhere. At least he could eat well, and if he put his money into the food business, the customers would be putting their money on the tables instead of him.

The temptation of rolling the dice just one more time with his newfound riches was making his hands twitch on the steering wheel of his pickup truck as he neared the exit to Las Vegas. He was approaching the exit when he noticed the woman sitting next to the interstate highway. She was apparently sobbing with her face held in her hands. He couldn't see her face, but he noticed her large upper body heaving up and down. Franky's hands were anticipating the right turn toward Las Vegas, but now all they wanted to do was stop the truck.

Franky rolled down his window and asked, "Do you want a ride?"

The woman uncovered her beautiful tear-streaked face and asked, "Where to?"

"Is Montana far enough?" asked Franky.

"No place is far enough away from here," she sobbed. She opened the door and said, "My name is Bonnie. I don't have any money to pay for anything! My husband lost everything last night at the tables. All I need right now is a ride in this truck. If you have any ideas about anything other than a truck ride together, then move on. Right now, I hate men, and I would rather ride with a billy goat so that I could castrate him and not go to prison for mutilating his manhood and making him bleed to death. If you understand me, then I'll throw my suitcase in the back."

Franky was very nervous as he pulled out onto the interstate highway and headed toward the Utah state line. All he could think about was castration and a lot of bleeding. He wondered if she had a knife hidden somewhere. His hands began twitching on the steering wheel again, and he felt like he had to pee, although he'd just gone at a rest stop a few miles back down the road.

Franky tried to make small talk with the woman as they journeyed northeast toward Utah, but the woman only sobbed occasionally and bounced her chest up and down.

"I've got me a good stake, and I'm going to open up a nice, big restaurant in Montana. That country is really going to grow in the next few years, and I'll need a hostess and manager to help when things get rolling. There might be a big opportunity there for somebody who gets in on the ground floor of things."

Bonnie sat back in a daze. "I just can't believe this has happened to me! I told my husband last night that it was time to quit. We were starting to lose at every game we played. It was late when we both went up to the room, and I had several of those free drinks at the tables. I must have passed out. When I woke up this morning, my husband was gone, and the hotel and casino managers were both there to tell me that our credit cards were maxed out and that I had to leave. When I looked into my purse, all of my credit cards were gone. My husband lost everything last night, including the inheritance that my dad just left me."

Franky drove all night toward Montana and only stopped to fuel up the truck and use the restroom along the way. He told Bonnie his entire life story while she leaned motionless against the passenger side door. He couldn't tell if she was asleep or not, but living alone in the desert for several months and the sound of conversation, though one-sided, stimulated him to narrate a larger-than-life image of his greatness and gallantry in a world where fate often did him an injustice. Just having a beautiful woman next to him that he could lie to and who didn't doubt him or question his greatness encouraged him up the highway toward new and better things in Big Scratch, Montana.

Everybody in Big Scratch was talking about how Franky Meyers bought out his brother's old Grab and Grow Café—a.k.a. the Roadkill Café. Nothing ever seemed to change much around town from year to year, and this was big news. Folks were saying that the new owner traded a gold claim in Nevada to Lefty and that he was remodeling the old café into a first-class restaurant. Folks couldn't tell what they were doing inside the old place for many days. The new owner covered up the glass from the inside, and it was about to drive some of the town ladies insane.

Bonnie had the idea of bargaining for the wood from a dismantled barn and pole corral from down the street and using the old barn wood to cover some of the white plastered walls on the outside. She told the local carpenters on the job to use the corral poles for a veranda with a southwest image on the front side of the building and to keep some sections of the exterior plaster just as it was. With borders of large pine support and framing beams from the old barn, a southwest-style hacienda was in the making.

Clyde rode by almost every morning on one of his young horses, and what he saw pleased him greatly. Finally, somebody was building something that was as pleasing to the eye as the log trading post that his relatives built many years ago. It was about time somebody built something new, with an image of the Old West and the good old days.

There was something else new, exciting, and spectacular! Fleebit said that her name was Bonnie.

Clyde assumed that the man she'd arrived with was her husband or boyfriend. But by casual observance of riding past on a different horse several times a day, the man and the woman didn't appear to be connected in intimacy or by ambition. The woman appeared to be doing most of the work and seemed to avoid the man. She was extremely beautiful, and there was an air of courage and self-confidence about her. She held her head high and walked like a Lakota woman. Her long, brown hair, dark eyes, and olive skin reminded him of his mother.

The town gossips were speculating about the new man and woman who arrived in town, and everyone was watching as they worked on the old building each day. Helga called Marty at the hardware store and said, "Yes, that man, he sleep in one room at the hotel, and the woman, she sleep in another room at the other end of the hotel. That woman, she work all the time, and that man, he just watch that woman while she work!"

Franky spent a lot of money on the new sign. It was a huge sign, and it was very colorful. It took a lot of paint too! Bonnie was an art teacher at one time, and the sign was of her original creation. It was the biggest and the brightest sign on any building in Big Scratch, and it got a lot of attention.

Finally, it was time for the grand opening, and everybody in town was ready to see what they had done to the inside of the building and what was on the menu. Every housewife was hopeful for some progressive cooking from some source other than their own kitchens, and every man needed a place to shoot the bull and drink some coffee with his friends. Even the wolf and bear people were hopeful for some good salads, steak, seafood, and pasta, and they were even more hopeful that a new proprietor would be friendly to them.

Franky was a pretty fair hand around a kitchen, and he knew how to cook and prepare different dishes to please a variety of different customers. He knew that a truck driver liked greasy french fries, burgers, and gravy, and he knew that housewives would want some salads and dishes that had some color and creative flair. The problem was, Franky couldn't cook and do anything else at the same time. He had a short-sighted, single focus on one thing at a time, and anything that might divert his attention away from the present task at hand could be a disaster. He could barely chew gum and walk at the same time.

Franky's attention was distracted from the first time that he laid eyes on Bonnie Barker, and it was driving him crazy. Since they arrived in Big Scratch, he'd tried everything to get her to move in with him. He said, "Bonnie, we can save a lot of money by both of us staying in the same room. Let's be partners!"

Bonnie just looked through him with cold eyes and said, "I told you that I would help to get this restaurant thing started and that I don't want to start anything else with you. If you can't handle that, then I'll hitchhike out to the interstate highway and get inside another pickup truck that's headed to nowhere."

"These two rooms at this hotel are expensive," said Franky, "and I've given you some advances already."

"Yeah, you've *made* several advances already," said Bonnie. "You will get your money's worth out of me after we open, but you will not get it in any hotel room. I might decide to go and moonlight at another job down at the veterinary clinic on weekends if I start feeling like getting my hands bloody. If I start thinking about my husband, I might want to castrate some bulls for these ranchers around here."

Franky's right hand started twitching, and he suddenly felt like he had to pee.

Bonnie hand painted many menus of creative design in her hotel room each night, and she often stayed up all night at the restaurant painting large Western murals on the interior walls. Bonnie told the small construction crew what she wanted done on a day-to-day schedule and produced many blueprints on a cheap nightstand with poor lighting that were better than anything the crew had seen on some of their bigger jobs in Missoula and Great Falls. When Bonnie wasn't on a ladder driving nails or using a screw gun, she was telling someone to get with it and to do it over, because it wasn't in the plan that she gave them. The two local carpenters were trying to watch Bonnie while they worked, and they often smashed a finger with a hammer or tripped over something.

Bonnie finished painting the big welcome banner that announced opening day, and she felt like it was the signature to her biggest, brightest work.

Bonnie felt proud of her inventive remodeling, decorating, and hard work. She felt more empowered and somewhat daring. She hadn't felt this way in a long, long time.

I can't believe that shy, handsome cowboy has been riding past here for three weeks and hasn't stopped to introduce himself yet. He smiles at me and sometimes tips his hat as he rides by, but today, I'm going to introduce myself, Bonnie thought. *Around 4:00 p.m., he often ties the bay horse to a hitching post behind the café, picks up his feet, and combs his mane and tail.*

Clyde rode all seven young horses on a ride in the foothills surrounding the town that day. The last turn toward home took them down a hill and past the new restaurant. He tried to ride up to Bonnie several times and introduce himself, but something always went haywire with his plan.

The young sorrel gelding wouldn't stand still when he rode closer, and he had to turn him in tight circles. He became skittish when he heard the sound of pounding hammers and refused to venture closer. Clyde didn't want to create a scene.

Bonnie was standing outside all alone when he rode up on the fancy palomino. He was a quiet horse and coming along fine in his training. Suddenly, an air compressor blew off pressure and began rattling. His horse snorted and jumped sideways. He bucked twice as Clyde held on and turned him back toward home.

The black gelding was always frisky when they started out, but he tired quickly and became lazy on the return ride home. Clyde pushed him harder and farther than usual. By the time they reached the café, he was out of breath and sluggish in his step. Bonnie was standing on a ladder hanging the new banner when they rode up. A strong gust of wind suddenly tore it out of her hands, and it flapped wildly in the wind. His horse suddenly became a Pegasus with wings, and he flew high into the air and bolted sideways. Clyde rode it out and stayed in the center of him, but it made him angry. He pounded his lazy ass in a hard gallop all the way home.

He quickly unsaddled the black and threw his rig on the back of the bay. Grabbing the saddle horn with both hands, he swung in the air and landed in the middle, catching both stirrups on the run. He raced back to the café as fast as he could. When the café came into view, Bonnie was gone, and the construction crew was finished for the day. He was too late!

He wasn't sure why he felt so disappointed, dejected, and defeated. He tied up his horse to the hitching post and pulled a hoof pick and a fine steel comb from his saddle pocket.

Bonnie came out of the back kitchen door and entered the alley. She walked toward the hitching rail and crouched down, using the row of trash cans to block her advance. The cowboy was picking up a front foot with his back to her, when she came up and peeked around the trash containers.

The horse saw her immediately. His eyes were wide, and his ears were pointed and focused upon her movement. He nickered a soft, friendly welcome.

Clyde dropped the foot and spun around facing Bonnie. "Hi! You surprised me. That don't happen very often. Are you an Indian?"

Bonnie laughed. "No, but I played an Indian princess called Pocahontas in a high-school play."

Clyde walked toward her and stretched out his hand. "That must be why you walk quietly like an Indian. My name is Clyde Deerhide."

"Hello, Clyde. I'm Bonnie Barker. It's my turn to ask: are you an Indian?"

Clyde realized that he was holding her hand longer than a normal, introductory handshake, and he quickly relaxed his grip, dropping her firm hand. "Yes, I am an Indian—half Indian. My mother was a full-blood Lakota."

Bonnie asked, "Can I pet your horse? He is my favorite one. I've watched you ride several others past the café, but he's the most beautiful one, and he isn't wild like the palomino, the gray, the black, the paint, and the two sorrels."

Clyde was startled. "Yeah, I'm real proud of this one. He acts calm, but he's all business. Sure, you can pet him. I could tell that he wasn't alarmed when you approached. When he nickered, he introduced himself to you like he wanted to be friends."

Bonnie held out her hand so that he could smell her and then gently stroked his neck. "What's his name?"

Clyde noticed how she did everything right when approaching a horse, and she knew the proper names of their colors, but he could tell she wasn't a horse person. "He doesn't have a proper name yet. I call him No-Name."

Bonnie seemed puzzled. "Why doesn't he have a name?"

Clyde was nervously turning the hoof pick over and over in his hands. "I never name the horses that I might want to sell. It would be like selling a friend. But I'll never sell this one! He's strong, fearless, and has more intelligence and guts than most people. I'm actually waiting for something to happen so I can give him a special Indian name. I believe that a powerful spirit name for a horse will give him special abilities. In olden times, war ponies and buffalo runners were always painted with their power symbols and given powerful names."

Franky came out of the kitchen and yelled, "Come on, Bonnie, it's time to drive back to the hotel now!"

Bonnie stepped away from Clyde and No-Name a short distance and yelled back, "Go on without me. I'll walk!"

She walked up close to Clyde and extended both of her hands. Clyde dropped the hoof pick in the dirt and took her hands. This time, it was she who held her grip and seemed reluctant to let go.

"I'm sorry about that! It would appear that Franky wants you to think that I'm his woman. He's a jerk! I'll never be his woman, and I've told him that. We have a business deal and that is all. I am married, but my husband deserted me in Las Vegas after losing all of our money. If I ever see him again, I might kill him. He's history! Franky promised me a business proposition in this restaurant if I could help get it running, and I might end up killing him first. Clyde, all I need right now is a friend. I've already found out that you are a bachelor, and everybody says that you enjoy the company of horses more than the company of people."

Bonnie released one of her hands and held her grip on Clyde while she stretched out her other arm and rubbed against the big bay's shoulder. "I don't like people very much anymore. They always seem to drain out my energy and let me down. Clyde, I really don't know very much about horses, but I can see how No-Name could become your best chosen company. I arrive early at the restaurant, and I've seen you ride around here in the dark mornings while the town is still asleep. I'm a night rider too! I'll be happy to buy you a cup of coffee in the morning."

Opening day was a big one! Everybody who pulled in, rode up, or walked to the new restaurant saw Bonnie's big colorful sign announcing the new Thin Vein Gold Strike Café.

Men from miles around had watched and waited for this day. It wasn't so much that they were hungry for hash browns and eggs over easy or that they couldn't make a cup of coffee for themselves. For the majority of local men, it didn't really matter what they served inside that fancy new place. The server inside was what mattered! Most of them had either seen or heard about Bonnie Barker.

As the people came inside on opening morning, Franky had a clear view of everything. While he managed the grill and kitchen all by himself, he could look out through a large, wide-open counter and food pick-up station that overlooked the entire dining area. Bonnie appeared to be everywhere at once. Bonnie took care of the entire dining area by herself, and nothing was behind or lacking from anything. In fact, Bonnie was a magnificent example of the female species defined as grace in motion. She moved quickly and fluently throughout the busy diner while her upper body bounced as she moved back and forth. Her upper bosom bounced in rhythm with her hips when she moved like a ballet dancer with skilled practice of performing on a stage. Bonnie was a star on a stage in front of uncouth men who stared.

Franky was doing okay until he noticed that men were staring at Bonnie's boobs. Then he noticed some truckers were staring at her and snickering between themselves over something that one of them had said. Then he saw a guy purposely drop his fork in front of Bonnie and look down her blouse when she stooped over to pick it up for him. Before long, the hash browns were burning, the toast was smoking, and the eggs were stuck like cement to his grill.

Two older cowboys came in dressed like something from the cast of a Western movie set and made themselves at home like they had done it many times before. Franky noticed out of his window that Bonnie laughed a lot when she came by this one certain table. Every time Bonnie came past this table, she stopped and laughed at something and then bounced on to the other customers.

Franky was trying to pay better attention to what he was doing at the grill, scraping off everything that he burned, and starting over again. He just couldn't believe how many men had come in here for breakfast on opening day! It was beginning to look like another gold mine. Now, if he could only strike it rich with Bonnie, this adventure would turn into a true bonanza.

It was lunchtime now, and Franky expected a different crowd. He could see through his serving window that more housewives and couples were coming in for lunch, and he thought he had it all figured out. Now was the time to put out a special with a little bit more color and flair. Anybody could fry up a breakfast and make some gravy to cover up a biscuit, but lunch and dinner separated the men from the boys. That was what would pay the bills and recover his expenses from this enterprise.

The cowboys who tied their horses out in back behind his kitchen were still there, and Bonnie was seated beside the man who everyone called Clyde Deerhide. It was true that business slowed down some, but she seemed to be enjoying herself a little bit too much.

"Bonnie, can you come back here and help me get this lunch ready?"

"Stuff it!" shouted Bonnie. "I am not the cook!"

Bonnie finally got up, greeted two elderly ladies, and seated them. They each ordered a taco salad. A big group of young people came in, and they ordered seafood linguini.

Franky was watching Bonnie to see if she would sit back down next to Clyde, and before long, the pasta boiled over into the big salad bowl. All of the salad was ruined, and the pasta boiled into a thick paste. Franky didn't have enough salad greens left for both lunch and dinner, so he drained the hot water off of the salad and dumped the hot, wilted lettuce on some plates. He threw some chunks of tomato and avocado on the salad, added some taco chips, and yelled, "Ready!"

He looked out and saw Bonnie talking to Clyde and laughing hysterically. This really upset him. He slopped the pasta paste onto some plates, threw some imitation crabmeat on top, shook some canned parmesan cheese over the whole thing, and yelled,

"Ready!"

It seemed like everything was a disaster. One of the old ladies carried her taco salad back to the counter, slammed her plate down, and confronted him personally, saying, "This taco salad should go back to Mexico to feed the swine!"

Bonnie seemed to be jubilant, and she was spending more time flirting with Clyde between customers. If a customer seemed dissatisfied with something that was prepared by Franky, she sent them back to him personally carrying their plates.

The lunch crowd was thinning out, and Franky was able to catch up by frying cheeseburgers on the grill for some truck drivers. He overcooked the french fries, though, and they came out of the deep fryer brown and crisp. As soon as he caught up, he stormed over to Clyde's table and demanded, "Are you going to order anything to eat today? I don't get rich off of coffee, ya know!"

Clyde retorted, "When I come in here, you always start burning something back in that kitchen. They ought to move the fire station next door to save money on telephone calls and gasoline. I know what burned eggs and toast smell like, and it ruins my appetite."

"Well, I'm starting to get tired of shoveling up all of that horse shit out in the back of my establishment," said Franky. "If you want to buy this place, then you can do what you want to, but I happen to be in charge right now."

Clyde said, "Fleebit, let's go stretch our horses' legs."

Dinner passed by without any incident or calamity, and Franky associated his good luck with the absence of Clyde Deerhide. After everyone left, Franky asked Bonnie, "So how much did you make in tips today?"

"That is none of your damned business," declared Bonnie.

"Well, it looked like that cowboy left a big pile of greenbacks on the table when he left. That reject from an old Western movie sure isn't rich. I'll bet that he don't own anything except that horse that stays tied out back there and shits all day long. He can't afford to buy any food in here. All he does is drink coffee and take up space where somebody else could sit when things get busy in here. He probably gave you a big tip because he has a small one someplace that wants more than just coffee. Come on, Bonnie, some of these guys just want to jump you!"

Bonnie said, "Yeah, like you haven't tried? The difference between you and Clyde Deerhide might be a few years, but there is a much bigger difference. Clyde makes me laugh, and that was something I thought I'd forgotten how to do. You get me pissed off every day, and that is something that I am real good at remembering!"

14

IT WAS LATE SPRING IN THE FOOTHILLS ABOVE BIG SCRATCH,
Montana, and Clyde and Fleebit were returning to town after riding
several miles on their saddle animals. Cabin fever had drawn them
out of their winter headquarters in the town house, and they were
looking forward to moving up on their high summer range where
the old cabin stood, still cloaked in deep snow.

Clyde looked out over the wide mountain range covered in
white. "It's been a long winter cooped up in town, and I feel like
those elk that we saw today. I'd like to keep heading north, but
Mother Nature won't let me until it's her time to decide when I can
move on. My horse is looking forward to his summer home as much
as me. He wanted to push on up through that deep snow and keep
going. He wanted to go where there is some freedom and where
he remembers that times are worth living. Animals are not much
different from us, really. They have desires and wishful thoughts in
their heads, just like us."

Fleebit nudged his big riding mule ahead, and Clyde followed
on his horse until they stopped on top of the flat, sandy hill that
overlooked the center of downtown Big Scratch. From this one high
spot, you could look over the entire town and every street coming
into it from each direction.

"Look, Clyde, those bear people are on their way into town from the west. I'll bet that it won't be long until the wolf people come driving in from the east. You can tell that it's springtime when those tree huggers all show up and start running around in the mountains. Yep, I was right! Here come the wolf people in from the east side of town. Can you tell me how those two groups of people can leave here every day in two different directions, spend all day somewhere in the mountains, and then all show up at the same time just before sundown?"

Clyde answered, "Some things Mother Nature plans, like when the snow line lets you move forward, and some things people plan together to make things work out."

Fleebit became excited. "Look, they're going to meet up at the hardware store like usual, and then they'll all go inside the store and buy some more cable and clips to make snares out of. I'll bet that they buy some more rolls of that fluorescent tape too so they can mark where they are tomorrow and they can find that spot again the next day."

Clyde said, "It sounds like Marty sells them things out of his hardware store and then tells the whole town what their business is. How would you like it if you went into the bank and deposited some money, and then the banker told everybody who came into the bank how much money you had or didn't have?"

Fleebit continued, "Yep, after the hardware store, those two groups of environmentalists are going to go through town like a flock of chickens. They'll all stay close together until they find what they need, and then they'll all end up at the Thin Vein for their dinner. They show up early to eat so they don't run into anybody that hates their guts and might want to get in their face. And then they'll all leave town together and split up at Route 6 and then go back their separate ways to their hidden tent camps up near the snow line."

Clyde turned his horse facing Fleebit. "It almost sounds like you are spying on those kids who are doing research on those wolves and bears for the Fish and Game Department. How would you like it if someone was spying on you? Why are you so worried about when those kids arrive in town, what they do in town, and when they leave?"

Fleebit shifted in his saddle and spit at the ground. "The whole town is saying that those tree huggers are going to ruin this whole country by spying on everything around here. Nobody likes them or trusts them very far. Folks in town say that they're going to stop logging, mining, and cattle ranching before it is all over. Clyde, I'm just telling you what everybody thinks."

Clyde said, "Well, you know that I'm a free thinker, and that means that I think things for myself as I see it. That also means that I don't think what the general public wants me to think until I sort it all out and reach my own conclusions on the issues at hand."

"You've been a cowboy all the years that I've known you, and I never figured you for a tree hugger!" exclaimed Fleebit. "Hell, man, those types of people want to take the beef off your plate and the horse off your trail!"

Clyde gazed out over the town, but his memory was far away. "Those look like good kids to me, and I've seen them around town a lot. When I see those young men and women all grouped together like a flock of chickens, it reminds me of my kinfolk and me many years ago. When I see them arrive in town just before it gets too dark to shop and they all cluster together to eat before anyone else shows up for dinner, I remember how it was when us Indian kids all showed up in a town away from the reservation. We knew that we were the enemy and that white folks didn't trust us because we were different. White folks that saw us all together thought that we were going to steal something from them or do them some kind of harm, but we were just afraid to be alone in a redneck cowboy town. The townspeople thought that we were going to harm them in some way, and we thought that they were going to harm us. And that was the whole misconception in the first place. If the white people and the Indians had parlayed together to resolve their differences instead of killing each other over misconceptions about life, maybe we wouldn't have global warming today. Maybe it wouldn't matter if you lived in a round tent or a square house made out of brick as long as you all realized that the earth was round and that we all had to make it work together.

"When I see those kids around this town, I see myself many years ago. When they all show up together in the early hours before sundown, they planned it that way so they could support each other in the face of the enemy. They think that some of these local people are going to do them some kind of harm. Those boys and girls are living in tents up near the snow line where hungry grizzly bears are waking up out of hibernation, yet they fear their own kind more than a dangerous bear. Those kids are just like me, but now you see me as a cowboy, and you see them as the Indians. How can you explain that? I'm getting to be an old Indian now, but I see a new thing happening. There are young white people today who realize that things are not good from the way our planet has been managed. They are the New Indians!

"I see the federal, state, and local government wanting to bring in big money for jobs and development. They want strip mines, oil and natural gas development, and anything else that will bring in a buck for something that is sold off to the highest bidder. I see environmental groups come into our country who want to protect everything. Being the free thinker that I am, I have come to this conclusion: I see Mother Earth as a beautiful maiden. The New Indians—who you call tree huggers—want to protect her by putting a chastity belt on her. Our state and local governments don't care if she gets molested or beat up a little. The developers and the mining companies claim that they just want to date her. They don't want to marry her with the vows of "to honor and protect" and "till death do we part," but after they use and abuse her, they'll drive off and never look back. After they get what they want, they'll no longer have any respect or feelings for her. To me, that is called date rape!

That's why the environmental groups want to lock her up and throw away the key.

"Fleebit, you've rode with me since we were youngsters and seen what the timber and mining companies have done to our country. They've had their day and their way. There is no middle ground!"

Fleebit said, "I've heard that some boys are thinking about riding up on the mountain and scaring those kids off."

Clyde was getting mad. "Is that right? Well, maybe I'll put on some war paint and go join up with those New Indians. I'd like to talk with them, anyway, and I'll bet that we could share some of the same philosophy. A war chief always sized up his enemy by trying to understand how he would think rather than by how big he was or how many were in his group. The most feared foe is one who believes in their cause and is committed to their battle. I wouldn't underestimate somebody who traps wolves and grizzly bears and lives in a cold tent up in the snow. It takes guts to snare a hungry bear and put a radio collar on him. Somebody who learns the habits of wolves and bears doesn't get dumber. They get smarter! Fleebit, the hunter always becomes the hunted."

Fleebit was agitated. "What do you mean by that statement?"

Clyde took down his rope, made a small loop, and spun it at his side. "You don't know it, but you are being stalked and trapped every day. That cagey German woman that you say you help but do not date has a big loop snare set for you, and you don't even know it. She has it camouflaged and opened big right now, and you are stepping through it without tripping it. Every day that you come into the bait of her home cooking, she starts making it a little bit smaller. When the time is right, *bam!* You'll be caught around the neck. You are wearing one of those tracking collars around your neck too, but you don't know that, either."

"I'm not neither," retorted Fleebit.

"Yep, there isn't a big antenna sticking up, but it's there. That woman tracks where you are all day long. She calls old snoopy nose down the street to see if you've left the house in the morning. Then she calls her friend Gladys down the street two blocks and finds out if you went to the café or to the feed store. Then she calls Marty at the hardware store, and he tells her if you went to help that other widow across town. He tells her what you bought for that other woman's garden, how much it cost, and what he thinks you'll be doing next. She calls down at the café to see what you ate for lunch so she can fix up a different bait for your dinner so you'll be hungry enough to run through that snare without seeing it."

Fleebit turned his mule around and trotted away from him toward home.

Clyde sat there and watched him ride away. Clyde thought about how easy it was to distract him and change his focus away from those kids who just arrived in town. It should be so easy to change the mind-set of everyone else who resided here. His good friend was influenced by the local population who believed that everyone who did something good for the environment was a threat and a bad person.

There had been many environmental debates over public land uses during the past few years. Meetings over wilderness, wild and scenic river designations, restricting forest clear-cutting, and holding mining companies accountable for environmental damage had caused hard lines to be drawn in the sand. The local popular belief was, that outsiders—tree huggers—wanted to shut down everything, and they had no right to tell the local people what to do.

There were several peaceful demonstrations in the Missoula area over land issues, and throughout the legal process, wilderness and environmental groups had influenced federal land agencies to change the way they managed public lands. For many years, public opinion supported public land managers' decisions to develop and sell the land's resources without any opposition. History was beginning to show that some management practices were not well founded, and new interest groups were holding the government more accountable for their decisions regarding the nation's public lands. Not everyone was happy with these encounters for new changes, and many local groups had incorporated support for their private causes. Many of the locals were angry. How dare these outside tree huggers come to their hometown and try to tell them what to do!

Being "environmental" had somehow become a bad thing. History was repeating itself. The majority of people fighting for no changes were the old cavalry, and there was a Custer leading the charge in every Western town and on every board of county commissioners.

Environmentalists were the symbolic New Indians! The red niggers were now green niggers, and they should all be exterminated. It was the same mentality, the same earth. Another time.

Clyde decided then and there, *If some of these local people are going to attack those kids who work for the Fish and Game Department, they'll have to fight me too!*

Clyde also thought, *There hasn't been any news about the missing girl for a long time. If someone from this town did something to Katie Colter, so far, they'd gotten away with it, and they might be confident enough to attack again. Those are some real cute girl biologists living out there in tents. I'm not sure if the guys in their group could stand up to a gang of big, dangerous men. If they do run into trouble way up there in the mountains, they are on their own and far from the law.*

15

IT WAS GETTING DAYLIGHT, AND CLYDE WAS FILLING THE graniteware coffeepot with water from the kitchen sink when there was a big commotion outside at the corral.

Clyde yelled, "Get out of bed, and go feed your pet! Your longhorn steer makes as much noise out there at daylight each morning as a semitruck loaded with roosters."

Fleebit stumbled into the kitchen rubbing his eyes. "If you would just go out there when you get up and throw Cheyenne a flake of hay, he'd stop bellowing and clacking his big horns on those corral poles."

Clyde threw his hot pad down on the counter. "That old cuss is not my responsibility, and I've told you that many times! Why don't you move him to a pen away from the back door? If we lived an inch closer to town, you would be arrested for disturbing the peace."

Fleebit yawned and stretched out his big, long arms. "He knows that you don't like him."

Clyde said, "I'd like him a lot better with some of that new mesquite barbecue sauce. We'd get along fine with some fried onions and green bell peppers too! And we'd make out good with just some salt and pepper. I would love him to death in a roaster oven. It's been many years since I've eaten an aged, longhorn rib eye. It's the best marbled steak in the whole world."

"You better quit talking about Cheyenne like that," Fleebit said. "He's smarter than you think, and I believe he knows when people are talking about him. I've seen how he acts when you get close to him. He's always sizing you up and thinking. One of these days, you'll really tick him off, and he's gonna take a swipe at you through those corral poles and catch you somewhere down low and in the middle. Anyway, he earns his keep when some rancher wants to hire us to move a bunch of yearling heifers somewhere across the country. They'll follow him anywhere!"

Clyde reflected, "I can remember when we loaded him in the gooseneck trailer in front of our rope horses after the Cheyenne Frontier Rodeo. He was just a baby calf then. His mother broke her leg in a gate during the preshow of the rodeo, and the stock contractor gave him to you. How old is Cheyenne now?"

Fleebit yawned a second time. "Heck, I can't remember."

"I don't recall your memory lacking any! You can remember when your Swede girlfriend, Helga, is taking her warm sweet buns out of the oven in the morning. You remember when your other friend May has something ready for lunch in her Crock-Pot. You know when it's time for sauerkraut and sausage for dinner at Ellen Jorgenstein's German restaurant. You seem to recall when the church is serving cake and ice cream. And you seem to know when it's time to get on your horse and ride out of town because all of your girlfriends are mad at you for spending so much time away from them with another woman."

"Clyde, I've tried to make you understand. All I do is help those women fix up things around their houses. They don't have a regular man around that they can depend on to work on a door or fix some windows or leaky plumbing. I just help them out, and then they feed me something they have cooked up. That's all there is to it, and none of them own me!"

Clyde shook his head from side to side and went back for the hot pad. "They are cooking something up, all right, but each one of them has the private intention of having their own personal handyman.

They start learning when they are babies that if you own a man, the tools of work come cheaply. That's you! You are him! You are the big dog of Big Scratch, Montana, and they all want to own you. One of these days, all three, four, or six of those lonely women will trap a flea-bit Shepherd for tipping over their trash cans. Three of them will hold him down while one of them with a sharp knife performs a neuter surgery. Someday, you won't come home, and I'll find out that one of those women went crazy with jealousy and locked you down in her basement while she got her knife sharpened up. It's happened to other good men before when they thought they were doing a good thing by helping an old lady with some general maintenance around her house."

"I've tried to get you to go over to their houses with me," reasoned Fleebit. "They all ask about you. If you didn't hide from them and act so grumpy toward them, they'd all want to invite you over for meals or to the social activities at the church. May thinks that you are very handsome. She told Helga that it was such a waste for such a handsome man to spend so much time alone when there were so many available women in this town."

"No, thanks," said Clyde. "I'm not that old! I'll just stay in the shadows until I jump out of the darkness to pick up your pieces."

Clyde saddled up early and rode over to the Thin Vein just as Bonnie was getting there. She liked to arrive before Franky got there, start the coffee, and warm up the grill. Bonnie was really proud of her work on the transformation of the old building, and she didn't have to share it with Franky at this hour. Bonnie brought two steaming hot cups of coffee over to Clyde and sat down next to him.

"Clyde, the people from this town are so rude! These clodhoppers, truckers, and cowboys all stare at my boobs, but you never do. I'd know if you did, but you never do. When you look at me, you always look into my eyes, and I want you to know how much I appreciate that in this hick town. Why don't you ever look at my boobs?"

Clyde said shyly, "Bonnie, I'm not young, but I'm not too old, either! The fact is, I have a photographic memory. That first day I saw you out in front of the café, when you were painting your pretty sign, I took a picture of you on that day when I rode by on my horse. I captured a sexy, beautiful image of you in my mind, and it's stored there in a very private place. I don't feel like I have to stare at you because I know what you look like without having to rudely look again and again just to remind myself. It's like when I see some new wildflowers on the mountain. I take a picture of them in my head. I don't have to pull them up and watch them slowly wither and die in a vase. If I see some new baby ducks on a lake, I can store them in my mind too. I don't have to try to catch them, put them inside a coop, and take away their freedom. Some things in life are so special, and nobody can ever take them away from me."

Suddenly, Fleebit barged in and flopped down across from them. "Bonnie, what do you have for a terrible hangover?"

In an irritated reply, Bonnie said, "I have a bowl of cold, red tomato soup with a long black hair in it. To go with that, I have a freshly caught cockroach that I just picked up off the men's restroom floor, and it will be served on a stale Ritz cracker. That's so you can puke your guts up, get rid of all that poison, and remember to never do that again."

Fleebit's eyes crossed east and west.

"That sounds good," said Clyde. "That's what I'll order this morning."

"Is there anything else you would like to go with that, sir?"

"Yeah, bring me a strainer so I can sift out all of that black hair and a can of Raid to spray on my cracker."

Fleebit jumped up, spilled the coffee, and ran off. He swung around the corner and tripped over the hostess stand on his way fumbling out the door.

"That big boob sure knows how to interrupt a tender moment," said Bonnie.

Clyde laughed. "You didn't have to go through all of that just to get me alone. He took off like somebody just told him that all four of his girlfriends were setting fire to his house and Franky was butchering his pet longhorn steer. It sure was funny! Maybe we should both go on the road and start up a comedy act."

Bonnie laughed. "Yeah, we could call it 'The Bonnie and Clyde Comedy Show.' Clyde, if I didn't know better, I'd say that you use that line about a mental picture of the wildflowers and the baby ducks just to pick up women. But you're not that type! Instead, I can imagine you having a well-oiled line for getting away from women and haven't used a rusty one like that to pick up a girl in a long time. You get to me with your shy, sweet, rusty honesty.

"I took a mental picture of you one day too. It was when you rode past the restaurant on that beautiful bay horse. I stored it in my memory and recorded it there as the most handsome man I'd ever seen on a horse. You both blended together as one, like a perfect painting. I wanted you to ride closer so I could ask you to pose in front of the new restaurant for some photographs, but you always rode away. Sometimes your horses bucked or reared, but you always held on and rode away. I'll carry that first picture of you with me until I can record it on canvas with an oil painting. I'm not as good as you at remembering a special moment. When something is very special to me, I want to look at it all of the time. That's the good thing about being an artist; you can preserve a memory that remains distant from you.

"Clyde, I want you to know that I enjoy your company when you come into the restaurant. I'm glad that you still come, regardless of Franky's jealous, rude behavior toward you. I think that when he sees a man like you, someone who is his own man, he feels like he's been kicked in the crotch. I just want to tell you that when you are near me, I feel happy. If we should never see each other again, I'll always remember that there are lights out there in the darkness. I found a light during my darkest hours somewhere in the middle of Montana."

"Bonnie, I feel real good when I'm around you too. When you approached me at my hitching rail, I thought, 'Here we go again! Another girl who wants to be a real cowgirl! Someone who wants to run away under that big Montana sky!' When I meet a lady, I always think about that song by Chris LeDoux and Garth Brooks, 'Watcha Gonna Do With a Cowboy.' When I think about the words to that song, it always reminds me that a relationship is meaningless if it's based on fantasy or deception. For the younger women I meet, it's always about the fantasy. It's not easy, living a cowboy's life like mine. It isn't the romantic version in songs and movies. It is self-sacrificing and hard! And for the other women, it's about deception. If a woman runs off with me and abandons her husband and children, she will deceive herself and somebody who depends on her over a dream. But Bonnie, you are different from anyone I've ever met. When I ride off the top of the hill in the dark early mornings and see a light on inside this place, I know you are here, and it lights up my life.

"I'm going to ride up to my cabin tomorrow, and I might be gone for a few days. I've seen how good of an artist you are and how you can decorate and fix things up real fine. I would like to hire you to help me and Fleebit change some things around in his old house where we spend the winters. And I want to hire somebody to paint Fleebit's portrait soon so I can send it to his daughter in California. He thinks that his grandkids don't appreciate him, but I think they might realize someday that they missed out. I would like to get a painting of him all dressed up in his cowboy work duds he wore back when we rode the range together long ago. I'm afraid Fleebit might not be around forever, and I'd really like to get this done as soon as possible."

"Is he sick and going to die?" asked Bonnie.

Clyde laughed. "Yeah, he's sick, all right! He's sick in the head right now because he tried to drown his fears with whiskey last night. There are several women in this town who might want to kill him. Fleebit Shepherd from Big Scratch, Montana, is an old cur dog that has been eating out of too many bowls and digging in too many different flower beds, and he might end up getting neutered in the pound. I've told him that being president of the Widows' Lonely Hearts Club was a risky office to hold."

Clyde gently pushed sideways against Bonnie and looked her in the eyes. "I want to advance you some money so you can find another place in town that's farther away from Franky. Fleebit and I will be moving out and heading south to begin our work soon, and his old house will just sit empty until winter rolls around again. You can stay there until you find another place or decide what you want to do. I would like to see you stay here, but I know that you'll probably move on. This is way too small of a cage to hold a bird with big wings. I don't care if you never pay me back, and I don't want you to feel obligated to me in any way. We'd be obliged to you for watching the house while we're gone. Fleebit is gone most of the time on his girlfriend route before he says good-bye, and I'll be spending more and more time in the hills getting my horses legged up before we leave town."

The back door slammed shut, and Franky started banging things and slamming pots and pans.

Bonnie glanced back over her shoulder and saw Franky glaring at them through the pick-up window. She rolled her eyes in the amazement at his audacity and turned back around with Clyde. She put her arm around him, turned, and kissed him firmly on the cheek.

"He is acting like the performance of a teenager just told he was grounded. Or maybe he dropped those pans because he feels like he just got kicked between the legs by a mule!"

Clyde put both hands on the table and bent over, silently laughing. He managed to catch his breath and choked, "Oh my, I thought Fleebit was the only one who could make me laugh this hard! 'The Bonnie and Clyde Comedy Show'! I really like that! Instead of robbing banks from a car, we could do it out of a horse trailer with chain saws. Instead of carrying guns, we could kill everybody with laughter!"

Finally, Clyde turned in the booth and said, "Bonnie, stop laughing and get serious!" She panicked, became frozen, and turned to face Clyde.

Clyde was serious. "Follow me outside!"

Bonnie followed Clyde into the alley where his bay horse stood tied. No-Name whinnied to him as they approached. Clyde spun around and took Bonnie into his arms, and they kissed passionately. He held her firmly, and she pushed forward into him. She kissed his eyes, each one over and over again.

Clyde kissed her ear softly and whispered, "I've got to get going now, but Fleebit will be in every day, and he'll tell you everything you need to know about the house. You'll be safe there!"

Franky watched out the back window of his kitchen and saw Bonnie embracing Clyde. Insult added to injury when Clyde's horse raised its tail high up into an arch and shit a big green pile onto his property. Franky became enraged. He slammed the meat cleaver down into the chopping block.

Bonnie walked back into the kitchen and announced, "I've found me another place to live, so I'm moving out of the hotel."

Franky yanked off his kitchen apron and began wadding it up, spinning it tightly into a ball. He threw it into a sink filled with dirty dishes. "So you're rich now, huh? You must be making more money serving cowboys than I make slinging hash back here!"

"I am grateful for you advancing me some money, Franky, but I'm not as appreciative of your other types of advances. I worked my buns off transforming a pigsty into a work of art for you while you tripped all over yourself and didn't do squat! If you are so worried about how much I make in tips, then maybe you should go out and try to wait tables. You stand in one spot all day while I run over a hundred miles back and forth through this dining room. I don't mind saving you money by doing the work of three waitresses, because it beats the Jenny Craig diet, I get to laugh once in a while, and I get to earn a buck."

In a rude, snide tone of voice, Franky asked, "So are you going to sleep with him too?"

Bonnie grabbed up the meat cleaver and slammed it down with a loud *wham!* on a row of breakfast sausage links on the chopping block. The ends rolled off and onto the floor.

Franky spun around and ran toward the men's restroom.

When Bonnie unfolded the note that Clyde stuffed inside her

apron pocket in the Thin Vein, she caught her breath and started to cry. There was a personal check from Clyde Morgan on account from the First National Bank in Missoula, Montana, for $10,000.

Dear Bonnie,

I think there is enough money here to buy a used car or a good bicycle and some new clothes. You can also buy some things for the old house if you decide to stay there. It looks pretty drab inside from two old bachelors living in it who are accustomed to living outdoors. I told Fleebit that I'd be back in a day or two, but it might be a lot longer than that, and I don't want him to start worrying and come looking for me. He knows that I like to make a big trip by myself every spring, and he'll worry more about his mule than he will for my well-being.

He also knows and agrees that you are in charge of the old house, and you have free rein to run with whatever you decide to do. He'll probably stay at Ellen Jorgenstein's house at night since I'm not going to be around to embarrass him about going over there so much. Fleebit will come by every morning and every evening just to feed the young horses and his cow herd. He likes to tell people that he's a rich cattleman, but he only owns one head, and it's a longhorn steer named Cheyenne. Please be careful of the big steer named Cheyenne, because he's getting grumpy with age, and his long, sharp horns could seriously hurt somebody. Good luck!

A friend,
Clyde

16

A WARM CHINOOK CAME BLOWING IN DURING THE NIGHT, melting deep snowdrifts and hanging ice left from the endlessly long spring blizzard. By midmorning, water was running everywhere around Big Scratch.

Clyde loudly announced to his sleeping friend, "I'm ready to ride this morning! I can probably make it to the cabin today through just a foot of snow. If you want to stay here in town and go on your breakfast, lunch, and dinner route with four different women today, can I borrow Blue and pack me an overnight rig on him? I'll have to pack a shovel so I can clear out around the cabin and pack some food and my bedroll. I'll be back in a few days."

Fleebit stammered, "I wasn't counting on that chinook last night, and I'm not quite ready to go to the cabin yet. I still have a few things to finish up here in town."

"Yeah," said Clyde, "you have to finish up a bunch of leftovers that are sitting in four different refrigerators in downtown Big Scratch, Montana. While I'm packing your mule up into God's country, you'll be a pack mule for Ellen Jorgenstein. I swear, one of these days, a bunch of German and Swede women are going to get into a big catfight in this town, and somebody is going to ride away with some scratches. And it sure won't be me! One of these days, you will realize what a big mess you've created. One morning, you'll hear a bunch of sirens on Main Street, and a big red fire engine will be spraying water on several women in the center of town who are pulling each other's hair and trying to scratch each other's eyes out. You'll run to the corral, saddle the first horse you can catch, throw the spurs to his guts, and hit for those hills up yonder. You'll think that you are free and clear like Butch Cassidy after a train robbery, but the Wild Bunch will be blocking your trail before you can get out of town.

"Fleebit, you don't need to worry about going with me now, because I want to make this ride alone. Besides, if I was to take you away from here before you said good-bye to all of those women, that wild bunch might block my trail and try to lynch me on my way up to the summer range. They're all going to blame me, anyway, for dragging you away from town against your own will. Miss Jorgenstein has never liked me from the start. She knows that I know how she sets a snare and baits a trap. You never told me what happened to her husband. Did he die from founder on too much cabbage, or was he just worn out from toting too many heavy buckets of soapy water while juggling a mop and a broom?"

Fleebit looked at the floor with a mournful expression. "She told me that he became weak and then he just died. He was one of those German mining engineers they shipped in here to separate the gold from the rocks and gravel."

"Well, that says a lot!" says Clyde. "Like I told you about that magazine article I read in one of her magazines, all of those German men are worn out from being worked to death by German women. Maybe you should think about taking a double dose of vitamins and stock up on some of that Viagra! Your girlfriends hate me because they think I'll drag you away where they won't see you for five months. But not to worry on their part—they can rent a storage unit and store all of their junk in it until you come back here in the fall to haul it off for them all winter long. They can socialize together again without wanting to kill each other after church. They can all enter their cakes and muffins in the county fair and get a fair and objective first place without you telling them that they are all a winner.

"I'm ready to ride. Can I borrow Blue?"

Clyde caught Blue and his saddle horse called No-Name. His big bay gelding was five years old, and he'd ridden him a lot the summer before on roundups and while hunting for wild cattle in northeastern Utah. He was becoming a powerful rope horse, but he was still young and fresh and sometimes unpredictable with how he might react to something he'd never seen before. He was chosen over several of Clyde's more dependable horses that were accustomed to encounters with wild animals of the wilderness, as well as wild fighting cattle from the prairie and brush country. No-Name performed excellently with wild cattle, but he still had yet to encounter a big black moose or grizzly bear in his path. There was a great difference to a horse, and many of Clyde's past experiences with young horses and a moose or bear became a rodeo. It was just something that a rider had to eventually face if his horse was going to become worldly. The gentlest horse could become the craziest, most terrified beast upon first glimpse of a big, black bull moose. It was a gamble whether they were curious and wanted to know more about the animal or whether they would try to run away and buck you off.

It most often didn't pay to take chances on a fresh, young saddle horse when you were alone far back into the wilderness or when you were leading pack animals. It was also a gamble during severe spring blizzards and slick, dangerous terrain. No-Name was the best bet because he was young and strong enough to withstand the high altitude, deep snowdrifts, and some very long rides. He was also very surefooted, but there was still a lot to know about him.

Clyde was carrying the saddle blanket and packsaddle around the corral to where Blue was tied when Cheyenne made a swipe at him with one long horn. The sharp-pointed tip slightly pricked the fabric in his coat sleeve and temporarily stopped him in his tracks, causing him to drop the packsaddle.

"Hey, you old burger! This Fourth of July, you might not be leading the parade. You might be *feeding* the parade!"

Clyde loaded up two big sacks of oats, his food, and his bedroll onto Blue and then tied a box hitch to secure the load with a forty-foot lash rope. He then placed the shovel and axe on top of the pack with their handles held underneath the tight lash rope where he could pull either one out quickly. He saddled up No-Name, shoved his Winchester .30-30 rifle into the boot, stepped into the stirrup, and swung on. He headed northeast out of town toward the summer cabin. After riding about two miles above Big Scratch where the sun had melted the snow off the gray rimrock, he turned back to the west and rode in the opposite direction of the cabin toward the camp of the New Indians that the townsfolk called "the bear people."

Clyde left the well-marked main trail and covered the country going west with a discriminating eye that was alive and perceptive to everything around him. He could with ease of habit look for tracks and easy passage on the trail below and in front of him while scanning the country far off ahead and as distant as the eye could see.

It was perhaps a day-and-a-half ride to where the bear group would be located, and that was only a time factor, because Clyde's chosen path was a meticulous route. It wasn't easy to stay in the rocks where there was no snow. It was slow going and tough at times, but his trail would be hard to trace and challenging for someone else to follow.

Clyde was sensitive to what he asked his animals to do for him and where he made them go. In other words, if his horse became injured from something that he made it do, it hurt him a whole lot more. The only snowless terrain was where the rocks attracted the heat from the midday sun. For a man who never worried about anything for most of his adult life, Clyde worried the most about losing a shoe and laming his horse.

He always instinctively tried not to leave his sign on a trail that would tell other people that he'd passed that way, but now he was more particular about covering his trail than ever before. He wasn't sure who might be planning to attack the kids who were at the bear study camp, because there were a lot of people from town that didn't like them or want them around. Since Fleebit knew that something was brewing up, it was probably going to happen. He was like a sponge that absorbed up all of the town's gossip. His many girlfriends carried the words of mischief, and locals openly discussed environmental issues in his presence.

The same people would clam up and remain silent when Clyde appeared. He was recently sitting in the Thin Vein and overheard a teenage kid tell his friend about Bobby Strickler and his gang terrorizing some tree huggers when they were coming into the café. It could be them, or it could be the son of the lumber company and his friends. It could be some farm or ranch kids who shoot at every bear on sight. Their parents had influenced all of them to feel threatened by and to hate anyone or anything that was associated with the environment.

Clyde thought, *These kids who work for the Fish and Wildlife Department are state employees and biologists. They are not some unemployed rich kids who are on a mission to halt all commerce. Discrimination has placed everything green into the same basket.*

The American Indians were all put into the same basket. There were many peaceful Indian camps where innocent women, children, and old people were massacred just because they were Indians. The American Indians started the environmental movement, and they were subdued by the whites. Now it seems like the whites who defend the environment are the Indians.

The local people considered Clyde to be a redneck cowboy until he made outspoken comments favoring wilderness designation at a public meeting. Now he was a distrusted Indian. He was a Lakota cowboy who was covering his back trail and trying to reach a peaceful camp of New Indians before it was too late.

Clyde got off to a late start because Fleebit hung around and paced back and forth throughout the house with indecision on his feeble mind. He was torn between his commitments with several elderly ladies in town and going with his partner up into the wild high country.

Fleebit thought about the ice cream that would be served up at the church that night, where some attractive, single women would attend from throughout town and the next county. That would be totally awesome! Then he thought about the ice and snow up where Clyde was headed and how cold, dirty, and miserable the cabin would be after it had been abandoned for several months. It would probably smell like the skunks that hibernated beneath the floorboards all winter. That would be awful.

Spending time with Ellen Jorgenstein had really changed some of his dirty ways. He was beginning to enjoy cleanliness, and Ellen instructed him that it was Godlike and a very good thing. But he was torn up, because his partner was leaving without him and taking his best mule too! It was almost too much for his brain to handle at one time.

What if Clyde got hurt way up there or his mule Blue got hurt? What if a hungry grizzly bear attacked Clyde? What if it attacked Blue? They'd experienced several close calls with mad and hungry grizzly bears during the past years, but Clyde said they wouldn't hurt him, and he wasn't afraid of them. Fleebit wasn't ashamed to admit that he was terrified of them, and they always seemed to appear before him when Clyde wasn't around.

Why was he so worried about Clyde, anyway? Clyde always wanted to get back into the high country before fair-weather riders and hikers ventured up there. He liked to be alone in the high country after spending a long winter in town with other people. *The fact is Clyde isn't as young as he thinks. He hadn't slowed down any, though! He could outride and outwork most men half his age. He often remarked how the women in town who were his age were old people.*

Then Fleebit thought about how Clyde's adventures were never easy and in fact often came with some great risks. Clyde was always having his own fun, it seemed, involving other people being at risk—namely, Fleebit!

It was a stressful situation, so he decided to get some ice cream over at the church that evening and think about it later.

It was getting late, and the sun would set very quickly up this high. It would become cold that night, because the sky was clear, and the moon was full. A sudden campsite presented itself by way of a thick, deep snowdrift close to the trail. Clyde decided to make camp for the night.

Clyde unpacked Blue and unsaddled his horse, and he placed all of the tack inside the manti tarp and covered it up with a tight fold inside a neat, protective package. Then he used the shovel to dig out a cave in the steep bank of snow where he laid out his waterproof bedroll. The deep snowdrift was solid enough to build a spacious room connected by an entrance that turned away from the prevailing, nightly wind gusts.

He staked out his animals by using a stake rope and the long lash rope to secure them close to his makeshift shelter. Then he poured out the oats onto the edge of the snow and gave them each a generous helping. Clyde rubbed their backs and silently thanked No-Name and Blue for their participation and then placed the pack boxes inside the snow cave and got comfortable. He opened up a sack of jerky, uncorked his canteen, and stretched out.

Sometime in the night, Clyde had a dream that left him shaken and soaked in sweat. He seldom remembered his dreams since leaving the Indian reservation as a young man. The dreams that he encountered after his grandfather prepared him for vision quest were always good and meaningful in some way. Those peaceful dreams involved eagles that soared with and above him. Somehow, it felt like they were guiding him in a direction. They often felt strict and intent.

One night, he dreamed about a large grizzly bear with scars all over his face. He roared and frightened all of the people and animals away and then came back to him and became like a big, playful dog that sat up and rolled over. Clyde rode on his back and traveled with him. He could still remember how safe and secure he felt there.

Oftentimes as a boy, in the dream state, butterflies were his companions when he was not traveling but sitting alone in meditation on a hill or in an open meadow. The butterflies were not serious like the eagles. They liked to have fun dancing and clowning around. They were happy spirits that made him feel less serious about life.

Clyde took out his handkerchief and wiped the sweat from his brow. *When I left the Indian way of life behind me, everything changed, including my dreams. This wasn't no Indian's dream in a nature film! This was a white man's dream, and I don't have a clue what it means.*

Clyde's breathed in deeply and suddenly inhaled the awareness of where he was inside the snow cave. He turned his attention from panic to speculation. This dream was unlike anything he'd ever encountered.

He'd dreamed of a woman who had her back to him, and he couldn't see her face. She was asking for him to help her and then pleading for him to rescue her. She was lying on her side next to a large aspen. A young white man stood nearby, waiting up ahead in the trees. He was holding a white elephant by a long, golden chain. A tall, dark shadow approached the helpless woman from behind.

Clyde suddenly awakened, and it was still dark outside with the deadly stillness just before dawn. He peered out from the snow cave opening and could see the darkened images of the horse and mule resting and sleeping peacefully upon three legs.

It was just a dream, but could the helpless woman be Katie? Where was she? Was it too late to help her? Or could it be one of the girl biologists who might become threatened? Did something happen, or is it going to happen? Who is she?

Clyde crawled out of his cave at first light and grained his animals. While they ate, he curried their backs and then saddled up for the journey ahead. He had everything packed and ready to go in a short time. He collapsed the snow cave and used a pine branch to brush out all sign of his camp in the snow. When the new sun came up, by midday, every trace of his presence there would have melted away.

Clyde rode on west, staying to the rocks and bare places for about a mile, when he came upon the tracks. They were the biggest bear tracks he'd ever seen. He followed the bear tracks for a short distance before they cut off into the deeper snow leading off toward the northeast. After a few more miles, Clyde found some fresh snowshoe tracks and an old snow-covered, cross-country ski trail that would surely lead him to the bear camp.

It was impossible to sneak up on their camp, and it wasn't a polite thing to consider. A polite person always announces his or her presence by yelling, "Hello, the camp!" Blue announced their arrival before Clyde had the chance with a loud, *"Ee-Aw, Ee-Aw!"* That was one of the reasons Clyde preferred horses over mules. A mule always told everybody where you were. But the good thing about a mule was that it also told you where someone else was.

When Clyde rode up closer to the tent camp, he could plainly see in the new snow where three people left on snowshoes and one person ran out behind a tent and into the thick trees. He could sense that this one person was circling around behind him, and Blue was looking off into the trees, following the hidden movement.

Clyde announced, "Hello, the camp!" toward the empty tents, even though he knew that the person who ran away from the camp was behind him by now. Suddenly, he heard the *shuck-shuck* sound of a pump shotgun at his back and a firm female voice say, "What do you want, mister?"

Without looking behind him, he said, "My name is Clyde Deerhide, and I'm the welcome wagon from Big Scratch. I've only got the horse without the wagon because I couldn't find anyone else to ride up here to welcome you folks to this country. It looks like I'm the only one on the committee who wants to meet you folks, and I baked you a cake in my dutch oven to give you for a housewarming present."

The cold, stern voice in the trees behind him said, "Okay, step off your horse real easy like, and don't make any quick moves, because I have a twelve-gauge shotgun with slugs in it, and I know how to use it. Just move over there to that pack mule and take out that cake! If you really baked a cake for us, I'll believe you and put down my gun."

Clyde took his time unpacking Blue without looking directly at the young woman with the shotgun. He unlaced the box hitch, coiled up his lash rope, and took off the pack box straps. He opened up one of the packs and took out a cardboard box. He opened up this box and took out a smaller box. Then he took out a fourth box and opened it up. Inside it was a cake that was perfectly intact from riding on a two-day mule trip.

The young woman began trembling and crying. "How did you know that it was my birthday? Hi. My name is Maggie. I'm sorry for not trusting you, but we had some visitors up here who were not the friendly types. While we were all gone checking traps, someone came and destroyed some of our equipment. You really scared me! I stayed here today because the Fish and Game Department said there wasn't any money left to buy more tracking and monitoring equipment. Our supervisor said that someone should stay around camp or else the study group might be terminated until next year. The guys didn't want me to stay here alone, but I insisted. I didn't tell them it was my birthday and that I needed some time to reflect on things by myself. I was feeling pretty sad and lonesome from being so far away from my family today, but you sure brightened up my spirits. Mr. Deerhide, are you a real Indian?"

Clyde smiled. "I'm a cowboy and an Indian. I'm what you call a breed. I'm half and half, you might say. I rope like a real cowboy, and I think like a real Indian."

Maggie said, "Two of the guys on my survey team are part Cherokee, but they don't look anything like you, and they don't act any different from anybody else I know. I come from Virginia. I guess I am a breed too! I have German, Scot, Irish, and American blood in my veins."

Clyde cautioned, "Maggie, it might not be safe here! How much longer are you going to be at this campsite?"

Maggie walked up to No-Name and petted his shoulder. "I'm not real sure. We are tracking a female bear with two cubs that we caught last year, and we need to trap her again and do some tests on the cubs. We need to find out if the female bear's milk is laced with arsenic and lead. Our tests last year showed that the same toxins that were found around the Strickler Clear Creek mine dump are showing up in the bear cubs. This could mean that there's a high mortality rate in the younger bears.

"We've also been trying to catch a large male grizzly that we trapped last year, but he's too smart for us this year. He won't go inside another culvert trap to get the bait. In his anger and frustration, he bites all of the tires on the culvert trap trailer and flattens them. We haven't had any luck at catching him with snares, either. We think that he's the same bear that we called Scarface. His face indicated that he'd been in a lot of bear fights over the years. We put a tracking collar on him last year, but he must have lost it, because we can't track his signal."

Clyde said, "I wish you and your friends would move over on the east end of this range where the wolf study group is camped. There's safety in numbers, and I'm afraid that those folks might receive some unwelcome visitors too. I have a summer cabin over there where you can camp, and I can help keep an eye on your camp and equipment while you are all out in the field."

"I really don't think we can leave this area," replied Maggie. "But I'll talk with my group about it when they come back this afternoon."

Clyde was eager to leave. No-Name and Blue were tugging and pointed toward home. "Maggie, I can show you where there are some bear dens over there, and you won't be all alone way up here. I can't stay here long to visit and meet your friends right now because I need to ride back to my cabin tonight, and it's a long journey. Try to call your friends on your radio, and tell them to consider my offer. I'll be in touch with the wolf study group sometime tomorrow afternoon. They'll know how to find my place. I think those people might come back here again in the near future, and things might get rough. If it's who I think it is, you could be in serious danger. There is one girl missing already!"

Maggie glanced around nervously. "All of us girls know about Katie. I'm afraid they might come back here again too—to look for this!" She handed Clyde an envelope.

"When they got out of their truck in the dark, they must have kicked out some of their mail. Maybe if you read this, you'll understand who is messing with us."

The letter was from the Billings, Montana Law Firm of Morris, Fitch and Cronwell.

Morris, Fitch, & Cronwell, Attorneys-at-Law
116 N. Broadway St.
Billings, MT

Strickler Resources LLC
PO box 92
Big Scratch, MT

Dear Mr. Strickler:

I am writing you in reference to the recent meeting at our office on October 1 in regard to your concerns about recent litigations against the Strickler Gold and Mineral Development Corporation. These litigations are seeking claims for the destruction of public lands on the Lolo National Forest.

The two law firms who have filed charges in federal court have succeeded in dismissing our standing on the statute of limitations. However, claims seeking to penetrate and exact monies from your new company of Strickler Resources LLC cannot withstand. The assets of Strickler Gold and Mineral Development Corp. were transferred and filed to your new company name of Strickler Resources LLC on a previous date before suits were filed in federal court. It is very important that all of your personal records from your old corporation have terminated all connections to your present limited liability corporation.

In regard to the second issue of our recent meeting, the law firm of Haslem and Marstall have agreed to drop their charges of rape against your son Bobby Ray Strickler and have settled for the amount of $75,000. We will immediately notify you if we receive any new information regarding these issues. Please call my office when you receive this notification.

Sincerely,

Bill Morris
Senior partner of Morris, Fitch & Cronwell
Attorneys-at-Law

17

THE STRICKLER GOLD AND MINERAL DEVELOPMENT
Corporation was founded in 1969 by an enterprising man named
George Strickler from Maryland. George was out west with some
buddies from the East, hunting elk in the fall of the year of 1968,
when he wounded an elk that ran over a rock outcropping and into
the dark timber. George tracked the blood trail over a hard rock
surface where the color of red blood was contrasted by the color of
bright gold.

It took a couple of years to file his claim with the Lolo National
Forest and register his claim throughout the government channels before
he could begin to extract the gold. George took several ore samples in
for analysis from the surrounding area, revealing that the strike of
gold was in a concentrated area in the vicinity of Clear Creek. With
some deep-core drilling samples, it registered an assay of one-half
ounce of gold to the ton. Over the next fifteen years, the once pristine
mountainside surrounding Clear Creek was reduced to a heap of rubble.

The local government, city council, the board of county
commissioners, and the local merchants were all very happy with
this new addition to a destitute place with a forsaken economy. From
a territory to statehood, Montana was nicknamed the Treasure State
by early political hopefuls.

During the next fifteen years, it was estimated that over $20 million net worth of gold was taken out of the Clear Creek mine. When the gold played out, the mining operation closed down, and once thriving boom towns with names like Big Scratch and Lucky Haven were reduced to their once normal flow: a trickle of occupants who survived by ranching, timbering, and retail merchandise.

George Strickler invested his riches in land, a wildcat oil drilling company, and several businesses in and around his hometown in Maryland. He owned several factories and warehouses in New Mexico, and he bought and sold businesses on a monthly basis.

George bought out two big ranches that totaled about fifteen thousand acres bordering the Lolo National Forest. This property was located about four miles north from where Clyde's property joined the same national forest boundary on the south side.

For many years, George Strickler was a celebrated man. Everyone for miles around knew that name, and they congratulated him for his contribution of advancing their kinfolk through some tough times. However, in recent times, headlines in all of the newspapers portrayed a bleaker image of the man George Strickler and his enterprise. It seemed that the many tons of tailing piles surrounding Clear Creek were contaminated with lead, arsenic, and a vast array of leaching chemicals that were left behind. Water samples from Clear Creek indicated that the snow and springwater runoff had leached these contaminants into the creek below and killed off a once thriving trout fishery and ecosystem for many miles downstream.

The Strickland Corporation was now being held accountable for millions of dollars' worth of cleanup and restoration by several groups of people. The state of Montana claimed that it would take at least $20 million to haul off the thousands of tons of contaminated mine tailings, dispose of them, and stabilize the water source of Clear Creek. Another group, called the Montana Wilderness Alliance, enlisted the support of some big-city political representatives and out-of-state sponsors. Both the State of Montana and the Wilderness

Alliance Group filed separate claims in court against Strickler Resources LLC.

The Strickler legal council claimed several things that would exonerate them from this liability. First off, they claimed the statute of limitations. They claimed that too much time had expired before anyone made a claim against them of any wrongdoing.

Secondly, they claimed that their corporation was bankrupt and void of any monies left in the corporation. They were now out of business and were a limited liability corporation that was no longer involved in any kind of surface mining operations.

Headlines in the newspapers were often ripe with other news involving the Strickler name. George's son, Bobby Ray Strickler, who managed the ranching operation near Big Scratch, was often arrested for possession of cocaine, methamphetamine, and accusations of rape, poaching of protected wildlife, and the beatings of local residents.

Bobby Ray was on his way back from a seven-day spree in Miles City with four of his friends who lived at the ranch with him. It was quite a party! He reserved several rooms at the Sleep Inn and Suites Hotel and invited everybody from miles around. Miles City, Montana, was the favorite party town, even though it was a long drive from Big Scratch. There were so many old Western bars all over town, and you could gamble in most of them. Many of the bars still had the original old bar settings with antique, hand-carved oak, mahogany, and cherrywood that was sculptured and imported from Europe, with intricate carvings of scenes from the Old West. Old brass railings and hardware had also been imported, and there were brass foot rails in front of the bars with flush spittoons at your feet. These old bar settings bordered giant lead-plate glass mirrors with intricate scroll work from a bygone era when Miles City was a brand-new, booming cow town on the new frontier.

Bobby liked to put his expensive, handmade boots up on the rail, spit at the floor, and look at his reflection in the big mirrors. He and the gang liked to feel like they were the cast from the movie

Lonesome Dove as they went from bar to bar dressed like real cowboys that were fresh off a big cattle drive.

Everyone around Big Scratch knew that they weren't real cowboys by any stretch of the imagination. They tried to dress up like they were real hands when they were having one of their parties at the ranch, when they went into town, or when they were on one of their road trip parties to Missoula, Billings, or Miles City. They wanted the party girls to believe that they were the real thing and that they worked on Bobby Ray's ranch all day long, breaking horses and tending cattle when they were actually loafing at the ranch in the big western lodge looking like California dreamers who built surfboards for an occupation.

An old Mexican gentleman named Pablo and his son, Arturo, did all of the work, and there were not that many cattle or horses to tend to. George Strickler decided long ago to use the fifteen thousand acres as a wildlife preserve rather than a working cattle operation. There were only about sixty head of the original cow herd left, and they'd been mismanaged by not culling old or inferior cows out of the herd. They also failed to change breeding bulls, and they missed castrating some of the bull calves every season.

There were calves that had never been branded and bull calves that were breeding their own mothers. Pablo did his best possible, but he could never get Bobby Ray and his gang of outlaws to help gather, brand, vaccinate, or to make any decisions that were required by an owner. They kept six head of old saddle horses that should have been retired long before. These were used to show off the ranch to George Stickler's important friends from Maryland or to impress the town girls by Bobby Ray.

The wildlife preserve sounded like a good form of management, but the Stricklers actually encouraged the wildlife onto areas of their property that had not been used for grazing so that they could poach them out of season. George Strickler often bragged that he and his friends never had to buy another hunting license after he'd bought the ranch. They could hunt all year long! Bobby Ray and his friends often chased and shot pregnant cow elk out of their 4×4 super trucks or from snowmobiles during the most stressful part of the winter and spring. They had an arsenal of semiautomatic weapons, and any wild game that appeared in their sights was considered as open season.

A lot of people showed up over the weekend from every surrounding city and town, and there were a lot of young girls who came that Bobby had never seen before. His invitation list seemed to grow each time that he had one of his big parties. His open-ended bank account didn't go unnoticed by all of the chicks who liked to do drugs, drink excessively, and follow his entourage of rowdy friends. They took over and made a big scene by pushing everybody around that got in their way.

Unlike most of Bobby's road trips to a party, nobody got thrown in jail this time. Bobby didn't like the way that a local cowboy was looking at him in a bar on Saturday night, so he sucker-punched the guy and then found out that he'd picked on someone who was a lot tougher than he appeared to be. Bobby's friends took care of that, though, and sure evened up the odds in that bar fight.

They usually held their parties at the ranch when his dad was out of town, and he was lying low from the law until things cooled down. His dad's attorneys insisted that he stay at the ranch and out of trouble until the charge of rape was settled. He still wasn't sure how that was going to go, but he was tired of being confined at the ranch, and his dad's law firm always seemed to do its job of getting him off the hook. That's what his dad paid those attorneys all of that money for, anyway!

Bobby and his gang had been driving for six hours, and they were feeling pretty hungover when they pulled the big Dodge crew cab down the main street of Big Scratch.

Bobby said, "I'm going to pull into the post office and pick up the mail, and then we'll stop at that new restaurant and get us some coffee before we head up to the ranch."

Bobby stopped at the post office and picked up a huge bundle of mail that was in the lockbox. He slid in behind the wheel and flung the mail into the backseat and onto the floorboard. When they pulled up in front of the new restaurant and saw the big new sign and the newly remodeled café, he exclaimed, "Look, boys! They've made us a new movie set right here in our own hometown! I hope they have some good drugs in there that I can shoot up in my thin vein!"

Everybody laughed.

As they filed into the Thin Vein, the sight of the waitress serving tables caught their attention right away. In a loud voice, Bobby Ray said, "Look here, boys! My, oh my! I was just going to order some coffee, but maybe they've got something on the special that I'll eat, after all!"

Bonnie was accustomed to men looking at her, but most of them just looked away when she stared them down. This crew of dress-up cowboys was much different from all the rest. Bonnie just ignored them and waited on two other tables while they sat down.

One of the big men had a long, jagged scar down the side of his face, and he said, "Hey, we've been driving all night! How long do you have to wait in here to get serviced?"

They all started laughing.

Bonnie brought the coffeepot over and filled their cups, slapped down some menus, and bounced away to the kitchen. She heard one of them say, "Boys, she bounces around like a mare that's been cinched up too tight." She overheard the big guy with the scar on his face say, "Yeah, I'd like to ride her and see her bounce!"

They ordered biscuits and gravy all around, and Bonnie tried to make herself scarce.

While she was serving the food, she leaned over the table to reach the scar-faced man seated on the inside of the booth, and she felt his hand roughly squeeze her breast. Bonnie swung back with all of her might and slapped him in the face with her open hand. She hit him so hard that his head snapped back and hit the oak border on the back of the booth. His head struck the hard wood railing with a loud *whack*. When his head recoiled forward, his nose was gushing blood. His friends started laughing at him.

Franky saw it all and came running out with the big meat cleaver in his hand.

"I'll call the sheriff if you guys don't leave right now!"

Bobby and his friends helped pull Sam out of the booth. Sam looked at Bonnie and said, "You bitch, I'll get you!"

They all loaded up and headed toward the ranch, laughing and teasing Sam. Sam said, "That's okay, boys, I'll get that bitch! Someday, she'll be broke to ride!"

Bonnie was shaken up. She'd always been able to take care of herself without things going this far. When she saw that man's face, she knew that she'd made a bad enemy. She'd hit him so hard that her hand was starting to swell up.

She turned on Franky, "Did I ask for your help? I'm sorry. I think I broke my hand! You should call two or three of those girls who came in here wanting a job. I'm going home to put some ice on this hand, and it might be a few days before I can come back."

18

BONNIE WAS TOUCHED BY CLYDE'S OFFER FOR HER TO MOVE
into his friend's house where they both lived part of the time, but it
sounded strange. Okay, it was not Clyde's house, but Clyde offered it
to her, and he was leaving on a horseback trip up into the wilderness.
His friend Fleebit owned the house and approved of her moving
in, because he wanted to shack up with an older lady uptown that
Clyde didn't approve of. Clyde drew a portrait of Fleebit being an old
stud that spent time in several different pastures. It was too bad that
she was gifted as an artist instead of a romance writer. This could
be a better story than anything fiction that you could write about.
It might also be a story that you didn't want to personally witness.

It was a sweet, considerate gesture, but it wasn't Clyde's house,
and Clyde was leaving. If it was Clyde's house and he wasn't leaving,
she might already be there by now. She also wasn't sure if Fleebit
would still be staying there part time. She was sure that he was a fine
old gentleman, but it wasn't in her upbringing to take advantage of
people if you could make it some way on your own.

Although she'd told Franky that she was moving out of the
hotel, she had second thoughts about Clyde's offer. Now the incident
happened with the man at the café, and she suddenly felt more
vulnerable. Clyde had said that it was a safe place.

After she broke her hand, Bonnie walked back to the hotel and called Ellen Jorgenstein's house to see if Fleebit could give her a ride out to his house at the edge of town. She packed up her few clothes inside a suitcase and gathered up the new art supplies that she had accumulated during the past six weeks, putting it all inside a big box. Her hand hurt some, but it wasn't unbearable. She found out real quick what she could and couldn't do, though, and it looked like she was going to be left-handed for a while.

Fleebit picked her up in the company truck that he and Clyde jointly owned and headed across town. Bonnie asked him to stop by the bank for a minute, and she went inside and opened up her new lockbox. She looked at the endorsed check from Clyde Morgan that she hadn't endorsed and put it inside the box. Then she put her diamond wedding ring and a registered letter inside the box and turned the key.

It sure felt good to put that hotel behind her as they drove through town. There were times when she'd almost left there in the middle of the night to start walking toward the interstate highway. If it wasn't Franky whining outside her door, it was somebody who came in late at night and banged around, banged each other, or got into a fight. The walls were so thin that she could hear people snoring two or three rooms down the hall. And the snooping and gossip from that place was something else! It was a gossip factory, and everyone around there tried to find out everything they could about her past, present, and future.

But the worse thing that she'd endured while living and working here was the men. The owner of the sawmill laughed with his workers and sons after she walked away. She overheard a comment that they wouldn't want their mothers to hear. When he came in alone or with his brother, he openly suggested that she and he should get together. His two sons came in one at a time, possibly ducking away from work, to catch her alone at a slow time, where they ogled over her and stumbled over their tongues. They were repulsive and made her want to hide or run away. Married ranchers made suggestive remarks about having sex with her when they were with the cowboys, but when their wives forced them to attend the Thin Vein for Saturday-night dinner, they became aloof and didn't recall her name.

Sheriff Tolliber became like a stalker. At first, he appeared as a friend, and she liked his friendship and casual manor. She kept her distance and never sat down with him. He always appeared alone, and she sometimes stood and chatted with him at his side when times were slow. Then after Clyde left, he appeared out of the blue one evening and said that he'd told his wife about the two of them. He said, "I'm splitting the sheets!"

Then he tried to grope and kiss her! Feeling angry and very frustrated, she pushed him away, and bluntly told him off. Then he started driving his patrol car back and forth past the diner. He circled around in the back alley and shined his spotlight around and over the building.

There were good people who came into the restaurant, and some of them were from the Midwest. Most of the local residents treated the tourists and the wildlife biologists badly. Bonnie overheard a lot of local conversation about getting rid of the tree huggers. The good thing about Franky was that he wasn't afraid to call the cops and break up a fight in his establishment.

Bonnie lamented, *I'm not accustomed to a living on the edge. I grew up in a family that lived safely in middle-class comfort.* Her dad was probably turning over in his grave right now. If the deceased could kill, her husband would already be dead somewhere by now. Actually, he could be for all that she knew!

When she met Lee Hammond, they were both with their personal friends on a cruise to Mexico. He looked and sounded like a man of some class and means. When he found out that her dad had just died, he must have anticipated that she'd inherited an enormous amount of money. He swept her off her feet with his good looks and charm, and nothing was too good for his Bonnie! He was a romantic, silver-tongued devil, and his soft talking, soft soaping, and scheming talked her into a marriage after only three weeks of being together. After they were married under the vows of sharing everything as one, he must have received a disappointing look at the money in the bank account and wished that he'd romanced some other single woman that night on the cruise.

Suddenly, Lee started acting differently, as though he were weighing his options. Then he told her that she needed to get away from Indiana with him because she seemed depressed. He talked her into going to Las Vegas with him to celebrate their wedding and to try to forget the hardship of losing her father.

Her father and mother had both worked at factory jobs all of their lives. They paid for their house, where she was raised, and put her through art school and college and saved all that they could. Their life savings after retirement and death from working in a polluted factory environment was $45,000. Lee lost all of that sometime in the middle of one night in Las Vegas.

Bonnie still had her personal things in her parents' house in Indiana. She'd called her uncle who lived just down the street, telling him what happened in Las Vegas. Her uncle immediately called the county sheriff, and together, they took all of Lee's clothes and personal items to a storage unit until they heard from him. They changed the locks on the house and watched it constantly. Bonnie explained to her uncle that she was broke but had an opportunity to get in on the ground floor of a new business that might work out better than anything she'd find in her hometown in Indiana. He offered to send her some money to get home, but she knew that he couldn't afford it. Franky offered her a 30 percent split on a business partnership in a restaurant if she could help get it going and make a success of it. He might just be another liar, but she knew that she could fulfill her part of the verbal contract.

Now she was in the middle of Montana in the wintertime with a broken hand, and she believed that everything had somehow happened for a reason. She often wondered why she still believed in fate, because so far, it hadn't been very kind to her. She wasn't sure where this fate or whatever you wanted to call it might lead her, but she was an artist, and artists were sort of weird like that. She believed that sometimes fate gave you a canvas, but you had to find your own paint and choose your own colors if you were destined to create a masterpiece from an uncertain and uneventful life.

She trusted in fate when she was out on the Pacific Ocean with a handsome man and nearly drowned because she'd fallen overboard for someone she didn't know. Now she was high up in the Rocky Mountains and still trusted in a fate that she wouldn't fall and break what little resolve, determination, and spirit was left inside her.

As Fleebit drove through a silent part of town and turned onto an isolated, unpaved road, she wondered where she was headed and if she could still find her way over to the interstate highway without getting lost or freezing to death.

The old house sitting at the end of the street didn't give much of a first impression. It was just a neat, square-framed house with white wooden siding. The front view of the house wasn't so impressive, but the view behind it was magnificent! There was open land behind the house for as far as the eye could see. Fleebit's small property joined up with thousands of acres of national forest.

Fleebit pulled around in back of the house, and it was like visiting a Western movie set. There was a log barn and a lean-to with a network of pole corrals that led north toward the open country beyond. There were numerous pine slab buildings that were connected with false-front architecture like an Old West town from the 1800s. There was an old storefront sign on one building signifying the blacksmith shop and another that portrayed the feed store. Another colorful building had an old sign that said Pink Garter Saloon.

There was a herd of young horses inside the big corral with an open gate leading out into the big open country to the north. In front of the big barn in a separate pen was a single animal that was the biggest cow with the biggest horns that Bonnie had ever seen.

Bonnie asked, "Where did you find all of these old signs? They look like they are original signs from Dodge City during the Old West days."

"They are old original signs. Me and Clyde collected them from our travels all over the country during our early days. When someone was tearing down an old store or building so they could build a Quick Mart or a new house, we appropriated the old building's history by bringing the sign or part of the old building back here. Clyde almost got us into trouble a couple of times by taking something late at night. He always said that historians carried nine-tenths of the law on their side. Anyway, it makes us feel at home by having a reminder of the old days in our own backyard. Somebody would have burned them if we hadn't begged, borrowed, or stole them."

"Fleebit, is that the cow that Clyde warned me about?"

"Yeah, that's him, but he isn't a cow. He's a longhorn steer named Cheyenne. Now you watch out for him! He loves me, but he doesn't like Clyde. Clyde is always telling him that his days are numbered, and he calls him names like T-Bone or Pot Roast. Cheyenne sure ain't stupid, and he knows who his friends are. Don't you worry about him and this stock back here! I'll take care of them every day, and you just go in the house and take care of that hand. Maybe you should go to a doctor and get a cast put on it."

Bonnie looked at her swollen hand. "I'll put some ice on it, and it will be all right in a day or two," she insisted. "You have a beautiful place here, and I appreciate you for letting me stay here until I can sort things out and find my own way."

"You just make yourself at home here," assured Fleebit. "And if Clyde comes back, please don't tell him that I'm sleeping over at Ellen's house, because he will tease me about it to no end."

Bonnie laughed and said, "It's a promise!"

As she entered through the back door and into the kitchen, it was the beginning of a tour through a Western museum. The kitchen was medium-sized with white plaster walls and worn, unpolished hardwood flooring. Aged yellow pine cupboards surrounded the perimeter of two old cookstoves. The newer model was a vintage 1950s' industrial-sized electric range of white porcelain, and it looked very clean and well cared for. The older stove was a breathtaking chrome-covered giant. It was an original wood cookstove, and it was a polished robin-egg blue. It had towering warming ovens on both sides of the black stovepipe that joined the wall chimney.

All of the visible graniteware pots, dutch ovens, and iron and copper cookware looked like they were unloaded from a chuck wagon and a historical past. Her next few steps took her into a large single room with walls paneled with aged knotty pine. The hardwood floors were covered with large, antique Navajo rugs that were priceless. One of them was a tightly woven black-and-white rug that was centered on the floor of the large room.

Two giant, leather-covered chairs with Spanish-carved wooden posters and borders sat on each side of a massive matching sofa. An old arched-style 1930s' cabinet radio was the only entertainment center, and it sat back in a lonely corner of the room. There were two handmade saddle stands along one wall, and they were stacked with four saddles each, resting on top of each other. The most visible saddles on top were stamped Champion Header 2011 and Champion Heeler 2011. A look underneath each saddle showed the same name with an older year.

The walls were adorned with old pictures of cowboys, ranch families, trail drives, and roping and branding scenes. There were several pictures of Clyde and Fleebit roping cattle and wild horses and even signed photos of old Western film stars.

On one wall was a very old mirror that was bordered by cherrywood posters, carved with scenes from a Texas trail drive on one side and scenes of Indians chasing buffalo on the opposite side. Surrounding the entire setting was a thick cherrywood panel with white-tipped cow horns that were mounted in rich leather and bordered with brass mountings. Hanging from the many horns were old rawhide braided ropes, quirts, and headstalls with intricately braided brow bands and reins.

The entire room was a testament to two strong men of beautiful character in a land of rugged history.

In front of the large sofa was a long, handmade coffee table made out of thick pine slabs that were mounted on large moose antler legs. The tabletop was covered with stacks of *SuperLooper, Western Horseman, Ladies' Home Journal,* and *Today's Woman Now* magazines.

The only new addition to the Western theme was a very important one. There was a modern bathroom with a new shower and good lighting. The old house was very accommodating inside. It was simple and basic with a rustic charm that needed no great improvements or changes. She could see that some curtains needed to be replaced and some detailed cleaning two bachelors would overlook, but it was a perfect place to gather yourself up, and it was an inspirational art studio.

There was a small single room that someone had cleaned out, and it was all hers. She suddenly felt like a little girl again with her first freedom. All she could think about was baking some oatmeal cookies. Bonnie was wishing that she'd asked Fleebit to stop by the grocery store until she looked inside the kitchen cupboards and discovered that everything was well stocked. There were so many baking goods on hand that she suspected there was a woman who spent a lot of time in that kitchen. She also wondered about the ladies' magazines.

There were so many things that she wanted to do all at once, but her priorities indicated that she should wrap her hand in some ice and then try to bake some cookies to celebrate her own housewarming.

Bonnie stepped outside on the back porch with a plate of oatmeal cookies and a sketch book. She sat down on a worn, wooden bench facing the beautiful Old West scene before her and tried to catch the image of 150 years ago. The big steer named Cheyenne came up to the log fence right in front of her and pressed his massive head against it. He stared at her with his big brown eyes and mooed at her with a gentle pleading sound while his long tongue licked the air. He pressed harder against the poles until they bent slightly outward, and he mooed and licked up over his nose. Bonnie got up and took her cookies over to the fence, where she held out her hand as far as she could reach. His size and massive long horns were intimidating, and she remembered Clyde and Fleebit's warning. Cheyenne reached out his long tongue through the fence, and it curled around the cookie. A transformation came over him after chewing on the oatmeal cookie. He begged and pleaded for more. Pretty soon, the cookies were almost gone, and Bonnie was scratching and rubbing his head through the fence. For Cheyenne, it was love at first bite.

She tried to sketch Cheyenne and the rustic background, but her right hand started throbbing. The swelling hadn't gone down, and it was colored with a tinge of black and blue on the outside. She tried to reflect on her situation but could only think about Clyde out there in those snow-capped mountains and wondered, *How could a person go off by themselves like that on horseback and how could you survive? Could you live without fear of wild animals, bad weather, and loneliness?*

Fleebit tried to assure her that Clyde was an expert horseman and mountain man and that he was more at home in the wilderness than most folks were who lived in town. He'd said, "Bonnie, don't worry about Clyde. He rides off alone every spring just to celebrate life at the end of winter, and he wants to be alone up there. Clyde is more Indian than white, and there's a lot that you and I will never understand about him. He becomes like a wild animal inside a cage by the end of winter, and now he's busted out of that cage and has to make a big run to see if the world is still 'round after living in a square box for six months. He'll ride back in here when he gets his fill of being alone, because he's a joker, and he'll miss teasing and aggravating me and Cheyenne. He'll start missing his young saddle horses out behind the house too, because they are like his children. And, Bonnie, he'll miss you too! He's giving you a chance to run."

Bonnie didn't sleep very well because she could hear something out in back of the house. With all of those horses and Cheyenne stirring around eating hay, the night sounds would be something that she'd have to grow accustomed to. They were just different sounds from the noisy hotel uptown that she'd finally learned how to sleep through. Each time that she heard something, she could imagine Clyde coming back and putting his horse and Fleebit's mule away. The noisiest time was at first daylight, when Cheyenne started bawling and clacking his big horns through the corral poles. He became demanding for attention and especially for an oatmeal cookie.

Fleebit said that he noticed a big change come over Cheyenne since she'd moved into the old house. He told her that Cheyenne had never taken to anybody like he had to her. He still advised her not to get inside the pen with him because the reach of his horns could hurt her if he only innocently decided to swing his head around to scratch himself. Bonnie found something consoling about being outside with Cheyenne. Something filled a longing she had buried deep inside. She noticed that he was very gentle and careful with his horns when she was inside the pen with him, scratching his tall back or hand-feeding him. She had no idea that a cow could display such feelings of emotion.

Her hand was getting better now, but it was still tender when she scrubbed the floors and tried to do some major housecleaning. She was spending more time doing sketches of Fleebit from memory and building a background scene of Cheyenne and the Old Western town image from behind the house. She'd made at least a dozen individual sketches, and now she was incorporating them all into one scene. When she had it all perfected, she would start on the painting. Her art school instructors would have died for the models she now had available out her back door.

19

THE MIDMORNING SUN GAINED STRENGTH OVER THE HIGH
mountain peaks as it was joined by a warm southwest wind. The
snow was rapidly melting away from all except the high places and
those that were sheltered from direct sunlight on north-facing slopes.
Clyde gave No-Name his head and encouraged him on. Horses and
mules always traveled faster when they were pointed back toward
their home range than they did going away from it.

After looking at the letter that Maggie found, he too felt an
urgency to move on more quickly. He was thinking about the wolf
study group camped somewhere in the vicinity of his property
near Big Gulch, over forty miles distant to the east. The wolf people
were much closer to the Stricklers' vast property that bordered the
national forest than Maggie's group had been, and he'd arrived there
too late to warn them about their first visit from the unwelcome
guests. It was only a matter of time before they came back.

Maggie was such a cute girl and so full of life and enthusiasm for
the bear study program. It was a lucky thing for her that Bobby Ray
and his gang of thugs hadn't caught her all alone up there. There'd
been no recent news about Katie Colter's fate, and the mob-like
mentality against the environmentalists continued in town.

If he rode all night, he figured he could reach his cabin in the early hours just before dawn. Then he could feed his animals, get some rest, and ride on to find the other group of kids.

His horse was in good shape from being ridden in the foothills around town. Many folks thought that Clyde's horses were only ridden to the café and then tied up, where he loafed around all morning drinking coffee with the locals. Little did they know that his horses were often ridden since before daylight on a big circle that covered several miles through a foot or more of snow. They were only tied up at the café to rest and cool off while he enjoyed some hot coffee.

Clyde knew how to get horses in shape, and he knew how and when to rest them, saving their strength for a time when he might need to call upon it. So many people these days had horses, but he noticed that they were never used until there was an immediate need for them. Then they were abused by their riders' impatience for a sudden burst of speed to get somewhere quickly or to gather up a few cows as quickly as possible. You could drive around any Western town these days and see good, well-bred horses standing in lots or in small pastures where million-dollar log homes now dominated the landscape. The horses were nothing but lawn ornaments to most of these owners, and their animals were treated with the same respect and emotion as a Honda motorcycle.

Clyde didn't care so much now about leaving his tracks, as he returned by the same trail that he arrived by the day before. He noticed that his tracks from early morning were disappearing into the melting snow. He could still see the giant bear tracks that left the main trail into a big snowdrift heading northeast. As he rode on and arrived at the place of his snow cave the night before, there was no trace of his camp being there at all, but there were fresh tracks all over where he'd collapsed the snow cave.

The giant grizzly had circled back around and walked all over his camp spot. These tracks were very fresh, and they were the same uncommonly big tracks of a huge bear. He noticed something about the right front foot of the bear's imprint in the snow. There were pink blood spots inside the track. This foot had recently been injured, and he was walking in a pattern that indicated that he was protecting it from his full weight. Now this bear was on his trail heading east and was somewhere up ahead. Not only that, he was injured!

A short distance up the Highline Trail, the giant bear stopped, stood up tall on his massive hindquarters, and faced the western landscape. He tucked his right front paw inward and licked it tenderly. He expanded his chest and opened up his nostrils wide, testing the wind. A familiar and most recent smell triggered a stored memory in his brain.

His instinct vividly recalled the snare trap where an enticing, half-rotten mule deer lay hidden through a break in the trail. When he reached for the meat, he was suddenly held there. When he jerked backward, he was injured but free.

He recalled another distant memory in time when he became trapped inside a small cave with the meat that lured him there. He awakened to the smells of man and metallic smoke. He was drowsy like awakening from the long winter sleep, but there was a feeling of danger and hopelessness from being trapped there.

There was something around his neck. As he stared off to the west, a low growl rumbled in his chest. With a loud woof, he spun around and lumbered eastward down the trail.

Clyde reached the summit above Big Scratch sometime around 1:00 a.m. He still had another four-mile ride to the cabin and chose to keep going in the dark. He could see the city lights and pick out the lonesome night light on the outskirts of town where he'd spent the winter. He wondered if Bonnie was down there now at the old house or if she'd packed up and left Montana.

He had an important job to finish, and when he committed himself to something, he always saw it through. He knew that Fleebit would come looking for him if he wasn't back within a week, and this was something that he had to do alone. If he rode down to the town place now, he would have to answer questions, and perhaps the old dog would want to go with him.

Clyde was heading in the direction where he felt something pulling him. Was it the dream about the desperate woman pleading for him to rescue her? Her voice seemed to ride in the wind and echo from the rocks, calling him from the distant mountain in the east.

The warm southwest wind quit blowing, and it was getting cold. Cowboy boots were never warm when you carried your weight in the stirrups during long night rides this time of year. The big iron spurs that were attached to his cowboy boots also drew in the cold to his feet, but they were a necessity. Clyde used leg pressure against his horse and seldom used his spurs, but there were times when spurs could save your life. If your horse refused to face something or move forward, they were used as a last resort to encourage your horse onward.

When he reached the junction in the trail leading to town, No-Name and Blue wanted to head down to the corrals and join their friends to eat, but Clyde dallied up Blue's lead rope around his saddle horn and used his spurs to encourage No-Name on past their desired destination and up the trail.

As he rode onward through the cold, still night, images of his grandfather appeared as short captions of a movie about his past. Flashes of memory portrayed scenes of his grandfather with his medicine pipe and his wisdom.

His grandfather could talk with the spirits inside the medicine lodge. If he were alive, Clyde could ask him to hold a sweat ceremony for Katie Colter and her family. Perhaps he could find out what happened to her. He might know the meaning of Clyde's dream and the significance of the white elephant.

Riding like this alone at night was a time for reflecting on serious thoughts about many things. He was always joking around when he was in town. Perhaps it was because life was more like a joke, being trapped by harsh weather in the company of so many town gossips. Fleebit was an easy target that took it without rebellion, and Clyde's inventive humor and private jokes were what kept his spirits up and away from the winter blues. Grandfather said that the clown used laughter to heal the sickness of the human spirit when it seemed that all was lost.

The moon was completely hidden now, and it became so dark that he had to trust his horse to stay on the trail. His thoughts became centered upon Fleebit. Lately, he'd been saying how good looking he was. What was that about? And now he was using a new favorite word—*awesome*. Where the hell did that come from? And why was he calling him *Captain* now?

Clyde said out loud, "I've hauled his sorry ass all over the Rocky Mountains with me for forty years, but I'll be damned if I'll carry his dead ass around in meat coolers. I still can't believe he thought his daughter would do such a thing! He probably fell asleep on Ellen's couch watching the final episode of *Lonesome Dove*, where Captain Call hauled Augustus McCrae's body in a buckboard wagon from Montana to Texas. You just never know anymore what he has stored in his head and might speak out loud!"

Clyde wondered if Fleebit was going to move in with Ellen Jorgenstein or marry her. He knew that his partner was afraid to tell him the truth about how he felt for her. He was afraid of ending their working partnership of so many years.

As Clyde rode on through the dark night, the light north breeze brought the smell of pine and horse. He thought about all of his young horses and which ones were responding better to their training. They were like so many children who had hidden talents not yet revealed. He even thought about Cheyenne and wondered if he was missing him.

When he thought about Bonnie, he knew that something was building between them, although he wasn't quite sure where it would lead. She was much younger than he was but seemed to want more of a connection than just a coffee shop laugh session. Maybe she looked up to him as a father figure. No, not that! A mature figure, but definitely not fatherly! When she touched and kissed him, there were undeniable feelings of stimulation.

From first glance, he never viewed her as a daughter figure. She was sexy, ravishingly beautiful, and beyond his wildest dreams. He thought of cute little Maggie as a daughter figure, but since he'd never had any children, he wasn't quite sure how the genetic connection was supposed to feel.

Bonnie might just take the money and run. He couldn't really blame her if she did. The way her husband treated her and the way that Franky held her hostage, it would be understandable if she hated all men.

He'd fought against the urgent desire of taking her home and into his arms. But her smell, the sound of her voice, and her touch when she leaned against him in the booth at the café made him want her.

He fought the desire because she consumed him, his thoughts, and—tragically—his ability to stay focused on his horse training. He wasn't paying attention to his natural instinct and perception of a young horse's need for correction or reward at an opportune time. He'd been faced with this battle before. He was losing it! If he couldn't focus on what he did best, how could he manage a relationship with a full-time woman that consumed him? Would he have to choose between his love for a woman and his love for the horses?

He had an ability to always find good horses, but he'd only found one Bonnie. What if she bucked him off a few years down the road and ran away? He didn't think he could ever bear the pain of lost love again. It had drained him the last time.

When he wrote Bonnie that big check and rode away, he knew that if she stayed, it wasn't because she was desperate. It was because she wanted him. It would be a cheap trade-off when he weighed his heart on a scale against a pan of gold dust. If she ran with the money, his heart would heal, and he would go on as before. What if she stayed? Better sooner than later to find out. Good horses and money were easy enough to come by. Love only came once or twice if you were lucky!

Clyde continued riding through the cold, dark night and thought about the Strickler gang and what they might be up to next. Pretty soon, he was at his cabin and wondered where the time had gone. When he stepped down from No-Name, his feet were numb from the cold, and he knew they would throb when the circulation started coming back into them.

Clyde removed the snow shovel from the top of Blue's pack and cleared the snow away from the barn door. He pried it open with a loud creak. He led both of the animals inside and unpacked and unsaddled them. He opened up three bales of hay and spread it around on the barn floor so that they could eat their fill and then lie down on the excess hay. Horses usually sleep standing up, but when they've been traveling many miles over hard, frozen ground, they become leg weary and need to rest lying down.

Clyde gave each of them a gallon of oats, and while they were munching the grain, he took two buckets out in back of the cabin and filled them up from the overflowing spring. His animals would be thirsty after they ate.

He carried his pack and the shovel over to the cabin and began removing the snow from in front of the door. The cabin had been completely covered up with snow, and the windows and door were always swollen after the melt. He kept a flat pry bar hanging from the back of an aspen near the door, and it was used specifically for this one job each spring. He took the bar and carefully slipped it between the door and the framing and pried outward from around the door until it snapped free from its frozen grip.

The cabin was left well stocked with firewood, kerosene, and dry goods. It wasn't long until Clyde had a fire going in the wood cookstove. As the dry pine splinters popped and cracked, the thick iron stove top started thumping with the sound of expanding metal.

Clyde had shut off the water coming into the cabin the previous fall so that it wouldn't freeze up. He took a big graniteware coffeepot out back and filled it up from the overflowing spring.

He opened up a jar of dried fruit and his sack of jerky and ate some breakfast while the coffee water heated up. Suddenly, his eyes became heavy, and he was in a deep, deep, exhaustive sleep.

"Hi, old friend, you've come back!"

The scar-faced bear stood up tall and looked directly at him and his mounted horse. Then the golden giant looked nervously over his left shoulder. He dropped down and spun away, chasing the other cowboys and their horses over the horizon. Suddenly, he was back and stood up tall once again, looking directly into Clyde's eyes.

Clyde's horse stood facing the bear, unafraid. Clyde yelled, "Roll over!"

The giant bear sat down on his haunches and stared him in the eye.

Clyde asked, "Can I ride on your back and see the world again? Just like last time?"

The bear stood up tall again and spun around, looking over his left shoulder. Then he sprang away and vanished from sight.

The sound of Canada Jays squawking outside the cabin window jolted Clyde awake. Clyde panicked and realized that he'd slept longer than intended.

Clyde felt troubled as he saddled up and rode northeast toward the Strickler Ranch. He thought about his dream. What was the bear trying to tell him? The scar-faced bear had come to him as a boy when he was called bad names and George Mountain Lion wanted to kill him. The bear appeared when he most needed security and confidence. When Clyde rode upon the giant bear's back, he no longer feared the lion.

Clyde thought, *The first time my friend came, he wanted to play and be happy. In my second dream, he was nervous and looked over his left shoulder. In the first dream, I was a boy in trouble. Now I am a man. Am I getting into trouble again? Maybe I should watch over my left shoulder!*

Clyde let No-Name have his head and guided him with both legs on a slack rein. Clyde guided him cross-country and away from the main trail. He first wanted to check the south gate to the Strickler property. It was a narrow cattle gate on a trail leading to Big Gulch, and it might be the direct route the gang would take if they were to attack the biologists at their camp. Although the isolated gate was heavily chained and locked, there were no spy cameras.

The day was warm, and the frost was pulling upward out of the mountain soil. The rich smell of spring was in the air. The ground was slick and muddy in the open places, and No-Name was careful and well balanced not to lose his footing and fall. Clyde was careful not to leave muddy tracks near the main trail, because they would freeze and leave permanent evidence of his passage.

It was obvious that no horsemen had been on the trail since the previous fall. He hoped that he could warn the New Indians at the wolf camp before the Strickler gang approached them.

Clyde decided to ride around the fenced property to see if there was any activity. He knew that the Stricklers patrolled it during summer and fall months to prevent hikers and hunters from crossing the national forest border onto their land. Their fence line was posted with Keep Out signs, and he knew that the front gate entrance was guarded with surveillance cameras.

It was at the back of their isolated ranch where he was most interested. The back-gate entrance joined the narrow gravel road leading to East Park. There was no electricity back there, and there were no spy cameras surrounding the locked iron gates. Clyde had earlier witnessed big men who patrolled the back entrance on ATVs or in 4×4 monster trucks. Sometimes he saw them walking around dressed in camouflage, carrying rifles slung over their shoulders.

As Clyde rode No-Name out of the thick pine forest and entered the gravel roadway, the sunlight reflected off of something shiny beneath the snow. He dismounted and picked up a piece of chrome lying beside the road. It appeared to be the shroud to a headlight, and there was a tuft of elk hair stuck inside it. Clyde continued walking up the road and leading his horse while scanning the ground for sign. There was still snow cover over much of the ground where sunlight was shaded by the forest canopy.

When he reached the locked iron gate, there were no fresh tracks, but there was a satellite dish mounted overhead with an attached camera. Clyde picked up a rock and threw it expertly into the lens, shattering it to pieces.

He mounted up and noticed another big camera. He took down his rope and threw a small loop up and overhand. He turned his horse away, and it snapped loose from the overhead arch. Clyde began riding back and forth through a large grove of aspens across the road. The large trees were marked with graffiti from years past. It always upset him to see where people scratched their names and initials into the bark of the majestic trees. Clyde thought that only the bears were entitled to leave their marks.

Suddenly, he noticed where someone had carved initials down low on a big tree. Unlike the other black initials carved higher up, where someone was standing vertically, these were carved horizontally, and the letters were still pink.

KC loves SI.

Clyde tied up his horse and sat down in front of the tree. He thought about how hard it would be for someone to make these marks. He lay on his side facing the tree and felt something under his hip in the aspen leaves. Clyde reached underneath him and pulled out a golden case with a long gold chain attached. He opened it up and saw the white elephant.

"KC ... Katie Colter!"

Clyde could hear the roar of a big truck speeding across the Strickler property and advancing toward the back gate. He quickly mounted his horse and galloped off through the trees away from the road.

Clyde trotted out of the dark forest and pushed his bay gelding into a gallop down a long, winding meadow. He didn't know who he could trust with this information or if he could count on anyone, including the sheriff and his bought-off deputies.

They might all be in George Strickler's pocket. They let his son Bobby Ray get away with all kinds of crimes. What if they might even let him get away with murder?

One thing was for certain—he had to get back and do what he set out to do. He had to protect little Maggie and those other kids at their camp.

No-Name was breathing hard as he came to the edge of the forest overlooking Big Gulch Canyon. Clyde could see the camp set up down below. Clyde took his time cutting diagonally down the slick, steep mountainside in full view of the camp, and he whistled a tune so that the camp's occupants could hear him and have plenty of time to see him coming. By the time he reached the canyon floor, the entire group was advancing his way.

A tall young man asked, "Are you Clyde Deerhide?"

"Yeah," said Clyde. "How did you know?"

"*Yah Te Hey!* My name is Fred. Maggie called us on their radio phone and said to be expecting you today. She and her group are coming over here tonight after the road freezes up."

Clyde grinned. "*Yah Te Hey!* You speak-um Native?"

"Oh no! I heard that greeting during a John Wayne movie. I'm part Miami. Maggie said you were Lakota. I can't speak my native language or yours. We all got excited, though, about the prospects of a Lakota warrior coming to help us defend our camps from the Big Scratch cavalry."

"You folks might be receiving some real bad visitors," said Clyde. "There might even be a murderer running loose around here. I'll come back in the morning when Maggie and her group have settled in, and we can all make a plan. I'll do some detective work and try to warn you in advance of their arrival. Please don't let any of the girls leave camp until I get back."

20

SHERIFF TOLLIBER AND HIS TWO DEPUTIES TRIED TO control the traffic on Main Street and keep order. Katie Colter's father was in town with a group of demonstrators and television crews. It was like a bomb had exploded in town. Bill Colter came into his office with a California film crew the day before, accusing him of sitting on his ass and doing nothing about Katie's disappearance. Bill had a lot of connections, and he used his influence to bring his missing daughter back into the spotlight. This event was planned months in advance. Environmental groups and the news media came from across the country.

Throughout the day and into the evening, more cars and vans with out-of-state license plates were lining Main Street and filling the motel parking lot. A tent city sprang up in the municipal park. A large Billings News van set up shop across the street from the local sawmill. A Salt Lake City Channel 2 News helicopter circled the town and landed at the courthouse.

At 10:00 a.m., he received a call from Franky at the Thin Vein. A fight broke out between some local boys and a group of men from Vermont. When the sheriff locked up the sawmill owner's sons for starting the ruckus, local ranchers and citizens swarmed into town with guns and tried to block off the town. The sheriff called in the state police.

Tim and his group of wildlife biologists were alarmed when they approached the town. They quickly loaded up with groceries and escaped down a side street ahead of an angry throng of local residents. They raced away toward Big Gulch Canyon. Two truckloads of men chased them out of town and then turned around and went back.

Fleebit left Ellen's house after daylight and saw the crowd forming. He drove around the traffic and over to his place, where he quickly fed and watered the livestock.

Bonnie came outside and asked him, "Is there going to be a parade or a festival today?"

Fleebit said, "It looks like some tree huggers are getting ready for a parade, but it sure isn't no festival! It might turn into a battleground on Main Street. Bonnie, don't walk uptown today. I don't know what might happen, but you'll be better off staying home."

Bonnie became alarmed at Fleebit's concern and the worried look on his face. "I wish Clyde were here. I know he's only been gone for three days, but I miss him."

Fleebit kicked at the dirt with his boot and looked up toward the mountain ridge to the northeast. "I hope Clyde don't come back and ride into town today."

"Why is that?" asked Bonnie.

Fleebit was very uncomfortable with his environmental conflicts with Clyde, and he hesitated to continue.

"If Clyde were here, his Indian blood would boil over, and he would join up with those tree huggers downtown. He gets real emotional when you threaten somebody who defends the earth. It was the way his grandpa raised him in the Indian way. If he were here, he might end up fighting some local people that he's known for a long time. Clyde has been worrying over that missing girl from California since he first heard the story, and Ellen told me that her dad brought all of these people into town. Clyde would get right in the middle of all this if he were here!"

"Fleebit, is he good friends with Tolly?"

Fleebit seemed confused. "They get along all right. Why do you ask?"

Bonnie smiled, "Oh, I just wondered if Clyde trusted him like a best friend, that's all."

Fleebit glanced out over the corrals at Clyde's young horses one more time. "Clyde don't put much faith in anybody from this town. He don't put any faith at all in white people who have power. Clyde's best friends are out there eating hay. He's up there today in those mountains, riding a good horse that he respects more than people." Fleebit smiled. "Like a good, faithful horse, it takes a while before you can earn Clyde's trust and respect. He's with his best friend right now. Oh, don't get me wrong! Me and him are close friends, but I'm not his best friend. If you can be patient with him and understanding and consistent in your dealings, there's not another man like him to have at your side and guard your back. You sure wouldn't want him for an enemy!

"Bonnie, I couldn't believe it when he told me that he wanted you to move in here! I didn't think he would ever trust another woman after he let Mary go. He hasn't said much to me about you, but you need to know how special this is. I know him better than anybody, and I can tell you this: he thinks a lot of you!"

They could hear sirens coming into town from the direction of the interstate highway. Loudspeakers echoed out across the town. Fleebit warned Bonnie, "Stay home!"

He jumped in the old green Ford pickup and raced back to Ellen's house.

Ellen ran to the front door and intercepted Fleebit. She wrapped her arms around him and kissed him. "Oh my, I was afraid that you went up town and would get into a fight. May and Helga both called me and said that there are fights breaking out in town. People are shouting and waving guns in the air!"

Fleebit took off his cowboy hat and hung it on the coatrack inside the door. "I decided to stay out of this. I've been in a lot of fights through the years, and I've learned that violence never wins. The law is hired to take care of things like this. Ellen, Bonnie just asked me if Clyde could trust the sheriff like a best friend. Why would she ask such a question?"

Ellen became distracted by Fleebit's question and turned away to attend a potted plant.

Fleebit took hold of her arm and turned her into him. "Okay, let's have it! Tell me!"

Ellen looked up into Fleebit's green eyes and said, "Marty, Helga, May, and Selma all talk about how the sheriff stalks Bonnie. They say that he told his wife that he was leaving her for Bonnie. They said that his patrol car was parked at the Thin Vein or driving around a lot after Clyde left town."

Fleebit became upset. "I don't believe that Bonnie would do this to Clyde. I think the reason she asked me that question is because she's troubled by Tolly's behavior but was afraid to tell me what's going on. Clyde told me a long time ago that he thinks Tolly is getting paid off by George Strickler. After Bobby Ray and the Strickler gang beat the hell out of those men who were taking water samples out of Clear Creek, Tolly turned that gang loose without charges or a court hearing! Clyde found a lot of things out about the Stricklers' activities while working for John Baxter's ranch next door. One time, he told Tolly about a bunch of dead elk they shot from snowmobiles. Clyde found a dozen dead cow elk spread out down through a long meadow. Nobody ever went in to check on it, and Clyde became frustrated with the law around here. He told me that he wouldn't tell the sheriff anything from now on. He doesn't trust him."

Fleebit thought about Bonnie's question about whether Tolly was Clyde's friend, and he grabbed Ellen's hand. "Clyde invites Tolly and his deputies over to the Pink Garter just because he enjoys winning all of their cash in fast-draw shooting contests over the bar. He told me, 'Those cops can practice all they want at that shooting range, but they'll never have the instinct of immediate, point-blank shooting!' I hope nobody ever tries to go up against Clyde with a handgun or a rifle. In his hands, they are just like his rope; when he lets go, it always finds the center of its target!"

Ellen said, "I like Bonnie a lot, and I trust her too. Maybe I can talk with her and find out if the sheriff is bothering her. Every woman needs another woman to talk to. I think she has special feelings for Clyde. I don't understand why, but she does! Fleebit, Clyde makes me very angry at times, but he's right about Tolly. I went to the sheriff after Henry died, and I took him Henry's journal." Ellen began shaking and cried, "George Strickler killed my Henry! And the sheriff betrayed me!"

Fleebit hugged her. "There, there, now

Ellen sobbed, "When Henry became sick, he spent more time writing in his journal after work. Then I didn't see it on the stand next to his chair anymore when I cleaned the house. When I was making our bed, I found it hidden beneath the mattress and feared that something was wrong. At first, I thought he was writing about another woman. I was afraid to read something that he was hiding, so I didn't read it. Instead, I asked him about his hidden journal. That was when he told me about the problems at the mine. He was afraid of someone stealing his journal. He was afraid that someone would kill us!

"The EPA officials who took soil and water samples were paid off with gold. George Strickler's son and his friends dumped chemicals into the ground after workers left at night.

"Safety gloves and shields became torn, cracked, and discarded without any new replacements. When Henry complained to George about the substandard operation, a giant man named Bubba came up from behind and lifted him up like a rag doll. He told Henry to keep his mouth shut or something might happen to me.

"Henry's young helper from Sweden became sick from mercury poisoning and died. That's what killed Henry! Fleebit, everything I told you was written in Henry's journal. I didn't think about trying to get money from Henry's death. I just thought that justice should be served. I gave Sheriff Tolliber Henry's journal. Months later, he told me that he didn't have time to read it, and it accidentally became lost."

The demonstrators organized at the city park to begin their march from the south end of town, in front of the Simple Log Homes and Lumber Company. They would march north up Main Street and rally on top of the hill in front of the courthouse and police station.

Bill Colter led the march with some of Katie's high-school friends and cameramen surrounding them. They led up the west side of the street, holding signs with Katie's enlarged photograph. They chanted loudly, "Where is Katie? Where's Montana law? Where is Katie? Where is justice? Where's our Katie?"

Behind the advancing group came the Montana Wilderness Alliance Group from throughout the state. They came in large numbers from the University of Montana in Missoula and from Montana State University in Bozeman.

They spread out across the street and marched north, holding large, wide, long banners. The leader of the group was dressed in a bear costume and carried a handheld loudspeaker.

"Welcome to George Strickler's town! If you are itching to kill your Earth Mother, come to Big Scratch, Montana. This is George Strickler's town, where you can scratch yourself away from any responsible actions. He took $20 million worth of gold out of our public lands and left us a death trap. Who is going to pay for the clean up on Clear Creek?"

Dozens of followers chanted, "Strickler pay! Clean it up! Strickler pay! Cough it up!"

Next in line was a group who had traveled from Utah. They held up posters saying, "Stop Hydrofracking!" "Protect Our Underground Water!" "Stop the Mother Frackers!" and "Patent Laws Protect Oil Companies, Not Life!"

The last group was a large contingent from the Sierra Club. Individuals, couples, and small groups from many states had come to the call for this demonstration. People who were casual associates of the Sierra Club and noncommittal members had all followed the tragic story about Katie Colter's disappearance. They filled the street.

The largest banner that covered the wide street in big block letters proclaimed "SAVE THE TREES! STOP THE TREE MUGGERS! NO MORE CHINA LUMBER!"

The large group that numbered hundreds surrounded a homemade coffin carried by pallbearers. It was followed by men wearing grim reaper costumes and wielding axes. Inside the coffin were small babies and seedling pine trees inside planters.

They all chanted loudly with loudspeakers and microphones in a deafening roar,

"Kill the trees and rape the land! Will your grandkids understand?"

Suddenly, an angry mob standing in the back of pickup trucks began shouting and throwing full beer bottles into the crowd of Sierra Club demonstrators. The bottles crashed into the hard pavement and sprayed glass and beer outward into the crowd. One bottle hit an old, gray-haired man in the side of the head, and it dropped him into the street. Another flung bottle broke against the casket, sending beer and flying shards of glass into the babies inside.

A deafening roar went up from the Sierra Club crowd when the small babies screamed out in fright and pain. The demonstrators became outraged. They turned and charged the tormenters across the street. The grim reapers took the lead and used their axe handles against the mob, knocking men down, while their followers tromped over them using boots, fists, and fingernails.

Sharp cracks of gunfire erupted from the state troopers. They fired smoke bombs and a canister of teargas into the crowd. A north wind carried the smoke down the street and over the babies and small children.

Bill Colter was joined by his wife, Sheena, after their group safely reached the hill north of town. They looked back down the hill at Main Street. People were running, screaming, and fighting. The news media flashed pictures of Katie's portrait and the mayhem down below. They quickly sent their documentary across the country.

Sheriff Tolliber stationed his deputies at two side streets coming into town. He told them to stay alert, stay out of the way, and let the state troopers take over.

He roared away from them with flashing lights and came to a stop on the flat hilltop overlooking the town. Tolly thought, *I'm sure as hell not going to be parked in front of those news cameras at the courthouse!* He shut off his engine, pushed back in his seat, and relaxed. He took out his binoculars and looked down upon Fleebit's house at the outskirts of town.

21

GEORGE STRICKLER WAS MAD AS HELL. HE'D BEEN TRYING
to reach Bobby Ray on the phone for several days now, but nobody
answered the phone at the ranch or checked messages. He knew
that somebody was there; the recording had been changed on the
ranch office phone during the course of several different calls that
he'd made.

The most recent recording was Bobby Ray's voice addressing
someone about the party. He sounded drunk on the phone.

George received two calls at his Maryland mansion from his
attorneys in Billings, who were very concerned that he hadn't called
them after he'd received their letter. The senior partner of the law
firm sounded very concerned about that letter getting into the wrong
hands. It seemed that a mistake was made during mailing, and it
was sent to the Montana ranch address instead of George Strickler's
resident box in Baltimore, Maryland. The letter was sent as registered
mail, and by tracking, it was confirmed that Bobby Ray signed for
it and took it with him.

He was facing a lawsuit for $20 million, and his attorneys couldn't
even mail a letter to the right address! The only reason he didn't fire
Bill Martin and his associates was because they were all in it too
deep. It was too late to start over.

Those overpaid sloggers know they wouldn't have anything without me! They know how much is in the pot, and they don't want it to boil over. If it boils over, it will quench their entire flame that I myself ignited. If they lose this case, they are washed up. I am their golden calf, and they will all worship a different reality if I'm gone! George thought. *There's always money! There has always been influence to direct issues with money. There are judges and politicians out there who hate tree huggers and can use more money. But I'd rather dig another gold mine out of the rocks than give it to the worthless, politician sons of bitches! None of their soft, lily hands ever touched a pick and a shovel. Those overpaid bastards all deserve a visit from Bubba!*

Now those goddamned tree huggers with the Montana Wilderness Alliance were on the Headline News channel, chanting, "Strickler pay! Twenty mill, now, today!" It seemed like things were falling apart. As top dog, he could only snarl and bite his only son, Bobby Ray, on the lips. But as the male alpha wolf, he could grab his lawyers by the throat and rip out their jugular veins.

Bobby Ray arrived home after a weeklong party and checked his phone messages. Then he slammed down the phone and shouted, "Oh shit!" He took a long drag from a half-empty Crown Royal bottle and slammed it down. "Boys, we've got to go back up the mountain to that tree hugger camp!"

Bobby Ray reluctantly called his dad in Maryland, but not before finding some courage from the bottle and thinking up some good excuses for being gone and for losing his dad's important mail.

"Bobby, where in the hell have you been?" demanded George Strickler. "And why didn't you call me and tell me about my letter from our lawyers? Do you have any idea how important this big lawsuit is against us? We could lose everything we have and more! How would you like to move back to Maryland into a little paperboard box of a house and go back to work at a Laundromat? You were supposed to stay at home and only go out to get my mail and a few groceries. I just bailed you out of one big mess!"

"Dad, we've been around here most of the time, and I just think this phone is messed up."

George said, "Well, it sure worked fine the night you left a message about the party!"

"Dad, we've been helping Pablo a lot around here with the cows and everything, and I must have misplaced your letter somewhere in the office."

George demanded, "I want you to find what you did with that letter, and I want you to stay home and out of trouble. I'm sending Bubba back there on a flight this evening. Send somebody to pick him up at the Missoula airport. And tell your other friends who live in my Montana house on my expense account to stay there, because I may need them to go on some other job. I want all of you to look around for that letter. Do you understand?"

"Yes, Dad. Good-bye!"

Bobby flopped down across a sofa and stared at the giant log support beams in the ceiling, thinking and planning. "Sway, take off for Missoula! You've got to pick up Beef at the airport tonight. There must be something important happening! Dad never tells me what he has planned for Bubba to do. Maybe Dad wants him to spy on us and report back to him."

Sam said, "Beef wouldn't rat on us. He's one of the old gang."

"I don't know," said Tony. "Maybe George bought him off. He's been gone a long time. None of us know where he's been or what he's done."

Sway started to light a cigarette.

Bobby demanded, "Put that out! You guys know that Bubba don't like the smell of cigarette smoke. Go outside on the deck! We've got to do things different." Bobby was worried. "I don't know why he's coming, but we have to be more careful around here with what we say and do. The party might be over for a while. One thing's for certain—we have to find Dad's important letter. Sam, Tony, Jeff, we've got to head back up where we raided that tree hugger camp. I think you guys kicked out some our mail where we parked that night. Grab some guns, and let's get going!"

They returned back to where they had parked the truck on the night they vandalized the bear study camp, and most of the snow had melted away. Bobby found a magazine subscription notice with his name on it, and it was wilted from the melted snow. There was an old cross-country ski track leading up toward the bear study camp in the distant aspen grove. They waited until sundown and started hiking up through the trees that circled around behind the camp where they'd visited over a week earlier. Jeff stayed with the truck, and Bobby followed the ski tracks, while Tony and Sam went around behind. When they met up at the camp, everything was gone.

"I'm afraid that someone on those skis found my dad's important letter. Dad said that if it got into the wrong hands, we could lose everything. They'll be able to trace that registered letter back to me for being up here that night and destroying their equipment, and if they read that letter, they could make a lot of trouble for my dad."

The next morning, Bobby Ray went into the hardware store and bought some coyote snares from Marty. It didn't take Marty long to mention the wolf and bear people who also bought snares, built traps, what they did with them, and where they went. Marty said that he overheard the two groups talking about sharing the same camp now over on East Ridge, near Big Gulch Canyon.

Bobby went home and told the boys, "Those bear people are a lot closer to the ranch now. They are camped with those wolf people just on the other side of the national forest from the ranch. We can ride the horses over there and watch them until they all leave. Then we'll go through their stuff and try to find that letter. We need to find out their routine. Sam, I want you to hang around town for a couple of nights and watch what they do and where they go. I want you to search both of their vehicles for my dad's registered letter without getting caught. Then when we're ready, you can call us when they all get into town and go to eat or into a movie. We can't let them see us near that camp, so we've got to be sure that they're gone before we ride in there. We can't mess up this operation!"

22

THE DRIVER LOADED UP BUBBA'S THREE BIG SUITCASES
into the back of the limo and sped away from the Strickler mansion,
heading for the interstate and the Baltimore airport. George reached
over and pushed the center window shut with a crisp, tight snap.

"Thanks for coming, Bubba. I have a special job for you to do,
and it won't require a lot of heavy lifting like when you first hired
out to me. You've almost been like a son to me since we all packed
up and left Maryland to dig for the gold. I've always tried to take
care of my loyal workers and keep them on the payroll with easy
jobs and higher pay scales."

Bubba loved to ride in the big limousine. He could stretch his
long legs outward and kick back. It was the only car made that fit
him for comfort. He didn't get to ride in the company car very often;
it was only when George had a new job for him. Then he would be
sent away to an island somewhere for several months. Bubba could
have imagined himself owning two or three of these cars a few
years ago, but George had talked him out of that full-ride football
scholarship.

"Boss, you've always been good to me, and I do what you tell
me to do."

"Yeah, that's right!" said George. "You've always done what I've asked you to do, and now I want you to do something else for me. I want you to answer some questions for me about Bobby Ray. I want to know if he is leaving the ranch and getting into more trouble. Is he doing drugs and partying with underage girls in my house? What in the hell has he done with some of my mail? Pablo told me that he's never around the ranch to help out with the cows, fencing, or to make decisions required of a manager."

Bubba suddenly felt less comfortable, and he pulled his long legs inward. "Boss, blood is thicker than water! If I start telling you what Bobby does, then you'll get on his ass because I told you, and pretty soon, I'll just be the water underneath the bridge."

George slammed his right hand down on the seat next to Bubba. It smacked hard upon the leather seat with a *crack*. He became very irritated and shook his head from side to side. He mixed himself a drink from the mobile bar and became silent as they hit the off-ramp and sped into the inside lane. "Beef, you've been real good at taking care of my special business and keeping quiet. I've always hated a rat! You are a smart man! If you won't tell on Bobby to me, then the way I understand it, you won't tell on me to Bobby. Am I right?"

Bubba relaxed and breathed deeply. He stretched his legs forward again. "Boss, you got that right!"

As they approached the airport, George stared out his side window. "I'm not sending you back to the ranch to spy on my son. Hell, I have investigators hired to spy on my investigators. I know what Bobby does! I just want you to keep him in line. I can't have him getting into more trouble and adding more problems to the ones I already have. I'm sending you back to take care of that other special business that you do and never talk about. There are a lot of people trying to stir things up and create problems for me. They are getting together, and I'm afraid that soon they'll form a strong chain. There is a group who is demanding $20 million. If I don't negotiate and lose this lawsuit, a federal judge might hit me for $100 million. Private investigators and small interest groups are out there right now prowling around and trying to get something on us. Beef, I want you to take charge of the ranch and find out who is out there walking around and causing trouble. Find out who is the strong link in the chain, and weaken it by snapping it in two! There are a lot of places where somebody can become lost.

"I have a new surveillance system set up for you. Bobby and the gang don't even know about it. Bobby thinks I installed a new satellite system for his birthday so he could pick up the sports channel. What he don't know and can't know is that I put in a new, high-tech surveillance system all around the ranch, and it is undetectable. New cameras are in place. The big, obvious cameras on the front and back gates are almost obsolete. Bobby can still check the monitor in his room and see someone parked at the front gate, but that's all he'll see. Since he's never around the ranch, I'm not sure what he's missing. There could be trespassers all over us. Find out! The new cameras are so small and hidden that you'll never see them, but you'll recognize the location of them when you see it on video. I'm sending a personal control system with you, and there are simple instructions. I told Bobby that you were taking over my office. Keep the door locked! Under my desk is a bunch of new, color-coded cables. That is where you will plug in your monitor and report back to me.

"Bobby has turned my workforce of men at the ranch into a bunch of partygoers who no longer look after my interests. Bubba, you are different from them. Don't let the old gang suck you down with them! I guess I should've spent more time with Bobby Ray, and maybe we could talk about things and I could trust him more than I do. I know that he lies to me. Beef, I hate to admit it, but I trust you more than my own son."

23

THE GIANT, SCAR-FACED GRIZZLY BEAR MOVED ACROSS THE

Strickler property, dragging a half-frozen cow elk carcass out of an open meadow and into the thick, dark pine forest. His heavy, silver-tipped coat and lean, long frame glistened like a mystic shadow under the pale moonlight of early morning. His large extended nostrils puffed hot, white vapor into the frost-laden air, and steam billowed up from beneath his sweating, powerful undercarriage. He held his head up high and slightly tilted to one side as he gripped the neck in his massive jaws and strode forward, his momentum easily pulling the five-hundred-pound weight across the heavily frosted ground.

Springtime usually found him roaming over a vast, one-hundred-square-mile area in search of a meal or a mate. He had gone into hibernation much underweight this season because the winter had never come when he was in his prime physical condition.

The past few winters had arrived late and mild. It was a change that he became adapted to, so he stayed out longer and roamed over a vast area. This year, he traveled far to the east until he came to the barren, windswept antelope country. Very little was found to eat there, and it was a great distance back to his winter country where he depended upon winter survival. The later that he stayed out foraging, fewer and fewer high-protein meals became available, and his distant foraging had burned off most of his midsummer weight. Then it suddenly became cold and started snowing, so he dug a den into a north-facing slope and went to sleep. The early spring suddenly became a harsh winter, and deep snow covered the north slopes with bone-crushing cold temperatures.

The thaw came late. He came out of the den weakened, lightheaded, and very near death from starvation. He was very hungry and overly dehydrated. His only salvation was to head straight downhill, letting gravity and momentum carry him down toward water, new grasses, or anything else directly in his path to survival.

The main trail above the timberline, called the Highline Trail, was a central highway that most all bears crossed when coming out of hibernation. The trail along the high ridge rose up to an elevation of nine thousand feet. From this high trail, air currents carried the scent of food and potential mates from many miles around. During the night, wind came out of the north and blew down from the high, snow-covered peaks. After daylight, the warm air currents came up from the south and southwest, sweeping low over the dry country and hugging the ground. The warm south wind rose up and up, trying to lift over the high Rocky Mountains with a renewal of the seasons, carrying dust, seed, and scent from far below. His instinct dictated that the wind would tell him where to go. Scarface traveled up the Highline Trail and detected the smell of decaying elk flesh coming down with the northern wind. He followed his nose in a direct route to the back end of the Strickler Ranch, where he found a killing field of many dead elk. The find was a smorgasbord to a very large and hungry bear.

After dragging the first elk carcass over half a mile away, he started eating. He soon found a special treat inside the cow's bloated stomach cavity. He relished the life-giving meal of a baby elk fetus. The giant grizzly bear dragged the carcass a few yards farther into a sunken depression beneath a small hill. He scratched pine needles, grass, and dirt over the partially eaten elk and then went back for another one. He worked all during the next two nights, dragging the many elk carcasses out of the clearing and into his hiding place. Full and exhausted, he strode up on the small hill and dug out a hollowed bed where he went to sleep with his nose pointed into the wind.

After becoming full and well rested, he stood up on all fours and shook himself vigorously all over. He sat back and scratched over his left shoulder at a flea.

Then he sniffed the wind coming over from the southeast, wheeled around, and loped back toward the Highline Trail toward a special scent.

Female bears with cubs did not stay on this east-west trail. They quickly passed over it and into the immediate thick cover of brush and slide rocks, where they could avoid an adult male bear that might kill their cubs. This season, there were several female bears without cubs that were potential mates, and his nose detected the scent of other females, who would soon be available after their weakened cubs died. Scarface could tell from the scent of every animal whether it had long to live. The smell of death to others was the smell of life to a huge, hungry grizzly bear. The smell of death on cub bears also meant a potential mate. If there were no cubs, the female bear would soon become ready to begin the reproductive cycle all over again.

Scarface encountered a large, old female who'd lost her cubs, and she was a bad-tempered date. She viciously dug him across his scarred nose and face, backing him up until he nearly fell over a ledge before allowing him to mate with her. She was restless and angry.

After mating with her and after both of them were well rested, the wind changed. Scarface smelled something blowing down with the northern wind and bounded away through the trees. She followed him until he was near his hidden lair, and then he suddenly turned on her viciously, chasing her back in the direction from where they had come.

He advanced cautiously and sniffed the wind. Then he made his charge. A large male black bear was eating one of his hidden elk caches. The rival bear rose up and defended his claim to the rotting flesh as Scarface charged straight at him. Scarface attacked with a powerful killing force.

It was too much for the rival bear, and he decided to give it up and run. Scarface was relentless in pursuit, running him down and viciously attacking. He bit down into the back of the bear's neck with his massive jaws and pinned him while he raked out with his powerful claws that ripped down below the rib cage and through the lower belly. In a heightened fighting frenzy and with the rush of adrenaline and anger, he let out a tremendous roar. The rival bear lay motionless now, but he attacked again and again. He slashed and slashed at the dead bear, flinging his internal organs and intestines into the air and covering the surrounding pine branches and brush with blood and gore.

Scarface didn't cover up the dead bear as he had his other trophies. He scattered its scent and left it so that other bears would know the danger of trespassing upon his domain.

With over a dozen different stashes to guard now, he found himself chasing off smaller bears nearly every day. He gorged himself and rested, filling his lean frame with flesh and power.

On one of his regular journeys back to the Highline Trail, he encountered a medium-sized young female who was very receptive to him and a very playful mate. She was chestnut in color and missing the tip of her right ear. When she followed him back to his daybed, he accepted her company. After they'd both eaten their fill, she scooped out a bed next to his on top of the lookout hill. She was a protective fighter, and Scarface watched her chase off wolves, coyotes, and many kinds of birds. Now the only time he was forced to leave his bed was to attack another rival bear or more than one wolf. There was no reason to leave this area now. He had food, water, and a pleasant mate.

24

CLYDE DEERHIDE WAS NOT AROUND, AND IT WAS MOST
enjoyable to look out the back window each morning and not
have the day ruined from seeing fresh horse shit all over the back
parking lot. It was a blessing not having Clyde around. Franky
wasn't distracted by Bonnie doting on him, and he was able to
focus on meal preparations and get into the rhythm of cooking on
a professional level. It seemed like a curse, because Bonnie was
in a foul mood. She threw gravy all over a truck driver and hit
a cowboy in the face. She didn't even speak to him, and he often
thought about how violent she was with that big meat cleaver. He
hid it behind a shelf in his kitchen. When he complained about the
horse shit and threatened to cut down the hitching rail in the back
alley, Bonnie became very upset and yelled, "Get over it! Clyde
Deerhide might scalp you over something like that!"

Franky was uncertain when Bonnie would be back since she
had hit that guy and broken a bone in her hand. He found two
young girls to replace her in the dining room and a part-time cook
that allowed him some free time. With Bonnie and Clyde both
gone, it looked like a good time to make a trip to the hardware
store.

Franky got into his pickup truck and sat looking across the alley at the old hitching rail on his property. He became mad as hell. He drove up town and went into the hardware store.

"I want to buy a new light-duty chain saw," said Franky.

"Are you going to cut some firewood for the hotel to help pay for your rent?" asked Marty. "If you are, they burn a lot of wood, and you might want to buy a bigger model with more power."

"No, I'm not going to cut firewood for nobody!" snapped Franky.

Marty became very curious. "Are you going to use it to cut down the backbone of a big steer? Lefty used one to saw up a big moose and some elk, and folks say that's one of the reasons why he left town, and did you know—"

Franky hefted up the saw and gripped it in his hands. "If you really need to know, I'm going to use it to clean up some horse shit. I've tried a shovel but the shit keeps coming back. I think a chain saw will eliminate the whole problem. If there isn't any place to tie up a horse, it will probably shit someplace else."

"Are you by chance referring to the hitching rails behind your restaurant where Clyde Deerhide ties up his horse?" asked Marty.

Franky turned toward the checkout counter and pulled out his wallet. "Yep, that's the one!"

Marty suddenly felt giddy and light on his feet. He was overcome with a surging and unbound joy. He couldn't wait for Franky to leave so that he could make some phone calls.

It wasn't long until the whole town of Big Scratch knew what was about to happen, and people were listening for the sound.

The elderly ladies all over Big Scratch were excited with what was unfolding in this mostly uneventful town, and the phone lines were all busy at once. This was a better story than was recorded on all of their worn-out Western movie cassettes of *High Noon*, *Gunfight at the O.K. Corral*, and *High Plains Drifter* all rolled into one script. Everyone was speculating about when the showdown would occur. Where was Clyde Deerhide while all of this was taking place? Boy, when Clyde came back into town, there would be hell to pay!

Helga called Ellen and said, "Ellen, there is going to be a shootout, I think, behind the Thin Vein pretty soon!"

Everyone was waiting for the sound. Finally, it came, and it echoed out like a shot heard all over Big Scratch. When Franky fired up that STIHL chain saw and it idled for a moment, all ears listened for the beginning. It idled and it purred for the longest time, it seemed. The loud roar of power and the cloud of smoke from burnt oil were much anticipated. That would be when the ultimate catastrophe would occur.

When Franky finally poured the gas to that powerful little machine and the sharp, new chain bit into that solid old juniper stump, it was a lustful sound of domination and conquest. The ultimate crime against John Wayne had just occurred! It was only a matter of time before John Wayne rode back into town and found that Franky had raped his wife, burned his crops, set fire to his cabin, shot his dog, and slapped his mother around.

The gossip spread like wildfire throughout town. Marty used his hardware store as the central headquarters of Operation High Noon. All of the locals either called Marty to ask what he knew, or they stopped into his store to browse and act uninterested until he volunteered out a meager amount of information. Business was so good at the store that he had to hire a couple of people to help sell things and order more merchandise so he could manage the telephone line.

People on a budget came in every day, and they bought things like a new handle for their snow shovel or a couple of screw-gun bits that cost twenty cents. Many of them just bought a package of rubber bands or tie clips. It didn't matter what they finally purchased; they hung around the checkout counter for as long as they could. The excited locals listened to Marty on the telephone and anticipated the unfolding story by what they overheard or by watching his vivid facial expressions and highly exotic hand movements.

It didn't take that long to commit the crime, do the deed, or—as most people feared for Franky—to commit suicide. Everyone was asking, "Where is Clyde Deerhide, and why isn't he back here yet?" For some unknown reason, everyone in town kept glancing at a clock.

Ellen finally found Fleebit and said, "Oh, my! Your friend Clyde, he will shoot Franky and kill him for sure! Everybody is saying it!"

It seemed like after the sound, everyone began evacuating Marty's hardware store because they were hungry or because they just had to have a hot cup of coffee in the middle of the day. Franky's Thin Vein Gold Strike Café was doing as much business this afternoon as it had done on the first day of his grand opening.

Franky noticed that everyone who pulled into his place drove around back through the alley, circled around, and then parked out in front. He looked out the back window of the kitchen and watched people file past the old sawed-up hitching post like a funeral procession. He also noticed that everyone who came into his place looked kind of wild-eyed and scared.

The customers all tried to make eye contact with him through the pick-up bar in front of his kitchen that overlooked the dining room. It was kind of spooky. For hell's sake, all he did was cut down some old wood on his own property! These town idiots sure acted strange over something that he had every right to do.

Jess Morgan from the feed store came in and walked over to the counter. "Franky, it sure has been nice knowing you. When you cut down Clyde Deerhide's hitching post, it couldn't have been worse than if you'd thrown a bomb against the last remaining wall of the Alamo!"

Stew Boren from the local post office walked up and said, "Franky, you couldn't have done anything more stupid than if you were at the US Capitol and used a cutting torch to cut off Lincoln's head!"

A punk local kid with earphones on and pants dragging the floor slouched over to his counter and said, "Man, talk about suicide!

It couldn't be more obvious! It's like you were on a US space shuttle, stopped at that Russian cosmonaut station, pissed all over their high-tech equipment, and left a note saying, 'Piss on Russia! Signed, the USA.'"

Fleebit told Ellen, "I've told him and I've told him to let everybody know that he owns that property over there! Heck, he's laughed about it all these years, knowing that he owned that land while people complained about horse shit on his own property that they thought they owned. Clyde thought it was the funniest thing that he could ever experience, watching Lefty and Franky shovel horse shit away from his own property. And when they complained about it every day, it just seemed to make his day even more enjoyable! Ellen, there's no telling what he'll do when he gets back here! We were at a roping one time in Cheyenne, and some midwestern cowboys who were top ropers showed up and thought that it would be easy pickings. Me and Clyde won all of their money at this big jackpot team roping, and one of them stole Clyde's silver-dollar saddle out of our horse trailer at the end of the jackpot. Clyde took off after that guy and went back east. He came back about a month later with his saddle, and everybody said that the guy never, ever showed up at another roping. Nobody ever saw him again on the Great Lakes Circuit back east or at any roping west of the Missouri River. Clyde never would talk about it. He said, 'I've got my saddle back, and that's all that matters.'"

Ellen Jorgenstein quickly called Helga and said, "Fleebit, he say that Clyde went back east after a cowboy one time for stealing his saddle! He say that Clyde came back a month later with his saddle and wouldn't talk about it. He say that man was never seen at the roping events again!"

Helga called Selma and said, "Yes, Selma, Ellen just told me that Clyde Deerhide did something to a cowboy that prevented him from ever competing in the rodeo ever again."

Selma called May right away and said, "Yes, May, oh, my! You are not going to believe this! Fleebit told Ellen that Clyde tracked and trailed a man across the United States and shot him like a dog!"

Everything that was said became distorted and enlarged, and it all came back to Franky until his hand was twitching so badly that he couldn't grasp a skillet or a big soup spoon. When he stirred something, he was shaking so badly that he slopped it all over himself and onto the floor. His concentration on cooking became lacking, and before long, he was burning things on his grill or boiling something over.

Franky overheard one of the sheriff deputies tell some cowboys, "I've never seen anyone faster on the draw or have such deadly accuracy with a navy Colt!"

At first, Franky thought the drama over cutting down the hitching rail was ridiculous, and he laughed it off. "This would be a slapstick comedy if it involved someone else. These town gossips like to build a mountain out of a molehill because there's nothing else to do in this one-horse town." He knew his rights as a property owner, and he could have Clyde arrested for trespassing and loitering. He could probably have him fined by the county health inspector over that horse shit piled up next to his eating establishment.

Franky quit laughing when he overheard his customers whispering to each other with hands held at the side of gaping mouths, their eyes wild and frantic.

The most compelling stories came from Clyde's only friend, Fleebit. Secondhand stories from his loose lips revealed a more serious situation. Fleebit told Ellen that Clyde had killed a man from the Midwest over a saddle and got away with murder. Fleebit told May that Clyde killed an Indian with a big rock when he was only fifteen years old. He ran away from the Indian reservation and hid out on isolated ranches. Fleebit told Helga that Clyde didn't like white people, and he tried to kill him once with a rock.

Paranoia soon made Franky jumpy at the anticipation of Clyde busting down the door at any moment and throwing down on him with a double-barreled shotgun.

Fleebit went to the county recorder's office and got a plot map. He was told that the property across the street from the Thin Vein was deeded to a Mr. Morgan from Fanbelt, Wyoming, and that there were no records of any existing survey done on that property.

Then he went to get the sheriff and a survey crew. It took the sheriff to get the county survey crew to leave their work across town and follow them to Franky's restaurant.

Sheriff Tolliber figured that he knew the half-breed as well as anyone around there ever could know Clyde Deerhide. However, he often felt like there was an exterior of wit and humor that camouflaged something about Clyde's quiet, deep interior. Clyde surprised nearly everyone who thought they knew him when he stood up at that wilderness meeting at the county commissioner's chambers and told the whole town that he would vote for more wilderness designation because they were "date raping" his Mother Earth. He pulled a gun on George Strickler's men and escorted those tree huggers into the courthouse that night.

Several people knew Clyde to be a joker, but they never learned anything beyond that social bullshit hour at the café. The sheriff was very concerned about what had happened, because he knew that Clyde would probably kill Franky when he returned, and there had never been a murder in his town. He was also afraid of Clyde finding out about his bold moves on Bonnie. Clyde could show up at any minute and start shooting.

When the local people found out that the sheriff and Fleebit were parked behind the Thin Vein, it suddenly became the most popular place in town. There were onlookers everywhere, and it took the sheriff and a deputy to control the traffic and keep people out of the way of the surveyors. The sheriff told his deputy to turn off his damned flashing lights, because it was like drawing moths to a flame.

The survey crew worked and worked. They took readings and

reference points from far away, surveyed, and then started all over again. It was several hours before they finally announced to Sheriff Tolliber that they were finished and that he should bring Franky outside.

Sheriff Tolliber told Franky, "I hate to tell you this, but that hitching rail that you cut down is not on your property! Your trash barrels over there are not on your property, either! In fact, four feet of your restaurant are not on your property! If anybody had paid for a title search before building here, they could've found out that most of this land belongs to a Mr. Morgan from Fanbelt, Wyoming."

Franky suddenly turned ghostly pale. "I went to the tax record office at the courthouse, and they gave me the owner's address. They told me that nobody in the courthouse had ever met him but that he paid his taxes on time. I sent him several offers to buy that lot across the street, but this Mr. Morgan never answered any of my letters."

"Mr. Clyde Morgan doesn't live in Fanbelt, Wyoming, anymore," revealed Fleebit. "He lives here in Big Scratch now, and he goes by the name of Clyde Deerhide. Why couldn't you just leave well enough alone? Clyde knew that he owned that hitching rail and that he owned the alley where you park your truck behind the restaurant. He didn't care if you used it, but he did care about that hitching rail over there that you sawed up into firewood. When he gets back, you're going to have hell to pay! And it looks to me like you have an unfriendly partner in the restaurant business now!"

Franky couldn't eat, and he couldn't sleep. Bonnie had left him and never came back. Now Clyde was going to show up at any minute and kill him.

The restaurant hadn't cost him much because he'd traded a worthless gold claim to his brother for some of the equity in it. Bonnie had done most of the work on fixing it up, and business had been good enough to recoup all of the money that he'd spent.

He figured that he had all of his original money left from his gold strike in Nevada.

Suddenly, he was overcome with a nostalgic emotion for the state of Nevada. He was thinking about the lyrics to "The Gambler," one of his favorite songs by Kenny Rogers.

> You've got to know when to hold 'em
> Know when to fold 'em
> Know when to walk away
> And know when to *run*

When the coffee-and-breakfast crowd showed up at the Thin Vein the next morning, there were no lights on inside. The shades were drawn, the door was locked, and there was a sign on the door that read Closed—Out of Business.

Lying on a table inside the darkened restaurant was a quit claim deed made out to Clyde Morgan.

25

THROUGHOUT THE NIGHT, A GENTLE NORTH WIND BLEW A
chill over the aspen canopy. A light frost covered the cabin roof and
forest floor. Muddy tracks from the day and evening before were
now frozen casts of mortal life beneath the Spirit plain.

Clyde slept restlessly throughout a dreamless night. Deep
emotions encompassed his innermost feelings and tortured him.
Somehow, he felt both love and loss. He felt a deep attachment to
Katie Colter. She was someone he'd come to know and let his heart
stake claim to. His feelings were not of personal desire but like a
strange bond of a tribal unity—almost like someone or something
he'd lost when he left the Indian reservation.

Finding the clues to Katie's fate had worried him all afternoon
and didn't give his subconscious mind a chance to rest and dream.
He tossed and turned all night.

He awakened in the darkness, wondering, *Should I ride back into
town and tell someone what I've discovered? Who can I trust with this
information? Certainly not the sheriff! If I have a best friend down there,
it is Fleebit! But if Ellen gets on top of him, he'll spill his guts to her about
everything he knows! A woman's affection is like injecting him with truth
serum; he could spill everything at once. When he gets with the gossip
crowd in town, he becomes a blabbermouth.*

Clyde knew that he had to contact Katie's parents, but that could take some time. If he asked the local law enforcement about a contact, it might arouse suspicion.

Since the weather was becoming mild, Bobby Ray and his gang might make their move against the kids in Big Gulch Canyon any time. Clyde decided to go back and circle the Strickler Ranch again. Maybe he would find more clues about Katie beneath the melted snow, where he'd found the headlight chrome and the elk hair.

So far, Clyde hadn't ridden onto the Strickler property. He rode around their high fences and checked their gates on the south, east, and west entrances. Their fences were high, tightly stretched woven wire. Three strands of sharp barbed wire bordered the top and showed evidence of hair and bleached leg bones twisted and held there. It wasn't a wildlife-friendly fence. It was a human-unfriendly fence, and without cutting through it with wire cutters, he'd found no way to get beyond the locked gates.

Clyde wanted to catch them coming off of their property. He felt like he should get inside their borders, but he also realized that things might be going on inside those tall fences that might get him killed. If he crossed over, they had the law on their side.

Fleebit cautioned him many times to keep his wire cutters inside his saddlebags and ride on.

It was getting more difficult to hide his horse's tracks in the soft, muddy ground, so he rode off a farther distance from the tall fence and stayed more hidden back into the maze of fallen trees.

Each morning after checking the south gate leading to Big Gulch, the strong smell of death and decay blew toward them from a mile away where he'd earlier found the poaching field of many dead elk. No-Name was shy of the smell at first, but he became more unconcerned each day while the stench worsened.

That morning, after checking the south gate for fresh tracks, it seemed that the bad smell no longer drifted down from the northeast wind. Clyde was dreading having to ride into that stench again today, because each day it became harder to bear. Now the smell was suddenly gone, but No-Name spooked, refused to go on, and was frightened by something in that direction. Clyde used his spurs and braced the sharp rowels firmly into his sides. He did everything to encourage the big bay horse onward, but No-Name refused. Then he started getting out of control.

Clyde knew that it was a long way around the big ranch, and he needed to make a direct route through here. It was a time factor, because he wanted to look for more clues about Katie along the road and get back to the biologists before sundown. He felt responsible for the young girls who could be in danger.

When Clyde became angry and tried to spur No-Name forward, No-Name snorted, jumped sideways, and then reared straight up into the air. Clyde was riding out the storm, but was shocked by a behavior he'd never seen before. He lost his patience with his horse and yelled, "What in the hell is wrong with you?"

When Clyde calmed down, No-Name began calming down. Clyde began turning his horse in slow, tight circles, both left and then right. Clyde spoke softly, "Whoa! Easy, now! Easy!" Clyde released the pressure of his legs against his horse's sides and then released his tight shortness on the reins. "It's okay, boy, we'll go around in another direction! We have to trust each other out here!"

Instead of riding east along the boundary fence, he turned south through the national forest and made a wide circle back around to the east. Clyde came out of the trees near where he'd found Katie's initials and the gold locket. He could see where tire tracks came through the Strickler Ranch gate and turned around. Large, muddy footprints had walked around the two broken gate cameras and went directly over to his horse's tracks in the aspen meadow beyond.

Clyde became alarmed. It was a rash act, breaking those cameras! He'd felt that he was out of video range when he roped one of the cameras from his horse and pulled it down. But when he shattered the other one with a rock, he took a split second of a chance being detected.

The broken cameras were still shattered on the ground. They hadn't been replaced, but Clyde felt like someone was watching him. He quickly turned his horse into the dark forest and vanished.

As soon as Bubba plugged his video monitor into the new cables beneath George's big oak desk, he rewound the tapes from the hidden cameras and saw the man on horseback. The man looked familiar. He repeatedly rode up to the back gate and looked around. The first day, he roped one of the dummy cameras with a trick overhead loop and tore it off the gate. He shattered the other one with a well-aimed rock. Bubba rewound the tape and played it again. "Wow! That was an amazing throw!"

The man scanned both sides of the road leading up to the gate and then rode across the road, where he looked around in the trees. The next day, he came back and rode around the ranch again, checking the locked gates and searching the ground. When Bubba realized that the man was at the back gate right now, he quickly jumped inside a ranch truck and tried to catch him there. He roared to the back of the property but was too late.

The muddy horse tracks were easy to follow. Bubba slung his sniper rifle behind his back and followed the fleeing horse's tracks on foot. They angled down the steep, slick mountainside for two or three miles toward the valley, leading into town. It appeared that the rider was from the valley or from town. Bubba turned around and headed back to the ranch. He repeatedly slipped backward as he climbed up the slick, muddy slope. He slipped several times and fell down. He'd been living at sea level for several months and had forgotten about the thin mountain air. He'd always had trouble breathing at this high altitude. It was almost as if his lungs hadn't grown big enough for his seven-foot frame.

Bubba realized that his long legs couldn't keep up with a mounted rider on a strong horse in this country. Bubba didn't like horses, and they didn't like him. There wasn't a big enough horse in the county that could carry him, anyway. He would have to wait for the man to come back and catch him somewhere on the ground.

This man seemed intent on being undetected, as he cautiously surveyed the ranch at a distance. It also appeared that he wanted to get inside the property and was looking for a way to get in.

Bubba hiked along the Strickler fence line wearing full forest-green camouflage and a face mask, lying in wait for the intruder. Each time the rider came near him, he seemed to sense danger and quickly melt away back into the forest. He could appear quietly from out of nowhere and then suddenly vanish like an Indian.

Bubba thought, *That's it! He's the Indian who won the fast-draw shooting contest in town a couple of years ago. He kicked the cops' asses with a handgun and a lever-action rifle.* Bubba recalled how impressed he was that day when the Indian shot clay pigeons out of the sky with a lever-action rifle.

Bubba recalled, *He is also the Indian who sided with those tree huggers at that wilderness meeting in the courthouse that evening. George ordered the gang to stay outside the courthouse that night and discourage any tree huggers from entering the building. The cops did their part and stayed away, but that Indian showed up and escorted that bunch of tree huggers into that meeting. When we ran up behind them, that Indian flashed a big pistol and cocked the hammer. He had a wild, crazy look in his eyes, like he didn't have anything to lose. That's him!*

George Strickler told Bubba to find the strong link in the environmental chain and snap it in two. *Now I know who the mouse is. I'll wait for him to come through a hole, and I'll get him!*

Clyde rode back to the wolf and bear study camp at sundown. Maggie ran out of the camp and over to his side. Tim and Fred walked out of their tents and approached him.

Fred asked, "Do you think it's safe for us to go back into the field again? We will lose our funding if we sit idle for too long."

Clyde looked down from his horse at Maggie. She was such a pretty girl. "All I can tell you is that the people who raided your camp the first time are living four miles from here, and there's nothing but wild country between them and you. I hate to tell you what to do, but I'd advise you not to go north of here yet. There might be a murderer who preys on young women running loose, and the girls shouldn't get separated from your group."

Tim asked, "Is there anything special that we can do?"

Clyde laughed. "Yeah, you could practice setting traps around the perimeter of this camp for some two-legged wolves. I'm going to go back to my cabin to feed my horse and get some sleep. I'll ride back here again tomorrow after I spy on the enemy. Since the weather is getting mild, they might be getting ready to pull something any time. I'll be back again tomorrow and report what I find out. If you see me come galloping back early, be ready for anything!"

Clyde rode back to his cabin in the dark. Blue heard them or sensed them coming from far away. Clyde could hear him through the distant forest, bellowing, *"Eeh-haw! Eeh-haw!"*

No-Name picked up a rapid, long pace toward his friend at the corral and the anticipation of a bucket of oats at the barn. Clyde unsaddled and curried No-Name's back. He picked up each of his four legs and felt the tendons for swelling. Clyde had pushed him hard through rough country leading downhill and southwest toward town. Then he'd circled back to the northeast and climbed back up the mountain. If someone had tracked him on foot, the muddy trail would discourage that person and mislead him from his true destination.

After his animals were attended, Clyde went inside the cabin and lit a fire inside the wood cookstove. He mixed up a batch of baking-powder biscuits and pulled a dressed pine grouse out of a plastic bag. He hadn't been eating much since leaving town and was losing weight. He always made sure that his horses had protein, but often neglected his own health. He felt hungry and the need to restore his energy. He would devour a good, hearty meal that night. Clyde thought about an old cowboy saying: "When a cowboy leaves home on horseback, he never knows when or if he'll ever eat again!"

Clyde took the golden locket out of his left inside vest pocket and set it on his pillow. He'd carried it all day inside his vest, resting centered over his heart. Earlier in the day when No-Name

217

became frightened, he felt something from somewhere in or near his chest. Then later on, when he sat mounted on his horse outside the Strickler gates, he felt it again, only stronger. Was the feeling of danger coming from the locket, or was it coming from somewhere deep inside his heart? Was he going crazy?

He might possibly deceive himself with paranoia, but what about his horse?

No-Name wasn't influenced by his dreams. His horse sensed danger on the trail that he had tried to ignore. He had to trust his horse!

In his dream, the scar-faced grizzly bear looked twice over his left shoulder.

His grandfather once said, "Death is always stalking a warrior over his left shoulder at arm's length. Sometimes, if he looks real quick, he can see it there. It is when a warrior looks death in the face that he becomes fully aware in the present moment."

Clyde finished picking the bones clean from the fried pine hen. He finished the can of green beans and covered up the remaining biscuits in the dutch oven. He filled up the coffeepot with water and put a solid chunk of pine inside the fire box of the cookstove. The coffeepot was placed at the edge of the fire and the biscuits on the shelf above the warming oven. Clyde placed the locket under his pillow and stretched out on the bed. He was soon in dreamland.

The new sun crested the horizon, and two Indian people stood outside their painted lodge, singing the morning song. The woman wore a white buckskin dress, with long, flowing fringes that danced in the wind. The man wore a long white shirt, leggings, and a headdress adorned with black and white eagle feathers. He held up a curved staff and pointed it to the edge of a long, open meadow.

As the morning sun cleared the ridge, their song ended. In the center of the meadow on a small rise was a giant white buffalo with radiant, shining pink eyes. The man and woman turned around and waved. Clyde realized that it was his mother and grandfather.

A golden eagle circled Clyde four times and then took off on a direct flight across a vast, open water.

A tribe of African men bearing spears and painted shields led their tribe away from a village of reed huts toward the edge of a large, open savanna. The men, women, and children were all painted, wearing headbands of brilliant-colored feathers and skirts made from bright strips of cloth. They followed behind a beautiful, young, dark-tanned woman dressed in modern English fashion.

Standing in the center of the open delta was a giant, white bull elephant with long ivory tusks and radiant eyes. He lifted his head up high and trumpeted loudly.

The young woman turned around facing Clyde and the two people standing behind him. He was unaware of the white man and black woman holding hands until now. The young woman waved to them and then turned to face a young white man dressed in a green safari shirt and short pants. He took her by the hand, and they vanished with the white elephant.

Clyde awoke in the early morning darkness with tears in his eyes. Deep emotion flooded through him, and he couldn't quit crying. *Now I know! It is all very clear now. My relatives are all with the sacred white buffalo and the Great Spirit. Katie is with her Native relatives, her guide, and the sacred white elephant!*

26

SAM SAT UP ON THE FLAT-TOPPED HILL ABOVE BIG SCRATCH
where he had a good view overlooking the town. Nobody had been up here except him for the past few days, and there were only signs of some old horse tracks.

He left his truck parked down on the backside of the hill and out of sight. He sat concealed between two tall sage bushes with a high-powered spotting scope and a case of beer. Since he'd been coming to this spot every day, he'd learned a lot, and there were dozens of empty beer cans scattered all over the ground.

The tree huggers all came into town every afternoon or evening, and they all came together in two pickup trucks from the east. There were four people in each truck, and there were five guys and three girls. The night before, they'd come in later than usual. Their trucks were splattered with fresh mud all over the side windows and front windshields. Each night, the two groups stopped in front of the hardware store and then pulled down in front of the Thin Vein to get something to eat. Since the Thin Vein was closed, they'd all gone over to the grocery store and done some shopping. Then they all loaded up and left town together going back east.

The first night he watched them, they all went into the small movie theater, and he ran down the hill under the cover of darkness and searched through their trucks. One of them was unlocked, but the other truck was locked, and he'd had to break a side window to get inside. He couldn't find the letter that Bobby Ray was looking for.

When Sam found out that the Thin Vein was closed, he wondered where the good-looking, feisty woman was who'd broken his nose and embarrassed him in front of the gang. While he was up on the hill looking around, he saw her behind an old house, messing around by some corrals. He knew it was her right away, and with his superpowered spotting scope turned up on the highest power, he could look down her blouse.

The night before, after calling Bobby Ray on his cell phone to report in, he went down the hill and had a look around. It looked like she lived alone and didn't go anywhere. She turned off the house lights at about nine o'clock.

Tonight was the time for the plan of attack on the tree hugger camp by Bobby, Tony, Jeff, and Sway. They had their horses all saddled and were ready to ride when he made the call. Bobby Ray asked, "Are you all set up to report back when those tree huggers leave town?"

"Sure thing, boss! They'll all go to the hardware store and shop around town. There isn't a new movie at the theater yet. They already watched the old one the other night, so they might not hang around town too long. The new restaurant isn't open, so they'll probably go over to the grocery store and get something to eat."

"Okay," said Bobby. "Call me back when they leave town. I told Beef that we were going on a horseback ride toward Big Gulch to hunt wolves and bears. I don't want him to know what we're up to. He knows that we don't have a horse big enough to carry him, and he seems content staying inside Dad's office."

The two government trucks pulled into Big Scratch an hour later. With all of the mud splattered over their windshields, Sam couldn't be very sure of his count on the eight tree huggers, but he was not paying as much attention tonight. His spotting scope was set up to focus on Bonnie all day, and he was ready to go back down there as soon as it got dark.

Bonnie brought Fleebit a hot cup of coffee out to the corrals while he was feeding Clyde's young horses. He was looking them over for any new cuts or scrapes that they might have received during the night. Young horses in a group could really get fired up with playing and stampeding around, and minor new injuries were not uncommon. Bonnie watched them every day, and she worried about them all as being potential suicides.

She asked, "How far is it up to the cabin?"

Fleebit answered, "Oh, it's five miles up that trail and maybe twenty-five miles by going way around on several back roads. But you can't drive up there yet! All of this snow runoff has made that road impassable to within a couple of miles to the cabin. You could get stuck in the mud halfway up there, and nobody would come along to help you out this time of year."

"What about the trail?" she asked.

"That trail leaves out of here just behind our place and goes up on that ridge to the north. It's easy to follow in the daylight, because there are Forest Service signs with names and arrows pointing where to turn toward Big Gulch Canyon. The trail to the cabin property cuts off of the main trail about a mile before you get to the canyon, and it isn't marked. It's just a cow path of a trail that cuts up through a thick pine forest. It gets so dark on that trail at night that you can't see your hand in front of your face. When you ride a horse through there on a moonless night, you just have to trust that your horse will stay on the trail. Horses and mules have better night vision than people do, and they have a sense for where to place their feet on a trail or worn path."

"Do you think that I could make it up to the cabin?" asked Bonnie. "Five miles isn't that far. I've gone backpacking that far a couple of times since I came here."

"No, don't you even think about going up there! Bonnie, those grumpy old bears are just now waking up from hibernation, and they haven't had anything to eat since last fall. Those female bears have little, bitty babies with them now, and they get real crazy about protecting them. Besides that, they travel on the same trails that we use to go up there. If you were to hike up there, maybe Clyde would be on his way back home by a different trail, and you'd miss him. He changes trails a lot, and he does that so people can't track him. Anyway, I have a sense for when he'll be back, and I look for him to be back here in two or three days. If he isn't back by then, we'll both go up there together to check on him."

"What about Clyde running into those bears up there on a trail?" asked Bonnie.

"Oh, I wouldn't worry about Clyde. Those grizzly bears are his medicine animals."

Fleebit left in the old green pickup, but not before warning her again about Cheyenne. She didn't tell Fleebit that she'd been getting inside the corral to feed him cookies and scratch his tall back. He was just a big pet cow! He was so slow and careful around her. One day, she climbed between the corral poles and dropped a cookie out of her pocket outside the pen. A few minutes later, she observed him reaching out under the fence with the sweep of one long horn and pulling the cookie under the fence. And yesterday, her cell phone was missing. She remembered leaving it on her art tablet next to the corral. She eventually found her missing phone inside the corral, smashed underneath Cheyenne. She would have to beg a ride into Great Falls and purchase another.

The urge to draw and paint was so great that Bonnie was using her left hand more and more. It was irritating that her work was sloppier, but it was unique for presenting a different style. Her perfection to detail by using her right hand now gave way to a new perspective—a roughness that her untrained left hand found accidentally. Her trained mind knew about balance and technique, but her two different hands each had different styles of portraying what her mind wanted to reveal.

Her right hand seemed to be mending, but it would cramp up

from holding a pencil or a brush too long, and a sharp pain would go down through the outside. She'd worked more with her bad hand than usual, so she turned in early just after dark and fell instantly to sleep.

Sometime in the night, Bonnie thought she could hear footsteps outside on the pine decking behind the house. She instantly thought that Clyde was home, so she jumped out of bed, threw a robe over her nightgown, and stepped out the back door into the dark, moonless night. She walked over to the corrals and tried to see if Clyde was back there unsaddling his horse. It was too dark to see very much, but there was nothing and no movement of any kind. The horses were far out into the pasture, and Cheyenne was behind the barn sleeping.

Suddenly, she was knocked down from behind with a tremendous force and pinned facedown by someone very heavy. With all of her strength, she pushed up and spun around, swinging her right fist.

Sam caught her right hand in front of his face and started crushing it inside his large, vice-grip hand. Bonnie screamed out in pain and agony.

Sam punched her in the face with a sledgehammer fist, knocking her head backward into the dirt. He slammed his knee down into her stomach and knocked all of the breath out of her. He pulled out a big knife and put it against her throat.

She could only partly see out of one eye and look upon the big scar-faced man from the restaurant.

"Remember me, bitch? Now you're going to get what you deserve!"

Bonnie thought, *Okay, this is it! Don't fight him anymore, because he has a big knife and wants an excuse to kill you!*

Sam used his knife to cut upward under her robe and slice the tie strap into. Then he grabbed the top of her nightgown and ripped it downward, exposing her nakedness.

"You made me look stupid in front of my friends, and now you're going to pay for that! See this scar on my face? That Sierra Club bitch did that to me with a sharp, pointed stick. Nobody knows about it except me and you. That's our little secret! But you broke my nose in front of all my friends and made a laughingstock out of me. I didn't spend much time on that tree hugger, but I'm going to take my time with you. I'm going to skin you like a deer. My dear, do you know where the tip of the knife is inserted when a hunter begins field dressing his trophy?"

Suddenly, her stomach was covered in a pool of hot blood. It squirted up into her face, stinging her eyes and blinding her. Then the crushing weight on top of her suddenly lifted up and away, and in that instant, she knew she was experiencing death. She waited for the journey back to her parents in Indiana. Where was the end of the tunnel? Where was the bright light? When would her pain end?

When nothing happened, she wiped the blood away from her undamaged eye and screamed.

Cheyenne had pierced the big man through his midsection with a giant horn and was pulling, ripping, and squeezing him through the narrowly spaced corral poles with a loud cracking of bones and gushing of blood.

27

CLYDE RODE PAST THE LOCKED SOUTH GATE LEADING TO BIG
Gulch and continued east around the tall fence line. He was near the
place where No-Name had become frightened the day before when
he noticed where a large, dead tree had fallen over the fence and
smashed it down. Clyde paused and sat quietly. He studied his horse
and then reached inside his vest pocket and touched the locket.
He jumped his horse through the narrow opening and entered the
Strickler property.

Clyde sat on his bay horse, No-Name, and secretly watched
the ranch headquarters from the seclusion of a distant stand of
thick pine forest. It was almost noon, and nobody had stirred
from the massive log house where Bobby Ray and his gang spent
their time.

He watched Pablo and Arturo work a Black Angus bull through
a small corral and into a squeeze chute, where they gave it a shot
and attempted to doctor its swollen hind foot. Clyde had visited
with Pablo and his son several times since they went to work for the
Stricklers, and he vividly recalled the time that he had found Pablo
badly beaten and his son terrified. He had found them hiding in the
log barn on John Baxter's place when he rode in to stay overnight
and look after John's cattle.

Pablo told him that Bobby Ray had beat him for telling his dad that he wasn't around to help him on the ranch. Bobby told him that if he ever found out that Pablo or Arturo reported on him again, he would kill them and then kill all of their relatives who lived in other nearby communities. Clyde took them to the cabin, fixed them up something to eat, and tended to Pablo's injuries. They hadn't eaten in two days.

When Clyde told Pablo that he should leave the Stricklers, he said, "Oh no, I must go back! Bobby will find me, or they will hurt my other relatives until I come back. I know too much. We can never leave there!"

Every time that he rode near here, he found something to upset him. This was once two of the best horse and cattle ranches in Montana. Twenty cowboys had jobs here during summer and fall seasons, and he and Fleebit were two of them. Now the ranch was just an unproductive playground for wild, late-night parties and a poaching field where big-game animals were slaughtered for someone's target practice.

The sheriff and local game wardens couldn't get beyond the big locked iron gates without a search warrant. The entrance far down by the main road prevented anyone from seeing what went on in the far reaches of the back property. Law officials didn't seem to care.

Clyde saw things that went on back there, and he knew a lot more than he ever reported to anybody locally. What they did on their own property was one thing, but when they left it and caused trouble, it was something entirely different. When they went after Maggie and her friends, they brought him into the fight.

They were doing something from this property late at night besides poaching. Clyde watched helicopters fly in from the far south and stay low over the treetops as they moved slowly over the national forest. They never stayed long after landing at the Strickler Ranch before heading back south at a much higher elevation and rate of speed.

Finally, someone came out of the log mansion and yelled at Pablo, who was opening the gate on the squeeze chute inside the corral. It was the one called Tony, and he yelled, "Pablo, Bobby said to get four horses caught and saddled up. Pronto!"

That was what Clyde was waiting for. It was time to ride back ahead of them and warn everybody at the camp in Big Gulch. He knew that it would take some time to catch their horses and get them ready to go. He also knew that their horses were too old and unconditioned to ride hard for many miles. Bobby and his gang only rode at one speed. They would have their horses winded and lathered by the time they reached the rim of the distant canyon. The Strickler horses were abused, spurred, and beaten so often that they were hard to catch. They well remembered the rough hands that cinched them up too tight and jerked violently on bits inside their sore mouths. They remembered being tied for many hours at a time without any water or a loosening of the saddle. Horses with these kinds of memories are hard to catch if they get away from you in the wilderness country.

Clyde quietly led No-Name far back into the tall trees and mounted up. The quickest way back was through the opening in the fence. As he rode closer, he felt something alarming, and his horse became frightened. Clyde quickly turned in a different direction and quietly walked away. He circled around for about a mile before coming back to the tall wire fence. He quickly dismounted, pulled out his wire cutters, and sliced through. Clyde headed cross-country toward Big Gulch Canyon and rode parallel to the trail that Bobby Ray and his gang would take. He was about a half mile from the canyon when he noticed a large pine tree leaning partway over the trail. He figured that it would serve his plan well when the Strickler gang rode back this way.

Bubba was late in getting to the hole in the fence. He'd pushed the big dead tree over it the day before, and it had crashed down. He could see where the Indian had jumped his horse through the opening early in the morning. The ground had been frozen when he'd gone through, and the horse's tracks were barely visible. He would wait here for the mouse to come back through the hole and kill him. After smashing the fence, Bubba set up an invisible blind a few yards from the tree next to the only path a horse could take. With one reach, he could easily pull the man off his horse and snap his neck. The opening of the blind was set up facing the fence where he planned to catch the mouse, but now that he'd entered the trap, he would be returning from behind the blind. Bubba practiced rising up and turning around several times. He was getting tired of that rotten smell. Bobby and the gang must have had a lot of fun last winter on their snowmobiles, chasing those elk! The first time he got a whiff of it, it caused him to lose his breakfast. It was still there, but not as strong.

Bubba sat down in the blind and waited. This would make the fourth mouse that he had exterminated for George Strickler. He liked the cat-and-mouse game very much, and the pay was extremely good. And after he killed a mouse or a rat, George always sent him on a paid vacation to a tropical island for several months. Bobby and the gang were always trying to find out what George hired him to do. They even hired hookers to pump him for information about where he'd been. But Bubba would never talk. He was afraid to.

It all started when George told him to kill that guy who wouldn't take a bribe over taking the water samples at the gold mine. He was told to kill him during elk season, take him far away, and make it look like he had fallen from a cliff. Then George sent him to New Mexico to kill a Mexican who was stealing from the company and threatened to report him to the IRS.

He'd broken arms and legs, beaten men to a pulp, and killed an African, a Mexican, and a white man. Bubba couldn't wait to kill his first Indian.

Scarface became fat and lazy while his chestnut mate ran up and down the hill, chasing birds and a persistent coyote away. The day before, there was a loud crash somewhere down below them, and she had become very restless. Now she was nervous again and huffed a warning. Alerted, Scarface awoke from his nap and stood up tall. He expanded his nostrils wide and tested the wind. He couldn't smell anything different, but his mate sensed the presence a rival bear. Scarface silently angled down the hill and circled around the unseen presence where the wind was more favorable. His mate followed him at a distance. Suddenly, he smelled the threat in the brush and charged up the trail.

Bubba heard the rider coming fast. The giant man jumped up like a cat from his blind and reached around for the mouse. The giant scar-faced bear stood up and towered over Bubba, roaring. He grabbed Bubba's shoulders with razor-sharp claws and held him a second and then quickly bit down with wide-open jaws, crushing Bubba's neck.

Clyde hollered out when he came off the ridge and angled his horse down to the waiting camp of the New Indians. All eight members of the group were present. Clyde was relieved to see that everyone was here. "They will be here in perhaps an hour, so let's go over the plan."

Fred Holliday was senior biologist for the entire group, and he insisted on staying behind as a witness. He said that he wanted to get evidence against the vandals who had wrecked their valuable equipment on the last raid. Maggie also insisted on staying with Fred while the others drove into town.

Clyde said, "They probably have somebody in town who will be watching how many of you show up tonight."

"We took care of the two missing people," said Maggie. She pulled out two manikins that they built long ago when they were afraid to drive into town alone. Each of them lived with the fear that he or she might be attacked by a sawmill owner who had lost a big timber sale on the national forest or by a stockman who had lost a calf to a predatory bear.

Clyde looked the manikins over and thought how, with their ball caps pulled down, they would look very convincing through a mud-splattered windshield.

Fred selected a high, rocky ledge up on the south-facing rim above the camp where two giant rocks leaned against each other, creating an open space underneath. From this high vantage point was a central view of the entire camp. This was where Fred and Maggie planned to hide behind their best high-tech zoom-lens camera.

Clyde looked up at the black hole between the big boulders above the camp. "If you stay up there, you are taking a chance. You'll be within viewing distance of your enemy, and if you do get spotted, you could become trapped under those big boulders. You should know by now that if you can spot a predator, he can also spot you. Although you do have the advantage of being at the top of the hill and them being down at the bottom. If you stay there, you can't move around or make any noise. You know that I won't be here! I'll be between here and the Strickler Ranch. I wish that all of you would just leave here together, because I won't be here to help if you get into trouble."

They both insisted that they would be fine.

Clyde walked around camp and inspected the hidden, spring-loaded snares that these kids had expertly set and camouflaged. He was impressed.

"You are good! I'm afraid to make a move around here! Maggie, take my hand and lead me out of this camp and over to my horse."

They all laughed.

Fred and one of the other guys from camp carried something out for Clyde to inspect. They each carried one end of a long metal box that Clyde instantly recognized. It was an old single locker like the ones he'd seen inside the old schoolhouse in Jordan, Montana, many years ago.

Clyde asked, "Where did you get that thing?"

"These were government surplus items from old buildings that were demolished on federal property," explained Fred. "We confiscated them to keep our personal items in while we live in a tent for five months out of the year. They are great for keeping your clothes, papers, and personal things in while keeping the pine needles and water out. All of us have one or two of them inside our big tents. We have removed our personal items out of some of these lockers and put something else inside them for our unwelcome visitors to inspect. We would like to show you our secret weapon."

They carefully stood the locker up and opened the door. Pointed directly at the face was a mounted can of bear pepper spray attached to the back of the locker with a hose clamp. There was a wire cable looped around the trigger that ran back through two small pulleys. There was a place to attach the other end of the wire to the door. When the door was opened, the cable would trigger the pepper spray directly into the face at eye level. When the door was opened wide, a second cable rigger was set to pull the pin on a canister of tear gas.

Maggie said, "Fred found a way to change the firing mechanism on the pepper spray so that it will activate from a slight trigger pull."

Clyde said, "I wish I could stay here to watch them receive this type of punishment, but my plan of action against them begins up the trail to the north of here a ways. I've always done my best work from horseback." Clyde laughed and exclaimed, "I think it's about time for you dummies to load up and leave here!"

Everybody laughed.

"Take some buckets of water with you, and mix up some of that red clay in it," said Clyde. "When you get down to the main highway, throw that mix all over your windshields and door windows. I'm afraid that one of those dummies looks a lot like me, and you might get shot at on your way into town."

There was more laughter from the group.

Clyde said, "When you get into town, just act as you normally do when you arrive and are afraid that some redneck is going to beat you up. Just stay together, and take your time. Cover up those two dummies in the front seats of your pickup trucks, and make them look like they are asleep. Just don't come back here too soon! I'm not sure when they will arrive. They might fall off and get hurt before they ever reach here. The serious side is that when they get here, they will be heavily armed, and someone could become seriously injured or killed. Now let's all go!"

Maggie said, "Clyde, please be careful out there. I'm getting real fond of your company, and someday, I would like for you to teach me how to bake in a dutch oven."

Just before sundown, four old, fat, lathered-up horses were jerked suddenly to a stop and walked the last few yards to the rim of Big Gulch Canyon. The four men tied their horses up to some aspens a short distance from the rim. They pulled the rifles out of their scabbards and stalked up to the rim where they peered over the side toward the camp down below. They watched and waited as the two mud-spattered pickup trucks rocked and weaved down the muddy ruts far below them and out of sight.

Bobby couldn't get a signal on his cell phone. Communication from Sam would be questionable, so they waited for half an hour until they were sure that the camp was vacated and quiet.

Bobby Ray ordered, "Sway, you go down around the camp and come in from the south. Tony, you go down and come in from the east. Jeff, you go straight down and come in from the north. I'm going to work my way down this ridge of rocks to the west and stay up high with my sniper rifle. From up here, I'll be able to see if anybody comes back up that road. When you all get down to the camp, go through all of their personal stuff and try to find that registered letter to my dad."

Clyde watched the four men disappear over the rim and start down the hillside toward the camp. He approached their horses and took out his razor-sharp pocketknife. Clyde made a thin, deep cut almost through the latigo leather where it rested against the brass *D* ring of the saddle. He knew that it would hold a rider's weight when he mounted and walked away, but if the horse expanded its chest when it jumped over something, the thin leather would snap loose, and the saddle would break free from the horse's back. As Clyde made the last cut, he whispered to the old, lathered horses, "It will be all right. You'll soon be free!"

Clyde rode No-Name north for about one-half mile until he came to a bend in the trail where the giant ponderosa pine tree leaned down from overhead. The four riders had passed underneath the big tree on their way to the canyon. Clyde attached a rope around it and encouraged his horse to pull it down over the trail. Now when they returned, their horses would be surprised and forced to jump over it when they suddenly ran around the curve in the trail.

Everyone was down in the camp now except Bobby Ray, who was trying to work his way around some big ledge rocks up near the rim. Suddenly, there was screaming and yelling coming from down inside the camp. Each of the three men triggered the pepper spray canisters into their faces and activated the tear gas bombs. They were stumbling around, falling down, throwing up, and cussing. Someone screamed out, "Bobby, I'm blind!

"Somebody help me! Bobby, where are you? Help me!"

Bobby was standing next to some big rocks when he thought he heard someone laughing nearby. He brought up his high-powered rifle and crept around the boulders. Through a small gap between the rocks, he could see two people crouched down.

"All right, come out of there, or I'm going to empty this gun into that hole!"

Bobby ran around the rocks and intercepted Fred as he crawled out from the hiding place. When Fred stood up, Bobby struck him in the side of the head with his rifle butt. Fred fell and rolled down the hill a few yards before he stopped and lay motionless on the hillside. Bobby smashed the camera equipment with a rock. When Maggie crawled out, he roughly grabbed her and twisted her arm behind her back. He shoved her down the hill toward the camp.

Tony was walking around blindly, trying to find his rifle. Sway was on his hands and knees throwing up. Jeff was pouring water over his head and coughing. He screamed, "Bobby, where are you? I'm blind!"

Bobby shouted, "I'm coming!"

Bobby let go of Maggie's arm and poked her in the back with his rifle barrel. The yellow fog from the tear gas drifted out of the tents and blew toward them. Maggie pulled out a handkerchief and tried to wrap it around her nose and mouth. Bobby grabbed it away from her and covered his own face with one hand while training the rifle on Maggie with the other.

"Sway, get off of the ground, and tie up our prisoner of war," ordered Bobby. "It sure looks like you guys have been in a war and lost."

Sway said, "Shit, man! I can't see, and I can't breathe! I opened up a locker in that tent over there, and it blew up on me! I think I have that bear spray in my eyes and tear gas in my lungs. What should we do?"

Bobby pointed his rifle at the center of Maggie's forehead and said, "Well, missy, I guess you think you're pretty smart now, don't you? I ought to just shoot you for setting us up like this! And I will probably do that after I let my boys take turns paying you back for what you just did to them."

"Man, what are we gonna do?" asked Tony.

Jeff answered, "I'm getting out of here before those others get back from town. They are on to us, we're way back here in the middle of nowhere, and it's going to get dark soon."

Bobby says, "We're not going anywhere until we get that letter! Little Missy Brown Eyes here is going to give it to us. We have about an hour before those other tree huggers show up, and she's going to go inside one of those tents and bring it out here to me."

Maggie pleaded, "I don't know what you're talking about!"

"Sure you do!" said Bobby. "If you didn't pick that letter up out of the snow about a week ago, then one of your stupid wolf boyfriends did! I'll bet that my dad's letter provided all of you with some good campfire entertainment." Bobby pointed the gun at her nose and asked, "Where is it?"

"I don't know!" she cried.

"Okay, say your prayers! I killed your friend, and one more won't matter."

Jeff said, "Man, did you really kill one of these tree huggers back there? I'm getting out of here!" Jeff tried to get oriented and focus on the direction back to the horses. Each time he rubbed his eyes, they burned even more. He finally focused on the south-facing rim and staggered off in that direction. Jeff stumbled off through a break in the trees and was suddenly flung high up into the air, feet first. He was suspended by his ankles from a tall, thin ponderosa pine sapling that bounced and swayed beneath his weight.

Bobby still had his rifle trained on Maggie. "Sway, do you think you can cut Jeff down?"

Sway said, "I think I can see him, but he's awful high up there!" Sway pulled out a large bowie knife and staggered over to Jeff, who was groaning and swinging back and forth. Sway stood on his tiptoes and tried to cut the cord on a moving target. Jeff swung, and Sway swayed as he reached and tried to cut the cord around Jeff's ankles. Suddenly, his blade connected with the thin cord, and Jeff fell on top of him headfirst. They both fell to the ground and groaned. They rolled over, got up, and staggered off in the direction of the steep hillside that would lead them up to their waiting horses.

"What are we gonna do, boss?" asked Tony.

Bobby shouted, "You guys aren't worth a shit! First you lose my dad's letter, and now when I need you, all of you turn into a bunch of babies and want to run home."

Tony looked around nervously. "Hey, man, those others are going to show up any minute, and it's a long ride out of here in the dark. And I'm not ready to go to prison for you killing somebody who works for the state government! I'm with Jeff and Sway for getting out of here quick!"

Bobby turned on Maggie and said, "I might as well kill you now, then. I've already killed your friend, and there won't be any witnesses left with you gone."

"Wait!" said Maggie. "You'll need me to get back home! There are traps and ambushes set up for you along the main trail back to your ranch. There are snares, deadfalls, and trip wires set up that you'll encounter on the way back in the dark."

Bobby said, "Sway, if you can see well enough, tie her hands together with some of that cord you cut off of Jeff's feet. Little Missy here is going with us, and anything that happens to us on the way back home is going to happen a whole lot worse for her. Hey, if we didn't run into any traps on the trail coming here, how can we run into any of them going back, unless somebody was trailing us?" He poked Maggie again with his rifle barrel. "If there's anybody else up there to cause us some problems, I'm going to get rid of the first problem in front of me, and that will be you. Now get up that hill!"

They each struggled to climb up the steep, slick mountainside in the crisp, thin air. Three of the guys still had burning eyes, and their lungs were full of the choking tear gas. They kept stopping to cough and wheeze in the oxygen-deficient air.

Bobby yelled at them, "It's getting dark on us, and we've got to move!" He became impatient with Jeff and Sway for stopping so often on the trail. He shoved Maggie ahead of him and said, "Go around those guys and catch up with Tony. I'm not waiting on anybody! If you guys aren't up that hill when we get there, we will ride off and leave you!"

When Jeff and Sway realized that they were being left behind, they struggled up the trail much faster. Tony reached the top of the rim and was bending over gasping for breath. Jeff and Sway reached the top after Bobby and Maggie, and they both vomited.

They walked a few yards through the trees and untied the horses from the aspen branches. Bobby said, "Tony, hold my horse while I put Missy on, then I'll get on behind her, and you can hand me up my rifle and the reins. Hurry up, you guys, and get mounted up! Little Miss Tree Hugger and I are going to bring up the rear."

Tony asked, "What about those traps that she talked about on this trail?"

Bobby said, "She's lying just to buy her some time! There ain't nothing on this trail except our old horse shit, so get going!"

After Tony's question, none of them wanted to head down the trail first. Jeff said, "I'm not going first! You all saw what happened the last time that I took the lead."

Bobby shouted, "You chickenshits!" He kicked his horse into a gallop down the trail ahead of Tony, Sway, and Jeff. The light was beginning to fade as the old horses galloped toward home where they knew they'd be free. The only direction where they ever showed any enthusiasm was toward home. For the first two miles, they always gave it all they had and more than they were physically capable of.

Bobby's horse galloped for about one-half mile from the rim and was running as fast as he could with two people on top of him. He was in full stride when he abruptly came to a fallen tree across the trail in front of him. He jumped over the hurdle, and something popped. He landed on the other side running, and the saddle started slipping off to the side. The saddle with the two people fell off onto the ground, and he didn't slow down. He was free!

The other horses were running close behind Bobby's horse on the darkened trail, and each of them vaulted over the fallen tree. They each spilled their riders and stampeded after Bobby's horse that was heading toward the ranch.

Maggie rolled, got up, and started running through the forest and away from the trail. Her progress was hindered by the fallen trees and her hands tied behind her back. She tried to jump over a tree and fell on her face.

Bobby Ray fell hard and punctured his arm on a sharp tree limb. He was pinned to a dead pine tree by the spike of a branch sticking up through the flesh of his arm. He struggled to grasp his rifle that was just beyond his reach.

Tony, Jeff, and Sway were getting up from the ground and trying to recover their senses. Bobby yelled, "Get your guns, and shoot the girl! She's getting away!" Sway found his saddle on the ground and pulled his rifle out of the scabbard.

Clyde charged out of the dark trees swinging a rope. His loop went around Sway and jerked him off his feet, making him drop his rifle. He spun his horse around, dragging him off into the darkness.

Maggie was running and tried to jump over another tree, but tripped and fell again. Without arms to support her, she struggled to get back up. Bobby shouted, "Shoot her!"

Clyde charged back and intercepted Maggie as Tony fired an offhand shot at her. Clyde reached down and grabbed the back of her Levi's, hoisting her up and in front of him without breaking his horse's stride. Clyde carried her off and out of harm's way. He cut her hands free and quietly said, "Just lie down and stay quiet until I come back for you."

Maggie pleaded, "I have to go back to camp to see if Fred is still alive. Don't worry about me, because I'm all right!"

"Okay," said Clyde. "Take my rifle with you, because it's just in my way." He handed her the lever-action .30-30 Winchester, took down one of several ropes that were buckled to his saddle, and rode off into the darkness.

Bobby yelled, "Somebody come over here and break this limb off before he comes back and I bleed to death!"

Tony came over with his knife and tried to cut the limb off below Bobby's arm, but the blade would not cut through the tuff pine limb.

"Just grab my arm with both of your hands and pull upward!" insisted Bobby. His arm came free just as Clyde came charging back toward them.

Tony yelled at Jeff, "Shoot him!"

Jeff cried, "My eyes are all blurry, and I can't focus on my gun sights!"

The rope shot out like a lightning bolt and caught around Jeff's rifle and his neck and right shoulder. The rifle exploded through the still night air, and fire flashed out the end of the barrel. The rope snapped tight as the powerful horse spun and loped away, dragging

239

Jeff over tangled pine trees and rock-strewn earth. Clyde dragged Jeff through the darkness until he quit moving. Then he unwound his dallies around the saddle horn and took the tail of his rope up over a high, stout-looking pine branch. Then he wound three dallies around his saddle horn and coached the big bay forward until Jeff was hoisted up into the big pine tree. Clyde rode his horse around a nearby tree two times and then stood high in his stirrups and tied off the rope to a distant limb.

Bobby wrapped a handkerchief around his bleeding arm and grabbed his rifle. He stumbled off and away from the main trail with Tony right behind him. They walked over deadfalls and through the thickest places where a horse and a rider couldn't travel. After two hours of walking, Tony asked, "Bobby, are you going to make it?"

"Yeah, I'll make it! I'll make it better than Jeff and Sway did back there. That cowboy was crazy! That was that Indian Clyde Deerhide! I'll bet he killed those guys back there, and he's probably trying to follow us through this thick deadfall."

"I think we're lost!" exclaimed Tony.

Bobby said, "I'm not lost! We've been working our way northeast, and we'll come out of the forest near that big meadow where we shot all of those elk this winter."

A short time later, the chestnut-colored female grizzly became restless and stood up to smell into the night breeze. She huffed and then rumbled a low growl from deep inside her chest. That was the signal to her scar-faced mate, telling him to wake up and pay attention, because there was more than one wolf this time.

28

BONNIE BUSTED THROUGH THE BACK DOOR OF THE HOUSE,
dripping blood all over the floor throughout the kitchen and parlor
to her back room. She quickly shed her housecoat and what was
left of her nightgown. She struggled with one usable hand to pull
on her hiking boots and warmest outdoor attire. She grabbed her
backpack and retraced her hurried steps out the back door toward
the mountain trail that would lead her to Clyde.

She didn't stop to take a breather until she was up on the first
high bench above the town. It was another half mile up to the second
prominent bench and the junction to the Highline Trail. When
Bonnie reached the high trail, she gasped for breath and looked
down over the lights of Big Scratch. She thought, *Okay, that's one mile!
I only have four more to go!*

Bonnie felt dizzy, and there was pain in her chest when she
breathed deeply. She sat down with the forty-pound weight of her
backpack resting upon a rock. She started thinking about what just
happened, where she was going, and how dangerous a trek she had
undertaken.

She was in shock when she went running out of the house. Now
that she was breathing deeply from the excursion of the steep climb,
her head was becoming clearer, and she started realizing her situation.

Bonnie wiped some dried blood out of her swollen eye and looked down at her bloodstained hands. She wondered why she hadn't washed off the blood or taken the time to look at her face. She could barely see out of her left eye, and she realized that she must look frightful. Her broken right hand was extremely painful and throbbing.

Why didn't she at least leave Fleebit a note? She must have been out of her mind! That poor man would worry himself crazy about what happened to her. Then she started thinking about the danger she was fleeing from. She feared that the man who attacked her probably had his friends waiting nearby for him. If they came looking for him and found him dead and her there, it was no telling what they might do to her.

Then she cried, "Oh, my God! He murdered Katie Colter! He said that only he and I knew, so he was going to kill me too!"

If she turned and went back, there wasn't a phone in the house. Her cell phone was broken, and she feared going to the sheriff. He gave her the creeps. When she was knocked down from behind, she first thought it was him. She was afraid to be seen on the streets, and Fleebit wouldn't be back again until morning. She had to toughen up and keep going.

Then she started thinking about hungry grizzly bears on the trail that Fleebit had warned her about. After what she'd just gone through, her worst fears were of returning to the house in the darkness. She only had four more miles to go.

Her imagination started seeing things in the darkness on the trail, and she became terrified that a bear was stalking her. She said, "Stop this! Just keep on walking, and think positive!" It was hard to remain positive, though, and she started feeling sorry for herself as she trudged up the high, rocky trail. She thought, *You are forty years old now, and what have you ever accomplished? You and your girlfriends met all of those guys in college, and your friends all got married to guys they met, while you held out and never found anybody that you wanted.*

She thought about some of the good-looking guys that she'd met and dated while she was in school. They were all so self-centered and immature. All they ever wanted was a jump. Those were the types that her friends married the first time. Their second go wasn't much better, but by this time, they had a kid or two, and they just hung on and made things stick together. At least they had some kids to watch grow up. *Bonnie, you are just a barren cow in a dusty weed patch. Your midlife is nothing but a crisis!*

She'd held out for a relationship with something more powerful and meaningful for the long run. It just never came her way. By the time that she met Lee, she must have felt desperate. After only three weeks, she married the worthless man, and look what happened.

She really didn't know Clyde all that well, either. He had a silly, joking side to him that was reckless and adventuresome. That side of him was similar to her left hand that substituted for her injured right hand when she painted or sketched. It was a side with an abstract portrait and ideology. You could call it a planned accident. Clyde also had a serious side that lay hidden below the surface and revealed itself in the fine display of his horses' training and his attention to detail. He and his horses' appearances both spoke of perfection and a serious attitude. That side of him was like her practiced right hand that was a master of fine art detail and perfection—a serious adventure of experience that displayed real life.

She often compared the other men in her life to Clyde and his example of what a real man should be like. He made her feel happy when she felt alone, sad, and empty. He'd offered a spark of hope when she was ready to return to Indiana. Then he gave her enough money to leave and start over again somewhere else or stick it out here somehow and make a new beginning. There were no catches or expectations. It was an unconditional gesture.

Tall, dark, generous, and handsome! Clyde sure was easy to look at, and her body felt a super sensation when they touched. A physical and emotional attachment had slowly developed. Then when she was ready for him to take her, he had suddenly saddled up and rode away.

Living in the house with all of his pictures, championship buckles, and saddles every day made her feel like she knew him better than she did or maybe ever would get to know him. She could tell from the pictures in the house that he was older than she was, but he didn't appear to be. He appeared to be timeless and someone who never aged, almost as if he had time traveled from a historical Western theme and into this modern world. She felt something much more for him than just friendship, but friendship should be timeless and something that never ages also. Maybe she had focused too much on finding an earth-shaking love without first seeking or finding a true friend. Clyde was the complete package.

Bonnie was walking along fine and then suddenly tripped and fell into the rocky trail. She tried to break the fall and instinctively caught herself with her right hand. Her hand gave way, and she absorbed the shock of the fall with her right arm and elbow. She tried to get up and instinctively tried to brace herself with the injured hand again. She cried out in pain.

Bonnie took off her heavy pack and took out a headlamp. She couldn't hold her flashlight with her good hand and protect herself if she should fall again. At least her backpack was well equipped. She'd purchased it and lots of survival gear when she'd first arrived in town with Franky. When he advanced her some money and then started harassing her every night, she'd prepared herself for a sudden departure. Her pack was heavy, and she probably had too many unnecessary things in it. She wouldn't need all of that food and gear because Clyde was only a short distance away.

It was deathly quiet on the mountain, and then suddenly something started howling off in the distance behind her. She was not sure of the difference between coyotes and wolves, but it scared her. She got up, started walking again, and wondered if the wolves were following her. She wondered if she had gone three miles yet.

Then something ran across the trail and crashed off into the trees below her. She started thinking about grizzly bears that had small cubs on the trail ahead of her and how protective they were of them. *Bonnie, stop this! Stop torturing yourself this way! You'll be fine, and you will find Clyde up here very soon.*

She tried to change her focus back to the few short times when she'd opened up the restaurant before Franky arrived, enjoying the southwestern atmosphere that she had worked so hard to design and decorate. Then Clyde would ride up on one of his young horses past the window and come in to sip coffee with her. Those moments were always short-lived before Franky and the breakfast crowd arrived. They laughed a lot and talked about happy things and good times. There was never a discussion about world news or each other's problems, and they never said anything negative about anybody or anything. It was as if they each knew that they only had those moments to live before their lives ended. Why wasn't life always that way?

Fleebit said that this trail would lead to Big Gulch Canyon. The last sign and arrows indicated that she was on the right trail. That meant that it was only two miles farther. He also said the trail that cut north to the cabin was one mile west of the canyon. That meant that she only had one more mile to go before she must find the unmarked trail on the left.

She was not sure if she had traveled a mile yet, but there was a trail on the left side of the main trail, and it must be the one. It was so dark in the forest, and her light was getting weak. The other flashlight was missing, and she must have left it back on the trail. She took off her headlamp and tapped it lightly. It fluttered and went out. Then it came back on, but the light was weaker. She tried to shine it down at the trail to keep from tripping over dead branches while looking ahead for advancing bears. There were many fallen trees over the trail now, and she had to climb over them. Her pack caught on a branch as she climbed over a deadfall, and it ripped open. She lost her balance and fell down. Her light went out.

It was so dark! Without a light, she had to feel ahead of her face with her left hand to keep from walking into a tree or a hanging limb. She took small steps to keep from tripping. Then there was a crash of breaking branches on her left as something ran through the forest. She was shaking with fear that she was lost in the wilderness and a grizzly bear was stalking her at that moment.

Then she came to a clearing and was finally out of the dense forest. She was terrified, lost, and exhausted, and her right hand was in terrible pain. She knew that if you were lost, you should stay in one place and hope that someone found you.

As she sat near the edge of the open meadow, she heard something and realized that a bear had followed her to this open place where it would attack and eat her. It must have smelled all of the blood on her, and she could hear it crashing through the forest in her direction.

29

CLYDE WENT BACK TO TAKE CARE OF BOBBY RAY AND TONY,
but they were gone. He found where they'd left the main trail and
headed northeast through the dark timber. He knew that last spring's
big blow-down had littered the forest floor throughout that area. A
maze of fallen trees made horse travel nearly impossible. It would
be faster to travel through that area on foot than on horseback. A
man on foot could climb over downed trees or step across them
from one to another. A horse could get boxed in and injure legs from
protruding limbs and branches. He thought about running them
down on foot. By the condition they were in, it probably wouldn't
take that long. If only he hadn't given his Winchester rifle to Maggie!
Bobby and Tony both had rifles. They could hide down low under
big, fallen trees and have a rifle pointed right at him, and he'd never
know it until it was too late. This would be a good time to have his
navy Colt pistol, but he never liked to wear it on horseback. It was
a heavy, awkward burden to carry, and it restricted his quick, fluid
movement when mounting a horse.

It wouldn't do much good to have a rope without a horse, but
he thought about trying it, anyway. If he could just get around
them and wait for them to come to him! Then he thought about the
possibility of them doubling back and taking his horse.

Jeff was hanging from the big pine tree with his feet barely off the ground, and nothing had changed. The rope was bound tightly around his chest and underneath his arms. He was conscious and looked beat up, defeated, and really worried about what his fate might be. Clyde dismounted, tied up his horse, and walked around behind Jeff. He used a pigging string to crosstie Jeff's left wrist behind his back, down through his belt, and to his right ankle. He performed the opposite crosstie to the other two limbs and left just enough length in the two ropes to allow someone to walk but be unable to run, kick, or fight back.

He lowered Jeff down slowly and let him just barely touch the ground with the tips of his toes. Clyde said, "If you try anything with me, I'll hang you back up by your neck while you balance on your toes. Then I'll ride off and forget where I left you. If you had injured Maggie or my horse, you would already be a swinging corpse."

It took a while longer to find where he'd hung up Sway. The forest was pitch black now, and it was nearly impossible to see where he was going. Clyde was sure of the direction, but he didn't want to take any chances on losing Jeff. He told Jeff to call out for Sway.

Jeff yelled, "Sway, where are you?"

Sway hollered back, "Over here! Come and get me down before I strangle in this rope!"

Sway was not as pleasant or nearly as peaceful as Jeff had been. It took longer to tie him up and give him the same demonstration of what it might feel like to die from hanging.

Sway kicked at Clyde, and Jeff said, "Don't piss him off, or he'll kill both of us and ride off and leave us. I thought he was going to hang me back there!"

Clyde took the handle of his shot-filled quirt and struck Sway with a hard rap between the eyes. "I don't like you, so you maybe you should listen to your friend."

Clyde had them tied together now, and with his lariat rope around the two of them, they shuffled down the trail ahead of his horse. If he wanted them to go faster, he rode up close behind and hit them over their backs with the ball end of his hard-twist rope. If he wanted them to stop, he held leg pressure against his horse until the rope became tight. If he wanted them to lie down, he firmly held his spurs until No-Name stopped and backed up, pulling them over backward. It was good practice for his horse.

It took some time to get his team trail broke. At first, they stumbled down the trail and often became tangled and fell down. The trail was only wide enough for one person in many places. It was a slow process, but they finally found a rhythm of walking together in unison and walking sideways between trees. As they approached nearer to the canyon, they slowed and pretended that they were too exhausted to go on. Clyde could tell that they were whispering to each other and planning something.

Sway said, "I need to get loose from Jeff and go to the bathroom."

Clyde said, "I don't see any room with a bath up here. Just go where you stand!"

"I can't go until you untie my hands," pleaded Sway.

Clyde wanted an excuse to hit the big man just one more time. "When they hang a man up by his neck, he loses control of his bowels. He makes a mess all over himself when his neck gets broken and he jerks around. Just feel lucky that you get to practice that while you're still alive. If you keep whispering to Jeff, I'll untie you from him and hang both of you. Then there would be a lot of stink swinging in the air!"

It had taken most of the night to get his pair of outlaws to the rim of Big Gulch Canyon. It was getting daylight now. The night remained warm and without frost, and the ground was soft and muddy where patches of snow had melted. As they stood near the edge of the canyon, Clyde could see several vehicles quickly coming up the slick, muddy road from the south. The south wind carried the sounds of roaring engines and spinning tires in 4×4 trucks. It told of their struggle as they spun out in deep, water-filled ruts and bounced over rocks.

Clyde said, "Okay, head down the hill real careful-like. I'd hate to see the pair of you get hurt. If you should fall down, you might scare my horse, and he might take off straight downhill through those jagged rocks. I had trouble stopping him when I pulled you through the trees last night."

Jeff and Sway had lumps, cuts, and bruises from the dragging during the night, and they were extremely careful during the trek downhill.

When they reached the camp, Maggie was outside a tent changing a bandage on Fred's head. When she saw Clyde coming, she yelled, "Hey, you guys! Wake up and get out here! Clyde is back!"

The roar of engines and the sound of multiple doors slamming, *thump, thump, thump,* echoed up through the aspens from far below the camp. Clyde held onto the long rope and herded his captives toward the throng of running men. He recognized Fleebit and the sheriff, but there were two state policemen and three men wearing suits. The three men in suits were ahead of the uniformed state policemen in the race up the hill, with the sheriff running in fifth place and Fleebit far behind.

Maggie and her group were running nearby toward Clyde.

Just as everyone approached Clyde, he spurred his horse a hop forward behind his captives, pulled the slack in his rope back, and quickly threw an overhand, half-hitch loop over and around Sway and Jeff. He yanked on the slack and locked his spurs under No-Name. The strong bay gelding crouched down and scooted backward on his heels, pulling the men over and onto their backs.

Maggie yelled, "*Wow!*" Her group began clapping and shouting.

The suits and the state police surrounded Jeff and Sway. A short, clean-cut man introduced himself as Agent Haslow with the FBI. He asked Clyde, "Where are the other two?"

Clyde unwound his dallies from around his saddle horn and handed the agent his rope. "They got away from me last night. They were on foot, heading northeast toward the Strickler Ranch."

Haslow ordered his men, "Get the helicopter up here immediately."

Another FBI agent read Jeff and Sway their rights. When he finished, he said, "Boys, we have a friend of yours in the morgue downtown. It looks like he tried to play cowboy with a big, mean cow!"

Clyde reached inside his left vest pocket and felt Katie's locket resting there over his heart. He'd often thought about what he would do if he found her, found her murderer, found her family, or when he finally found the proper authorities.

Clyde said, "Agent Haslow, I think I found where Katie Colter was murdered, and I found evidence there."

Sheriff Tolliber overheard Clyde as he approached the group of officers, and he pushed through them to Clyde. "Where?" he asked.

Clyde spat in front of the sheriff's boots and stared him in the eye. "I wasn't talking to you, you Barney One-Bullet! You couldn't catch a cold! You couldn't solve a crime, especially if it involved the Strickler name. And I sure wouldn't tell you where you could go to destroy the evidence."

Tolly shouted, "Arrest that man!"

The FBI agents surrounded the sheriff. They took his gun and handcuffed him.

Agent Haslow addressed Clyde, "We started this investigation to find Katie Colter a long time ago, and you need to turn over any evidence you have and any that you can show us."

Clyde said, "I want to see her parents first. I want them to tell me who I can trust!"

Haslow replied, "No problem! They are staying at the hotel in town. Did you find Katie's body? Why do you think she was murdered?"

Clyde said, "No, I didn't find her, but I found where I think she was killed. She left something that's still there. You might not believe me if I tell you the whole story, but her parents will!"

Fleebit stumbled up to Clyde, gasping for breath. "Something has happened to Bonnie! I found a dead man in the corral this morning. Cheyenne tore him to shreds. And blood all over the house! I thought Bonnie was killed or kidnapped until I noticed that her backpack was missing from her room. I went through the corrals to the north pasture gate and found a water bottle and a handkerchief. She was headed toward the Highline Trail, and I think she's lost somewhere up here on this mountain. I think she was hurt pretty bad! The search-and-rescue team was getting ready to start a search from our place when I came up here."

Clyde grabbed his rifle from Maggie, spun his horse around, and charged back up the steep trail leading west of Big Gulch Canyon. No-Name ran freely at incredible speed, galloping up the rough and rocky trail. All fear for himself and his horse abandoned, Clyde gave No-Name his head, leaned forward, and thundered up the wilderness trail. The big bay lunged ahead, leaping over fallen trees in his path, splattering through soft mud, and clattering over rock-strewn earth.

Clyde tried to slow him down with leg pressure. He wouldn't heed the well-trained cue. *He is running too fast! There's a dangerous outcropping of boulders up ahead! He won't stop in time!* Clyde pulled back on the reins and pulled the steel bit back into his horse's mouth. It was too late! He tripped and flipped over in the air, throwing Clyde clear and into the soft earth. The big horse landed on his side in the rocky trail. He lay there and groaned. Then he tried to brace himself and roll back up on his feet. He rolled free from the giant rocks and stood. He shook himself rigorously and then limped onward up the trail.

Clyde caught up to No-Name and grabbed the loose reins dragging beneath him in the muddy trail. Clyde stopped him and looked under him in the rocks. The Winchester rifle lay bent and broken in the trail.

When his horse fell on his side in the rocks, the rifle had saved his life, but why was he limping? Clyde picked up the foot and examined it. His horse had torn off a front shoe and half of his hoof wall. It was serious! He couldn't go on!

Clyde quickly checked the cinch, making sure that it wasn't too loose or too tight. He turned his horse around and led him back through the rocks and onto the dirt trail. He pulled the bridle and tied it onto his saddle. He slapped No-Name on the rump and yelled, "Go home!"

Clyde turned around and took off running west, up the Highline Trail. He was heaving and out of breath when he reached the cutoff trail to his cabin. There were no fresh tracks in the damp earth. He raced onward, searching for sign on the trail and outward into the trees.

A short distance ahead, Clyde found the fresh imprint of a hiking boot. He took the path off the main trail and raced ahead, jumping downed trees and carelessly crashing through brush. Suddenly, he noticed where a bear had recently broke open a rotten log. *There is fresh bear scat in the trail!* Then he saw some torn fabric suspended from a bush and a package of tissues on the ground. Then he noticed other articles scattered up through the trees and away from the trail.

There is bear sign all over this area! A bear came up from behind Bonnie and tore her backpack away as she was fleeing!

Suddenly, Clyde felt overcome with a powerful surge of adrenaline and worried, nervous energy. He took off, crashing through the thick brush like a madman, cracking and popping dry limbs and charging onward. He came to the edge of a small, open meadow, heaving and gasping for breath.

Clyde saw her lying on the ground and covered in blood. He was too late! He was always too late! Clyde ran to Bonnie and rolled her over. She was dead! He grabbed her into his arms and shook her. She didn't move. Clyde stroked her long brown hair and her soft face with his course and callused hands. He became weak and began shaking. He softy cried, "I'm too late! I'm sorry! I loved you!"

Bonnie suddenly opened her eyes and saw Clyde. She jerked around and looked wildly toward the trees. "Where is the bear?

Clyde, there is a big bear here! I just saw it charging at me through the trees over there!"

Clyde softly said, "Bonnie, I scared the big, mean bear away. There's just a big, soft teddy bear here now. Are you all right?"

Bonnie urgently persisted, "No! I just saw it! You must climb up a tree or play dead. It has been following me, and I heard it coming. I curled up in the fetal position. Then it charged me, shook me, and touched—"

"It's all right now. Cry all you want. I'm here, and you are safe!" Clyde held Bonnie closely as she cried and cried. She squeezed him tightly and gasped in pain.

Clyde said, "Uh-huh, broken ribs! We've got to get you to a hospital! There a lot of worried people headed up here to find you. Let's see if you can make it to my cabin. It's just a short distance through the trees. If you can go a longer route back to the trail, I can make sure that my horse also makes it safely home."

Bonnie sobbed, "The man who attacked me said that he killed Katie Colter! Wherever you go, I am going! I promise that I'll never let you out of my sight ever again!"

Clyde and Bonnie intercepted No-Name and slowly led him back to the cabin. There wasn't much time for them to be alone together before the search-and-rescue team arrived. Then the FBI helicopter landed in the broad open meadow near the small cabin. The helicopter search team unloaded and informed Clyde and Bonnie that they were unable to find Bobby Ray and Tony on or near the Strickler Ranch.

The FBI and the state police wanted to interview Bonnie and file a report. Her hand was severely broken, she was having trouble breathing, and one of her eyes needed some serious medical attention from a hospital. Before she boarded the helicopter, she kissed Clyde and started crying. "I don't want to leave you. I want to stay here with you!"

Clyde said, "You're not going to leave me, because I'm going with you. My horse is too lame to go anywhere right now, and he'll be fine here with Blue until we can come back together. Just tell those FBI agents to handcuff me, blindfold me, and force me into that flying machine. That giant black bug scares me as much as it does my horse."

30

THE FBI HELICOPTER LANDED AT THE MISSOULA HOSPITAL,
and Bonnie was taken inside for treatment of dehydration, minor
cuts, two cracked ribs, an infected eye, bruises, and a broken hand.
The state police interviewed her after the hospital staff took x-rays
and put a cast on her hand. Fleebit met Clyde down in the hospital
waiting room, and they talked about the recent events.

"You must have done some fancy roping up there!" exclaimed
Fleebit.

Clyde slipped a dollar in the pop machine and kicked it with his
boot. "Yeah, I wish you could have seen my bay horse in action. He
charged into the middle of that gang while they were shooting guns
off into his face and jerked them right off their feet. Roping criminals,
dragging them off through the rocks and brush, and then hanging
them up high in the pine trees is a lot more fun than roping steers.
I'd quit chasing cows all over the country if I could travel around
and rope stupid people for the FBI. They should make it a spectator
sport for family entertainment. PRCA could stand for Professional
Roping Criminals Association instead of the Professional Rodeo
Cowboys Association."

"Haw-haw-haw! I really like that one!" exclaimed Fleebit.
Suddenly, he blurted out, "Ellen and me are going to get married!"

Clyde yanked off his hat and kicked the vending machine a second time. "Well, that is just one more new shocking piece of information! I just can't believe that you let yourself get caught in Ellen Jorgenstein's trap! Did she propose marriage, or did you?"

"Now, Clyde, that don't matter! We are going to get hitched, and I've made up my mind. Things can change, and I can change some too. Clyde, you can change if you'll just give Bonnie a chance. She's in love with you! You might even be able to make a cowgirl out of her and take her with you on your adventures back through our old range country. I doubt that she'll ever rope well enough to help you win a championship saddle, but she's prettier than those models in Ellen's magazines and young enough to ride the big circle that's wearing me down."

Clyde pushed his hat back on and got into Fleebit's worried face. "I'm afraid that you have it all wrong, old buddy! I'm the header, and I've helped you win some championship saddles!"

Fleebit continued, "Like I said, I want to quit riding the range all summer, but I don't want to quit team roping with you. You'll get ornery if you don't have me as a heeler to help you win once in a while."

Agent Haslow interrupted the conversation between two old friends and pulled Clyde away. Clyde followed him down a hallway until he stopped and turned toward him in privacy.

"Clyde, Katie's parents, Bill and Sheena Colter, are here. I told them that you wanted to speak with them before anyone else. I've already given them Bonnie's testimony about a confession to her murder. They are real shook up! If Katie's killer is dead, he can't tell us where her body is located. Perhaps your clues to her disappearance can help me solve this crime and help her parents find peace and closure."

Clyde followed the agent down several halls in the new hospital, and he wasn't sure where they were going. The agent stopped them outside a door, and Clyde felt something over his heart. Haslow tapped lightly and then opened the door to the chaplain's meeting room. A handsome white man and lovely black woman rose from seats facing the shrine, hand in hand. They turned around facing him.

Clyde took off his hat and held it over his heart. The agent turned away and silently closed the door behind him.

The man looked at Clyde with sad, red-streaked eyes. "I'm Katie's dad, Bill Colter."

The tall, well-proportioned woman held her head up high and looked directly into his eyes. "I'm Katie's mother, Sheena."

Clyde came forward and embraced the couple. He put both arms around them, resting his chin on both of their inner shoulders. He found himself weeping with them, facing Jesus on a wooden cross.

Katie's mother sobbed, "So are you the one who found her?"

Clyde said, "Let's sit down together." Clyde took their hands and sat down between the couple, facing the cross and holding both of their hands. He quietly introduced his background of spiritual Native heritage and then told them what he'd found in the aspen grove.

Then he told them about his dream.

When he finished, Katie's parents both gripped his hands and cried. They sat there for a while in silence. Clyde released their hands and took the golden locket out of his vest pocket. He placed it in Sheena's hand. She opened it up and showed it to her husband. He fell apart and broke down in agony.

Sheena gave her husband time to vent his grief. She paused and became silent.

Clyde reflected how she was much like his mother during times of loss, respecting tribal custom and giving people all the time they need.

Sheena whispered, "Clyde, in your dream, you described my native family in Africa and where they live. Bill came to our village as a young man, working for the Peace Corps. He married me at our village in tribal custom with the approval of my people. He brought me here to the United States. My mother gave us this locket for our first child. It was our only child, and she was a baby girl. The white elephant is sacred to my people. He greets my people in death and guides them through the spirit world, where they become one with the Great Spirit." Sheena began crying and couldn't continue.

Bill choked and attempted to speak. "Katie ... she ... Katie loved wild animals and nature above everything else. When she was little, she couldn't wait to watch Steve Irwin on television. With his wildlife films and fun behavior, he became a role model that strongly influenced her. When Steve was killed during a filming, Katie took it real hard. She became depressed. Sheena and I thought we'd lost her way back then! When she became sick over the climate change news and refused college, we thought we'd lost her again. Then she became involved with the Green Revolution and came back!" Bill choked and attempted to go on. "Although we've lost her, she was doing what kept her alive. Those initials that she carved on the tree ..." Bill Colter broke down sobbing.

Sheena took control then and became strong, focused and alert. "Those initials, 'KC loves SI'? SI is Steve Irwin! I think he greeted Katie in heaven!"

Suddenly, Bill's and Sheena's tears became a flow of mixed emotions. They certainly cried for Katie's loss but also out of happiness and joy for the loved one they'd lost.

Sheena said, "Clyde, I told Bill that it would take someone special to find our Katie, and I believe that you found her in heaven. That's pretty special! We were told that you also saved some other young women from a terrible fate." Sheena embraced Clyde. "You tell us that you are a half-breed. I don't like that word! Katie was also a half-breed, but she found her oneness from both cultures. In your dream, you saw her with her native people and with God. Do you think people live on different sides in heaven because of race? I think not! Katie was only alive when she was one with nature. In my native culture, living as one with nature is living as one with God. You and Katie have a lot in common. I also think that she talked to you in your heart. She sent you to us with the true story. She made you her messenger. Clyde, you will always be a special part of our family."

Bill said, "You need to trust Agent Haslow. He has been working undercover since Katie first disappeared. Like you, he didn't trust the local law enforcement. He found evidence of bribes and corruption here. It has been very hard for him to penetrate the local population here and find any information or leads."

Sheena hugged Clyde and kissed both of his cheeks. Then she kissed him on top of his forehead. "Please take the FBI up on the mountain to that place and show them. Bill and I are not ready to go up there yet. Thanks to you, we now know where Katie truly is. Someday soon, maybe you can take us up on the mountain with you. We would like you to be the one who shows us the tree inscribed 'KC loves SI.'"

As soon as the hospital, the FBI, state police, and news reporters all finished with Bonnie, the town gossips started speculating and creating their own news and entertainment in the town of Big Scratch, Montana. Rumors and wild tales abounded!

The truth revealed that the Strickler Ranch was confiscated by the government because of drug-related evidence found on the property. When an underground stash of drugs and bundles of cash were located, a deep-probe metal detector was brought in to search the ranch. On a not-too-far corner of the vast property, a heavy metal target was located. A heavy equipment operator started up the big ranch trackhoe and retraced its old, still visible imprints to the location where the missing car with California plates and Katie Colter were unearthed by the FBI.

The testimonies of Pablo, Jeff, and Sway confirmed that Sam was alone at the ranch during Katie's disappearance and that he was the only one skilled to start and operate the big machine. A videotape from the gate monitor was hidden in Sam's belongings. It revealed Sam driving Katie's car through the big iron gates. Bonnie's testimony of Sam's confession brought closure to Katie's family and the world that had followed the lengthy, tragic story.

Jeff and Sway were charged with the kidnapping and attempted murder of Maggie.

There was a long list of indictments against George Strickler, including drug trafficking, false claims of entitlement to fraudulent corporations, income tax evasion, money laundering, and murder.

Bobby Ray and Tony were not located until fall, when some elk hunters discovered their remains. Their bones were mingled with the many other bones from the elk that they had wastefully slaughtered on the Strickler Ranch. Bite marks into their skulls indicated death by a very large grizzly bear.

31

CLYDE DROVE BONNIE BACK TO THE TOWN HOUSE AFTER
dark. He took her into his room, because his bed was much larger
than the twin inside her small room. He gently sat her down on the
bed and fluffed stacked pillows behind her. Her eyes were black
and swollen, her lips cracked, swollen, and blue. Her beautiful face
was almost unrecognizable. She gasped for breath at the slightest
movement.

Clyde kissed Bonnie tenderly on the forehead and quietly turned
away. He started to close the door behind him.

Bonnie cried out, "Wait! Don't leave me alone!" She sobbed, "I've
wanted you to hold me tight and make love to me. The first time was
when you rode away that morning and left me a note and a check. I
didn't want your money, but I wanted and needed you! Then I was
attacked by that vicious murderer!" she sobbed and cried. "Now
I'm ugly, and I'm a cripple. I'm afraid that you're going to close that
door behind you and ride away where I'll never see you again." She
began shaking and gasped in pain. Clyde sat down next to her and
wrapped his arm around her.

"Bonnie, if you hadn't stopped me ..." Clyde paused and thought
about his words before he continued. "Yes, I was going to ride away
again soon! I knew that Fleebit was quitting me, so I made plans to join

up with a world champion team roper who lost his heading partner. We were going to meet up in Prescott, Arizona, and I was going to join the PRCA circuit with him and try to win a world championship buckle this year. I'm in my prime as a roper, and my string of rope horses are the best I've ever had. And my new partner is almost as good as Fleebit! I figured it might be my last big chance without anything holding me down. I've already made plans to sell all of my young horses at a sale. I thought I had everything figured out until I met you. If you truly want me and need me to stay here with you, and if you think you could learn to love me, I need to hear that now."

"Oh, Clyde, I do want and need you. I already love you! I know that I'm ugly. Please don't leave!"

Clyde whispered in her ear, "Remember when I told you that I had a photographic memory? I don't see you as ugly! I still see you on that first day when you were painting your pretty sign. You turned around and smiled at me. I could remember your beauty if I was wearing a blindfold during the darkest night. One of the best things about you is that you don't know you are beautiful or that you're the fantasy of every cowboy who ever lived. I've wanted to take you into my arms for a long time. Sweet thing, you are bruised and broken now, and you need a lot of rest. I've waited all my life for someone like you, and I think I can wait a little while longer until you get well."

Bonnie said, "I need you to help undress me and take me into the shower. With these broken ribs, I won't be able to do it alone. That man's creepy blood is all over me, and I feel so dirty," she cried. "He killed Katie, and I feel like I have two people's blood all over me. I'm sorry to put you through this. Please help me!" she sobbed.

Clyde realized that his hands were unsteady when he fumbled with the buttons on her blouse and unzipped her jeans. He pulled them off and laid them on the chair next to the bed. He breathed deeply and began pulling off her stockings.

Bonnie whispered, "After you take off my bra and panties, I want you to take off all your clothes and take me into the shower.

The medication they gave me is making my legs wobbly. I need you to steady me and help wash me all over. Clyde, I've fantasized about undressing and touching you. I'm sorry that I can't do that now. I only have one good hand."

6:00 a.m.

Clyde was out cold. A faint *clack, clack, clack* sound disturbed his deep slumber. The sound intensified and became louder. Temporarily disoriented and lost, familiarity came with the loud bawling, clacking, and bawling of Cheyenne.

Clyde flinched and tried to move, but he was trapped. A naked woman had one arm wrapped tightly around his waist, and her breasts were pushed firmly into his back. Her lips were pressed against his ear, and one of her long legs was entwined around one of his.

Clack, clack, clack, clack, clack, clack, clack! The sound of hollowed horn against wooden poles had a rhythm and became a steady beat.

Jolted fully awake, Clyde realized that he wouldn't be making the Prescott rodeo the next day. Bonnie had a firm hold on him now, and she was quickly becoming a handful.

How wonderful! Yes! The wonderful sound of Cheyenne!

Two days later, Clyde rode up to the back porch leading his oldest pet horse, and he tied it up. Bonnie came out on the back porch and asked, "Are you taking me riding?"

Clyde was very blunt. "Not yet! But we need to get the hell out of this town! I'll bet a hundred cars and trucks pulled up our one-way street yesterday, loaded with snoopy, gossipy sons of bitches that gawked around! I should've stood out there and sold them all tickets to get inside the pen with Cheyenne! Before we can leave, you need to get in shape to travel. You'll need horseback therapy before you can ride over a rough trail to the cabin with broken ribs. You told me that your riding experience was limited to sitting on the picture pony at the Indiana State Fair. I'm not worried about your riding experience when it comes to riding this particular horse, because he'll be set on automatic pilot. A five-mile ride to the cabin doesn't sound like much, but you won't be able to stand up or walk after a five-mile ride uphill unless you begin to straddle a horse and stretch your hips and legs. It's called saddle-sore prevention therapy."

Bonnie reached up and tugged on Clyde's right earlobe and then kissed him lightly on his chin. "But, honey, that sounds like the therapy you gave me last night. It was so gentle. It don't hurt at all when I walk today!"

Clyde smiled crookedly. "Sweet thing, when you can ride this horse without gasping for breath when he trips over a rock or steps over a fallen tree, I'll be able to get more aggressive with that other type of therapy. Now get on and just sit on him. If that doesn't kill you, walk him up and down the alley. The end gates are closed, and he won't run unless you make him run by kicking him or hitting him on the rump with these reins. Since you seem to think that I'm a great therapist, believe me, when I say that you don't want a horse to run while you have broken ribs. I'll do some horse training in the round corral where I can keep an eye on you. If I see that you're in pain or if you're crying, I'll carry you back to the bedroom."

"Honey, I'm scared, and I think I'm going to break down crying!"

Clyde responded, "I'll know if you're faking it, but I'll probably fall for it, anyway. I'm afraid that if you don't let me help you get up on this horse real soon, I'm going to make you cry. Be brave now, or I might give you a spanking!"

Four days later, Clyde saddled his retired rope horse named Trio for Bonnie to ride and packed his team of graduates with enough food and gear to last them for many days in the high country. Clyde led them north toward the Highline Trail with six loaded pack horses.

They spent their days in the seclusion of the high country getting to know each other while riding over the mountains and witnessing the changes of spring. They watched and listened to the migrating geese and ducks come back over the north country and gently glide down to rest on the newly unfrozen lakes.

Newborn elk and mule deer fawns with spots all over them bucked and played in the big, open meadow in front of the cabin. Bears with small cubs crossed the clearing and rapidly disappeared into the forest. Sometimes at night, a wolf or coyote howled as Clyde and Bonnie lay in each other's arms inside the small cabin.

Clyde led No-Name and Trio up to the cabin, fully tacked and ready to go.

Bonnie said, "You're ready to go early!"

"Yeah," said Clyde. "We can go on a longer ride today if you're up to it."

Bonnie couldn't hide her excitement. "I feel a lot better today. Let's go!"

Clyde led Bonnie on a long ride across country. They rode down a marked trail until Clyde cut off and took them through a wilderness of fallen trees, around large outcroppings of boulders, and down a steep grade, following a small winding creek. They came out of a thick, dark pine forest into a small, green meadow full of wildflowers of every color. Clyde stopped them near the shore of a hidden, crystal-blue lake.

Bonnie exclaimed, "Oh my! I feel like I'm the first person to ever witness paradise. Thank you for bringing me here."

Clyde unsaddled No-Name and spread his thick, wool saddle blankets out on the lush green meadow. He took Bonnie's reins as she dismounted. "You're doing that a lot better than a few days ago. I can tell that it didn't hurt as much today."

"Yes, it still hurts some when I get on, but I'm getting better at getting off."

Clyde smiled. "Yeah, I've really noticed that."

Bonnie was immediately embarrassed and almost at a loss for words. "Oh, Clyde, you are a brat! You always think ahead." Then she kissed him and skipped away toward the small lake.

Clyde hobbled the two horses, pulled their bridles, and released them to graze freely. He walked over to Bonnie and lightly took two fingers of her left hand. He led her over to the makeshift bed near the lake.

Bonnie asked, "Is it already time for my afternoon therapy, Dr. Morgan?"

Clyde smiled crookedly. "That's entirely up to you."

Bonnie said, "I can always appreciate a good massage. How should I position myself?"

Clyde asked, "Just like last time?"

For Bonnie, no clock, no outside news, and no reminders of a modern world at conflict and counter to nature created a timeless sunrise and sunset that blended the days and nights together. Like the basic paint colors on her art palette—white, blue, green, red, and yellow—the natural brush of nature blended them all together and gently stroked them on a new canvas with each breath and every heartbeat of the present moment.

For Clyde, he was thankful for the wisdom of his grandfather, who had prepared him for a dance with life on earth with a beautiful woman who also knew her oneness with a love for life and a life for love.

32

THE WEDDING TOOK PLACE AT ELLEN AND FLEEBIT'S CHURCH in town, and it was a big affair. Fleebit and Clyde had a big circle of friends from many western states, and Fleebit was a celebrated bachelor.

PRCA cowboys who were past and present champions, ranchers, horse trainers, cowboy poets, artists, and movie stuntmen attended. Clyde served as best man and wore an original 1960s' Western suit that he'd only worn one time. With a slight alteration, it fit him perfectly. It made a full circle and came back into style.

Fleebit's brother, Leonard Shepherd, flew in for the wedding with his new wife, Marcy, and Fleebit was worried sick that Clyde would say something offensive. He pulled Clyde away and softly demanded, "Clyde, bulldog your tongue now, and don't start with any dog jokes!"

"Are you calling me Smart Elk again? Heck, old buddy, don't worry. I won't ruin your wedding! Besides, you'll be so hogtied now that I won't have to worry anymore about you. I won't stay up late at night worrying if the cops locked you in the pound for getting into trash. I won't worry about you crossing streets and alleys in the night and getting hit by a car. Your new wife will have you boiled so clean that you won't smell like a Flea-bit Shepherd that rolled around on a rotten carcass and—"

"*Clyde!*" Fleebit shook his head from side to side. "Could we go somewhere private and talk?"

Clyde looked puzzled. "Sure, friend, lets slip outside real quick."

"Clyde, you and Bonnie have made our wedding something special. I know that all of these important and famous people wouldn't be here today if it wasn't for you. I wouldn't even have any friends if I hadn't met you a long, long time ago. Everybody would have passed up a big dumb guy like me.

"And I want to tell you something else. That day when you told me what your grandpa said about the Indian who was a joker and a clown and saved the people from giving up when it seemed like all was lost. I've lived with a clown for most of my life, and I've met a lot of people through the years who were overworked and underlaughed. Thank God I wasn't one of them.

"Me and Ellen and you and Bonnie are going to take different forks in the trail after today, and I want to thank you for a wonderful life together, partner. I'm going to miss you!"

Clyde seemed to be staring at the toes of his boots, and the words were choked back. Finally, he asked, "Are you finished now?"

Fleebit nodded.

Clyde began, "You know that I always get the last word in. I have to tell you when I think you're wrong, and you are very wrong when you say that these people didn't come here because of you. If it weren't for you, none of them would be here today. When I first met you, I was a wild, reckless, smart-ass kid and I could have easily ended up dead or in prison. I could have ended up an alcoholic lying in an alley on the reservation or become a radical AIM member.

"Fleebit, you were a stabilizing influence for me to grow up with. You proved to me that you were big and tough enough to whip anybody, but you would rather walk away from a fight. I had a huge ego, and you were humble as pie. I wanted to be more like you, and you helped balance me out to be who I am today. You helped me find the middle ground of how I wanted to be and what I wanted to become.

"If I'd stayed the way I was before I met you, none of these important people would be here today, because they never would've liked me or wanted anything to do with me. And I know that you could have been with Ellen some time ago, but you felt like you would be deserting me. You waited until I found somebody that I could share my life with too. That alone proves what a special person and friend you truly are. I have one last thing to say to you. Don't tell me that you are dumb! Now let's quit blubbering and go back inside and join the celebration."

Fleebit stood watching Clyde as he walked away, confident of getting in the last word and having the final say on the matter. "I may not be too smart, but I sure am good looking, *Captain Morgan!*"

Clyde flinched and stumbled like he'd been jabbed with an electric cattle prod but continued walking away, unblemished and cool, back into the church.

The reception took place at the town house, and there was no need to decorate. The Old West town atmosphere between the house and the corrals was perfect for the big group of people who were a natural product of the American West. Pablo and Arturo were preparing a big barbecue out in back with a multitude of Mexican food and southwestern dishes. The Pink Garter Saloon was brimming full of drinks, laughter, and good-hearted people.

Fleebit's new wife, Ellen, was in the kitchen and asked if someone would take out some garbage. Fleebit and Leonard ran into each other, almost butting heads while trying to volunteer. Clyde started chuckling.

"Clyde, don't get started!" insisted Fleebit.

Clyde laughed. "I was only going to comment on how handy you Shepherd men are inside a kitchen."

Bonnie was dressed in a long, beautiful dress with a bright southwestern pattern. She arranged for a professional photographer from Missoula to capture the event, and she was paying attention to all details of the reception while visiting with guests and answering questions about her art. Her portrait of Fleebit was finished and displayed inside the living room between the two stacks of championship saddles. Fleebit's rugged Western image was silhouetted against the background of Cheyenne's yellow-and-brown-speckled coloring and bordered on each side by two of his favorite saddle horses.

Everyone was celebrating in the living room and viewing the painting when Clyde found a chance to slip outside undetected. There wasn't anyone around the corrals when he reached the pen behind the barn. Clyde walked up to Cheyenne and said, "You old meatloaf! All you do is stand around here all day and recycle good alfalfa hay into fossil fuel. You old rascal! Don't tell anybody that I'm giving you this cookie. I know that it's only oatmeal instead of my raisin cookies that you prefer, and it isn't my delicious banana bread that you simply adore! The only time that you get testy with me is when I don't have a sugar biscuit or a raisin cookie in my pocket. That's because I've spoiled you too much, you big baby! You boo-boo, moo-moo, you-you!

"Bonnie thinks that you like her better than me, but you and I know better, and that is our little secret. I've told you many times to act like you don't like me, and that has been our little game that we've played since you were a baby calf. We can never let Fleebit know the difference, because it would cheat me out of a lot of fun with him. Now I want to thank you for protecting Bonnie and—"

"Clyde, what are you doing? Did I overhear you talking nice to Cheyenne?"

Clyde spun around to face Bonnie. "I was just telling that old sow that his rib eyes were getting overfinished and he was looking on the flabby side since you showed up and spoiled him. Now that both you and Fleebit are attached to him, he'll probably cheat me out of a steak dinner and remain on a pension back here until he dies of old age."

Cheyenne reached out through the corral poles with one long

horn, catching Clyde around his back with the hollowed crook and gently shoving him into Bonnie's arms. She caught Clyde and kissed him.

Clyde said, "I think he approves!"

They held hands and walked toward the horses.

"It looks like you are in the restaurant business now," said Bonnie.

"No," corrected Clyde. "You, Pablo, and Arturo are in the restaurant business now. All I want is free coffee and a sexy waitress."

"It is too bad that Franky cut down your historic old hitching rail," said Bonnie.

Clyde laughed. "I was going to tear it down, anyway, when I found the time. Those old posts were rotten beneath the ground, and I was afraid to tie up a rank horse there. I was going to replace it with a welded pipe hitching rail that was buried in cement."

Bonnie said, "Franky was very lucky that you didn't bury him in cement!"

They walked down the middle alley that separated each of the pole corrals, and all of the horses came up to the fence for attention. No-Name pushed ahead to the front of the herd and nickered to Clyde.

Bonnie asked, "While you were out in the wilderness catching desperados and rescuing young maidens from danger, did anything happen that would give your beautiful bay horse his Indian name?"

"Nope, but I only wait for so long! If I don't receive a magical Indian Spirit name for my horses, I name them after somebody who I respect or after somebody who did me a good turn. I named him John after John Baxter, who left us the high country property. But I have another young horse that I named. He's a lazy, clumsy gray colt that's not too thick across the middle, and he's very narrow between the ears. He is much too thin down his neckline, and I think he was born with a thin vein of bad luck. I'm going to get rid of him, but I named him Franky."

Bonnie was still laughing as they continued walking close, holding arm in arm down the wide alley between the pens full of horses. It was the middle ground between the young and old, inexperience and understanding. It was a crossover where respect, friendship, patience, and love could master the maze of life's journey that continued out to the freedom and openness of the pasture beyond.

An overhead view from high above them witnessed the two human forms walking as one down the center alley, leading out to a wilderness trail beyond.

The golden eagle circled them four times, screamed, then caught a powerful updraft and glided up and over the distant horizon.

Wind River Mountains
Wyoming, 2014

A large herd of elk crossed the highway, heading north on their spring migration to the high country in the seclusion of the Wind River Range. The F-350 King Ranch pickup and custom, deluxe, live-in aluminum horse trailer rounded a curve and entered a beautiful, breathtaking, uninterrupted, endlessly long green valley studded with pinion and sage. The driver slowed down and coasted to a stop just past a large real-estate billboard sign.

Bonnie asked, "Just like last time?"